A Mentor and Her Muse

Mary
I hope you
enjoy!
Susan

Susan Sage

12/1/23

Published by Open Books

Copyright © 2017 by Susan Sage

Cover photo "Flower Door" © by Jay

Learn more about the photographer at flickr.com/photos/jryde/

ISBN-13: 978-0615722801

To the memory of my dear mother:
Joyce Lindahl Sage

"Every child needs at least one adult who is irrationally crazy about him or her."

—Urie Bofenbrenner

From Maggie's Journal

I wouldn't classify what I did as a crime, rather as a sort of vigilante justice. Some, I'm sure, will believe I should serve a prison sentence for what I did, while others will conclude that I was both her mentor and her friend. I admit that what I did almost a year ago was impulsive, but it is my hope, if not to convince you of the rightness of my actions, to at least make you see my side of what transpired. Perhaps in the light of my own analysis even I will have to eventually concede that what I did was unethical, and that even then I knew that I was crossing a line that should not have been crossed.

A couple years ago, I was in the early stages of planning what could be considered a kidnapping. Hardly more than a fantasy concocted on a tedious afternoon. My thoughts were fodder for a future book, or at the very least, a short story. Maybe it would turn into the flip-side of my first novel, *Pauline's Revenge*, which was told from a kidnapped victim's point of view. Little did the students or staff at Jefferson Middle & High School know it, but I was searching for the right student to mentor (or the *perfect* victim—it will be up to you to decide), not too young or too old—maybe going into ninth grade, which meant beginning to attend classes in the high school wing of the building. Someone sensitive, and perceptive, and most importantly, curious. Not necessarily an A student, but one with aptitude. If my choice were a girl, not one who wore heavy make-up, and certainly not yet into dating. Also, someone without too much attitude: spunky is one thing; hostile, yet another; and a reader, of course, or even better, a *writer*.

At first my list was so long, it seemed impossible to choose. Would it be Jackie DeLand, the underfed boy who smiled at me warily every morning before school? He always looked like he had a secret he wanted to reveal; at least it did before he fell asleep at a table before the first hour bell. Maybe someone else, a girl… Certainly not Lisa Peters—eleven going on seventeen. You know the type: short skirt, too-tight top, taller than the others. Friendless but friendly with adults; some might say provocative. She had a way of shaking her head and rolling her eyes that did more than simply suggest she'd seen it all. She really *had* seen it all. Sadly, her grades had slipped during the past year. There was Corey Banks. Sweet, with large, flying saucer-eyes, and the soles of his sneakers flapping away from the rest of the shoe… He always seemed like a clown in training. A nice kid, who would have been one of the smarter ones had he attended school more regularly. Others shunned him because he came to school dirty with hair uncombed. He didn't know he was smart or potentially attractive. I brought him granola bars almost every morning.

Then there was Taezha Riverton. How could it be anyone but Taezha? I knew her to be one of the four Riverton sisters; they were all half-sisters—same mother, but each had a different father (or so I thought at the time). Taezha was the most intellectually curious. It was her second year at Jefferson; before that she'd attended a gifted program at a school on the other side of the city. She was an older sixth grader when I met her two years earlier: twelve going on thir- teen (her mother hadn't sent her to school until age six). Her eyes were such a deep brown that the pupils and corneas seemed one and the same—two deep wells *her* victims would fall into if they weren't careful. Sometimes, depending on the lighting, there were gold flecks in them. Her skin was the lightest of all the sisters—a crème brulee or toffee. They all had similar wide-set eyes, but hers were the largest. They all wore their hair in long, black braids. Taezha's braids were the thickest. All four laughed readily, breezily, but their spirits, in contrast to hers, were flimsy and lethargic. When I would see them all together it was obvious that they were in her shadow—a couple of them were deeply resentful and no doubt would be secretly overjoyed when she left home on the road trip with me.

It wasn't her intelligence alone that was uncommon, for there were many bright students at Jefferson, and even a few this side of brilliant, like James or Montgomery. I've always respected a high I.Q., but never have I been fascinated by intelligence alone. Certainly her intellectual curiosity was appealing; I so enjoyed her keen sense of observation. As far as her looks, there were several girls more glamorous, more 'standard definition' pretty. She was all legs, had large feet, and a forehead that was a little too shiny. We both realized, without telling ourselves or each other at the time, that we needed each other as central players in our lives.

Tae gave me a knowing smile when we first met—one that I've seen cross her lips many times since. I think it's because she could see the free-spirit within me, just as I noticed in spite of her adolescent, awkward grace—my mirror image! Our spirits danced, spun and leaped in recognition.

Finding a way to meet when not at school proved to be no easy task, not only due to the bias against fraternization between unrelated adults and children, but, unfortunately, due to race. I knew her mother would not only think, "What does this woman want from my daughter?" but, "What is this *white* woman up to?"

When one turns fifty, one more or less realizes how life has turned out, even though it is (hopefully) far from over. Chances are it's turned out—so far—completely different than one's wildest imaginings. Such high expectations and hopes I once had! I was going to be a highly acclaimed novelist and travel the world. It probably hadn't helped that I'd published a novel at thirty-five, which sold reasonably well for about a year. That experience fooled me into thinking that my career was just taking off, and that I would be publishing a novel, if not annually, then every couple of years. I certainly didn't lack ideas. What I did lack was the necessary discipline—especially whenever my routine was thrown off. It would take days or weeks to get back on track with a project. Something big and I'd be derailed for months. Big: like losing both my parents at the same time... Big:

like beginning and ending six different relationships!

Often I have wondered how Taezha Riverton saw me at the time. Did she view her younger self as having been my captive? How does she view me now, years afterward? If she were to say "as an outlaw," my hope is that she does so with a twinkle in her eyes and one of those wide Taezha grins.

Last Supper

What they don't know: this is my last supper home
The cold pizza might as well be bone in my mouth
Wish my sisters and mom could come along…
No, I don't!
It's my time, high time—to strike out on my own…

"Can't we for once sit at the table like a normal family?"
Sprawled on the couch and broken chairs, they laugh and sass me:
"You sayin' you're normal?"
"Come now girls," Mom rises like the queen she should be
"Let's humor, Sis"

They lose their hiss and silliness at the table in the darkening room
Mom lights a candle since the light bill wasn't paid
Does she know somehow that this is my last supper—home?
My secret's safe with me, but I'll share this pizza
Cold as bone—for it's my time…I'm ready
To make it on my own!

—Taezha Riverton

Chapter 1

Tae crosses the cold tile of the motel bathroom floor and sinks into a deep bath. Sliding into the steamy water, she can't get over the spotlessly clean bathroom. What she doesn't like is the constant whir of the ceiling fan; if she turns it off, the lights go off, too. Not the fanciest bathroom she's ever seen, but way better than home where the toilet doesn't flush right and the drain is always clogged. Here, except for the fan, it's quiet, peaceful even. She knows she can't linger in the bath because Maggie is waiting for her—they have an important phone call to make.

Maggie entered her life a year after she lost her Aunt Serafina. In no way is she as wonderful, of course, as her auntie (a once almost-famous singer). And yet, like her aunt, Maggie is someone who has taken more than a passing interest in her. While Maggie is a little old-school, she's an eccentric type, and also a bona fide artist/writer like herself. (Word of the day: *bona fide*. Sounds like Latin. Tae doesn't know where she picked it up.) As much as Maggie is like an aunt, what exactly is Tae doing in a motel room with her on a road trip to meet Uncle Tyler? He isn't really her uncle. She's never met him, nor has she ever been so far from home, except to visit Aunt Serafina in New York (where Tae had slept in a luxurious hotel room and had the time of her life). Truth is, she can't wait to meet him and wishes they were going to see him tomorrow. They aren't. According to Maggie, they're first going to take a road trip.

Still, she can't help but feel a little confused about this adventure.

Maggie keeps telling her to consider this trip to be more about "developing as a writer," and that it isn't a vacation, but an "enriching and unforgettable experience." Maybe…We'll see about that. She knows she shouldn't be so quick to judge—they've only made it as far as Toledo, just a few hours away from Flint. (Maggie said that they could have gone further, but she's never liked driving more than a few hours a day.) Instead, Tae will "hone her powers of observation," as Maggie called it. 'Honing'…Now, that's a funny sounding word. What's wrong with the way she observes now? Once she's better at it, will she see more clearly, like Maggie?

When Tae emerges from the bath, squeaky clean and sporting a long Detroit Tigers T-shirt, Maggie is sitting at a large desk in a comfy leather office chair on wheels in the other room. She's wearing a worn blue terrycloth robe that ties at her waist. Her long, blond-gray hair is finally free from the loose ponytail she usually wears. Tae's friend looks way older at night than she does by day; not quite an old woman, but the frumpy robe doesn't help, nor does the more-gray-than-blond strands which end halfway down her back.

Maggie told her that this was a typical guest room—nothing fancy. It's large and clean. Some, Maggie claimed, would go so far as to call it stark. (She often liked Maggie's unusual choice of words). Besides the desk, there are two beds, TV, table with two chairs. When they'd first arrived, Tae got so excited that she jumped on one of the beds, her long braids whiplashing the air.

Maggie twirls around in the chair with wheels and smiles at her. "I know you're tired, but are you feeling a little more refreshed now?"

Tae doesn't answer, as she is thinking about asking if she can brush Maggie's hair. Instead, she plunks down on the double bed next to the desk. It has a purple and yellow design that Maggie called paisley. She wants to channel surf, but Maggie says first they must make calls—most importantly, one to her mom who still doesn't know that they've left Flint, though Tae did leave a note on the kitchen table.

Against the wall by the door, Maggie has aligned her sandals next to Tae's purple running shoes. Maggie's shoes are worn-looking and part of the back straps seem to have been chewed—probably by Maggie's cat. Her cat… Who's taking care of the black and white Lucy Lucinda? Has Maggie left her outside to become a stray?

"Don't be a goose! Didn't I tell you that Toby's mom took her in? She'll have a good temporary home." (Toby is the pesky boy who lives in the apartment below Maggie's.)

"Everything's temporary," Tae says, lowering her voice to match her gloomy mood, and staring at the blank TV screen. Where is the remote? Did Maggie hide it?

"Not true. Love is everlasting. Real love, that is."

"I suppose," Tae says, sighing. "I better call my mom now. Okay if I borrow your cell? Mine doesn't have any minutes left."

Maggie, rummaging through her over-sized purse for her phone, assures Tae that tomorrow she'll add thousands of minutes for her. At last she locates it, and hands it to Tae, who punches out the familiar number with her thumbs. Her mom doesn't answer until the fifth ring. "Where you got my girl, Maggie?"

"Mom, it's not Maggie. It's me, Tae."

"I saw your note. How long you plan on being gone?"

Tae thinks she hears a burp followed by a yawn.

"Have you been drinking, Mama?"

"Who are you? My boss?"

"Guess I'll go now."

"You do that! Get on with your bad-ass self! See, what I…"

Maggie grabs the phone. "Hello, Quintana. Tae just wants to let you know that we're taking the trip we'd talked about. Remember? She just called because she thought you'd want to know."

"Nobody told me about it. Point of fact, Tae lied in that note."

"If you could only try to understand and see the trip as a positive experience for Taezha…"

"Never did I give you my permission, but I'm going to say it like it is: I'm glad you took her. Less drains to get clogged, fewer mouths to feed. You just remember that I'm her mama!"

Maggie puts the phone back into her purse, unsure if Quintana has hung up or is still rattling on. She doesn't need to listen to insults or ultimatums.

"Maggie, what did Mama say?"

"Nothing, Tae. We got that call made. You call her often as you want, but that's it for me. Guess her reaction could have been worse, right?"

"You really don't know my mama, do you?"

But it really doesn't matter since Quintana can't do anything about them being gone. Not like Maggie has to mind her! Suddenly, it seems right for the shoes to be cuddled up next to each other. Strange how the sound of her mother's voice, commanding and ornery as ever, but now like it belonged on someone puny and trying to be tall. She throws herself sideways onto her bed. It's so much bigger than the one at home. There are two doubles in the room. The mattress is a little hard, but she's used to one that sags and squeaks every time she moves a muscle, so this one seems heavenly.

Except for the phone call, it had been a good day. Mostly, anyway. The drive from Flint hadn't been too long (just boring). Before getting to the motel, they went to the Toledo Art Museum. In each of the rooms—what was it Maggie called them—galleries?—they'd played a game: both had had to find their favorite painting and say why. It was okay if they said 'just because' twice, but no more than twice. Usually, Maggie liked strange paintings—surreal ones. (Another word of the day: *Surreal*.) Tae doesn't much care for that kind of art. Her favorites had been landscapes or seascapes because they looked like the background for true adventures, plus they didn't have people in them.

She's tired of most people, at least those inside the frame of her life. Her sisters, who mostly picked on her or got in her way, were more like evil step-sisters than actual ones. If not for Tamala, she'd be a modern-day Cinderella... And there was Jayvon, Mama's new/old boyfriend. He liked to stare, not only at Mama, but sometimes at Tae, too (for some reason he's never bothered her sisters). One time he'd touched her shoulder and kept his hand on it a little too long. The next time it was her breast, and after that he came up from behind when Mama was passed out. Probably he'd been about to dry hump her when he'd come up from behind, but she'd turned around fast and stomped on his foot. When she'd later told Mama about it,

Mama had only laughed and called her a drama queen. Tae could see Mama wasn't about to take her seriously, though if it happened again, she said she wanted Tae to let her know.

There in the background, by the outside edges of the picture of Tae's life: her mom's friends, her sisters' friends—all nameless and loud—and forever interrupting her. Trying to mix the colors on her palette—then trying to put themselves on her canvas... If there had to be other people in her painting, she only wanted LeAndra, Auntie Serafina, Maggie, and the mysterious Uncle Tyler. She didn't know about Mama. All she knew for now is that it felt right to be away from her. She felt free, *unfettered* (her other word of the day—that one she got from a song on one of Maggie's CDs.) Unfettered and alive.

She takes her clothes from the suitcase and begins to place them neatly into the drawers beneath the TV.

Maggie laughs and remarks how they're only going to be in Toledo one night, but if it makes her happy to unpack, by all means do so. Next, Tae arranges her notebooks and books on her bedside table: her hardcover journal that Maggie had given her, a notebook for story notes and another one for poetry. Also, she has *The Hunger Games* trilogy and an anthology of teen poetry. She tells Maggie to pinky-swear that she'll never snoop through Tae's notebooks without permission.

"No problem," Maggie responds, adding, "as long as you don't open my journal or notes without asking first.

"No problemo, Maggie!"

Maggie is more curious about Tae's writing than Tae is about Maggie's. As much as Tae enjoys talking to her, Maggie seems like such an open-book, so there really isn't much to make Tae feel curious about her. Well, maybe certain things...

From Maggie's Journal

4/1/12

I met Taezha over two years ago. At twelve, she was one of the older sixth graders. I was fifty, a young fifty, or so I told myself. On a bitter-to-the-bones winter morning, I took a job at Jefferson School, even though I didn't need to work. My inheritance is enough to keep me financially afloat for (hopefully) the rest of my life. I work because I enjoy helping young people, especially those classified as at risk. Must have been a Monday because the heat wasn't working properly and we had to wear our coats all morning. She was returning books and asked if I'd always enjoyed reading. First time anyone had asked me about myself in quite some time—a nice surprise! Usually, I don't allow students to check out more than three books at a time, but in Taezha's case, I allowed her to take home five or six. Not long afterward, she began visiting me every day before class.

There I sat on my stool behind the large counter in the school's media center, and she, as always, was in motion. It was Taezha alone who could make me forget that I was earthbound and ageing. In turn, I hoped that my sincerity in wanting to get to know her came across. She stopped by my desk in the media center every chance she could, usually once before school, after lunch, as well as when the last bell had rung. Sometimes she showed up when she got special privileges from teachers as a reward for being an exceptional student. Not many excelled academically at Jefferson, and because of this, the media center was rarely crowded unless a teacher brought an entire class.

She always asked me how I was doing before I had a chance to ask her. I loved the way she inquired: "Have any interesting dreams last night?" "Any news flashes for me?" Never the perfunctory, "How are you today, Ms. Barnett?" It just wasn't her style. Some adults might view her as being a little too assertive, but I always enjoyed her positive, exuberant energy.

To say she made my day would be an understatement. To say my enjoyment of the work day depended entirely on whether or not I saw her would be the truth. Is there anything wrong with that? I couldn't help myself. Days when she was absent, which began to increase toward the end of each school year, were the most difficult to endure. Not only because I worried about the reason for her absence, but without her, the sunny days were anemic blue, and the gray days were solid lead. I became angry at her whenever she was absent, experiencing emotions similar to that of a jilted lover. I took it all so personally, too personally.

One particular afternoon she let me in on her secret, and nothing since has ever quite been the same. She was staying late for an after-school program, but chose to stop by to see me first. A couple of times during the day she had eluded to a secret she was going to tell me. The air of expectation made the hands of the clock move more slowly than usual. I felt a zest and an overall interest in existence which I hadn't felt in a long time.

She sat across from me with that wide Taezha grin, and drew my sense of anticipation out even further by saying nothing for the next couple of minutes. So many students would just blurt their hearts out with little provocation. They were amazing, many of them, but none nearly as interesting as she. Could there be a new boy in her life? Could she have won a trip to somewhere exotic? Maybe she was going to ask me to go with her instead of her best friend?

"You're going to make me guess? No fair!" I pouted, but was immediately sorry for my facial response, as I'm sure doing the pouty-lip thing isn't exactly attractive on a fifty-one-year-old woman.

"Okay, Ms. Barnett, I won't keep you in suspense a minute longer!" (In those days, she hadn't yet begun calling me Maggie, nor did I address her as Tae.)

"My big secret is that we've got something in common: I'm a writer!"

After giving her a heartfelt hug, she told me that wasn't all: she'd won first place in a story competition in her eighth grade class. On Friday, she would be reading her story aloud. Only problem was that she was terribly nervous, so she didn't see it exactly as a privilege. Did I have any tips for standing up before the class? Had I read much of my writing aloud? I told her that what had always worked best for me was to picture some of the audience as various zoo animals. If that didn't work, I'd imagine them without their clothes. She laughed so hard she almost fell out of her chair.

That was the beginning of many subsequent times devoted to discussing writing; not only the craft, but the joys, and—at times— difficulties of being a writer. We also loved discussing what we were currently reading—the necessity for writers to be readers. She especially enjoyed the tidbits I told her about writers: how Sylvia Plath had died with her head in an oven; how George Sand had actually been a woman but had changed her name so that she could publish.

Then we talked about the best times of day for writing. Night was best for her, especially after everyone else had gone to bed (provided she didn't have to go to school the next morning). She loved nothing better than to write in bed: blankets over her head and a flashlight shining down on her open notebook. It made her happy to know, that like her, I enjoyed penning my initial drafts in a notebook, not on my laptop. (At the time, she didn't own one.) I told her how I often force myself to begin writing at 4:00 o'clock a.m., since there just aren't enough hours in the day; adding, however, that I could only write after downing at least two cups of coffee in my blue mug with a chipped handle.

Taezha shared one of her stories, "Tears of Blood," with me the very next day. (A man shoots his wife at his daughter's birthday party. She almost dies, but doesn't. The happy ending is that they re-do that party, but the wife is missing her left eye, which is found by the daughter after the second party.) Every sentence moved the plot along at a good clip; dialog showed her to have a good ear... Nothing better than a grizzly, murder mystery story, she claimed. I didn't show her—or even tell her—about my published novel until much later. My reason for not doing so remains a mystery. (At first I was going to include parts of my novel, *Pauline's Revenge*, in this book, but since this is mostly about my relationship with Taezha and her development as a writer, I have decided against it.)

How could a young teenage girl have such an effect on me? What if she hadn't revealed her passion for writing, so much like my own when I was her age? Would it all have turned out differently? I began having daydreams about introducing her to the world of writing and writers. We would go to a poetry reading and sit close to the poet at the podium. Afterward, we would hobnob with the poet, and then maybe discuss writing over coffee and pastries. She could hear how others got their start in writing… Or maybe we would wind up at a bookstore, and after much searching of shelves, we would hunker down in two plush arm chairs with our books. How much to expose her to? Too much too soon might overwhelm her, and even turn her off. Maybe bookstore visits were the best sort of writerly outings for now.

Chapter 2

Two and a half Months before the Trip

Maggie rapped at the door of 369 Appalonia Drive on a rainy, spring morning. She was grateful for the inclement weather because no one was out walking. Had they been, they would have noticed her: a white woman in an almost entirely black neighborhood.

At last, the door opened a crack. She could feel her chin quiver when she tried to smile. Quintana Riverton yanked her inside like she was about to fall off the deck of a boat. She was friendlier than the first time Maggie had seen her at school, for she immediately offered coffee. Even so, she hadn't asked her to sit down, so Maggie just stood in the doorway.

Tae had been missing from school for a week and it was Maggie's responsibility to check on her since the parent liaison had quit last month. The principal had decided to add 'truant officer' to her ever-growing list of job duties.

No sign of Tae anywhere. All she could see was a small, cluttered living room and a dark hallway leading into what must be the kitchen. Unopened envelopes and laundry baskets of wrinkled clothes. Overflowing ashtrays. Four or five cats sprawled on worn couch and chair cushions. Lowered blinds allowed only weak light to pass through a small window. She heard Quintana's voice arguing with what sounded like two other females. Quintana's was by far the loudest: "Don't sass me now!" Clearly, she had the upper hand.

Maggie shifted from one foot to the other. She had to pee. Why did her bladder always call at a time like this? Finally, Quintana reappeared and asked what she was doing still standing there, but then noticed there was absolutely no place for Maggie to sit.

"No need to stand on ceremony, Miz Barnett. Just throw those old cats to the floor. Reason I feel relaxed around you is cuz Tae's always telling us how 'Miz Barnett said this,' or 'Miz Barnett said that.' Lordy, you'd think you was the be-all and end-all in that child's life!"

Quintana wondered if anything was wrong with the coffee. Besides being lukewarm and too strong for her taste, it was fine. Maggie took a sip, smaller than the first, and thanked Quintana for her hospitality. The smells of cigarette smoke and cat urine competed for attention in her nostrils. Sadly, the aroma of coffee came in a distant third.

"Mrs. Riverton, we're hoping that Tae will soon be ready to rejoin us at Jefferson."

"Quintana to you, Honey. I'll call her in with us in a minute, but first I want to explain some things, Miz Barnett."

"Please, call me Maggie."

Quintana tugged down her sequined top as it was riding up over her waist, exposing a rather large muffin top. As she did so, it yanked down her already sagging breasts. She proceeded to explain how her sister, Serafina, had died less than three years ago—the sister who'd almost made it as a big-time jazz singer. Had Maggie ever heard of Nina Simone? Could've been her sister… She'd been especially close to Tae. No, not Nina, but Serafina. That was the main reason, Quintana went on to explain, that Tae hadn't been in school: they'd just had a memorial service in her sister's honor. Also, Quintana had recently been laid off and wasn't able to buy gas for her car, and *no way* does she want her baby walking to school by herself. Not down these mean streets… The other girls got out of school earlier because they attended the high school. It didn't pose a problem for those three since they were able to go to and from school with each other. Even though the two schools were attached, the school days began and ended at different times. What about the possibility of Tae taking the bus or having the parent of one of her friends pick her up? Quintana quickly changed the subject.

"It's been a few years since Serafina passed, but I had a real hard time with it," she informed. Not exactly a shock, but her sister had been in her prime. Because of her sister's death, Quintana suffered from nightly insomnia, smoked, and drank a little too much for her own good, which was the reason she had to drop classes she was taking at the community college. Tae, too, had taken her auntie's death hard. Some nights she'd just stay up with Quintana till the sun came up.

Maggie wanted to mention that while she felt sympathetic about their loss and the hard times they must have endured, their tragedy was now a few years in the past, not six months ago. She'd refrained. Since she'd lost her parents tragically, she could certainly relate. Sometimes she thought she might never get over losing them.

"Mama, you telling my business again?" said Tae, who'd been in the kitchen, eavesdropping, for who-knew-how-long.

After Maggie told Tae how sorry she was about the loss of her aunt, they spoke about the general ups and downs of life. Tae took the lead in the discussion, as Maggie pointed to the schoolwork she'd brought with her. "Think you could get some of it done over the weekend?" she asked Tae.

"You know me, Miss Barnett. Good as done."

"Will I see you on Monday?"

Tae nodded, grinning widely.

From Maggie's Journal

Two Months before the Trip

4/15

No one to blame for my lack of friends except myself—not counting my friendship with Jocelyn, though I only hear from her maybe three or four times a year. At Tae's age, we'd been best friends… Teachers at Jefferson keep me at arm's length, as I do them. No doubt my isolation is of my own doing—I've lived in too many cities, lived with many men, held too many jobs… At times it feels like I've lived in different cities with different men for each year of my adult life. Some relief there have been only six cities with six men. Will the sixth one be the last? Life with Andrew the Sixth was the worst. We always bickered and fought; the make-up sex wasn't even good. Only thing in common was our love of books. He's been a clerk at a used bookstore for several years. Sometimes we get together for coffee, but he always wants to go over and over what went wrong, when really it was just that—it—our relationship—was wrong. It lasted two years, which was longer than most of the others. Weirdly, we've remained friends. Not best ones…

4/16

For the first time in several days I had a decent day. Tae, LeAndra, and I decided to begin an after-school book club/writing group. Nice that Derek and Eli showed up, though they said they weren't sure if they wanted to do any writing. LeAndra doesn't write stories or poems either; she prefers drawing and plans on illustrating Tae's book when she's older. Can't get over how fast Tae reads and how much she remembers!

LeAndra's her best friend. They've known each other since they were little, though Jefferson is the first school they've attended together. (Up until the previous year, Tae had gone to a school for gifted students, then transferred to Jefferson because her sisters had gone there; also, it was close to home.) I sure wouldn't have picked out LeAndra to be her best friend. She's sweet, but too sweet, giggles a little too much, not nearly as mature as Tae... Sometimes, I wish they weren't so close. Of course, I'd never tell her this.

When Tae is with LeAndra she isn't herself. She becomes giggly, silly. It's not like she dumbs herself down, but just acts childish. I realize she's not an adult, but when we're alone she acts mature. But with LeAndra, she acts like other girls. I know it's so that she can connect with LeAndra. They're always whispering, lost in their private world. Jocelyn and I used to be like that. We wrote and sometimes spoke in code. My toughest days are when I talk to hardly anyone at school, and happen to see Tae and LeAndra together. It's different on the book club afternoons.

LeAndra isn't so sure of me either. She rarely meets my eyes, and still whispers in Tae's ear much of the time when they're in my presence. You'd think by now that she'd be past that stage. Her drawing ability strikes me as so-so, and perhaps she detects falseness in my praise. Today went a little better because we stopped for ice cream before I dropped them off at Tae's house. I'd get in trouble if Leroy Hardin (the Principal) knew, but the girls and I are keeping it, as Tae and LeAndra would say, on the 'down low.'

4/17

Tae came to me crying after third hour. She was late for school because she and her mom had had another argument. Quintana had brought yet another man home (there have been several this past month). They'd drunk quite a bit of wine and gotten really loud. She was pretty sure that her mom had taken pills, too. She'd also tried to get Tae and her sisters to join the party. Tyleena and Tasha actually did. The man, Jayvon, had flirted with all of them. When Tae had reminded Quintana that it was a week night and that she really didn't want to miss any more school, her mother broke down, apologized repeatedly, and finally, at 3:30 a.m., told Jayvon to leave.

Later, Tae and her mom fought again because Quintana felt like Tae was "up in her business." Quintana was the mother—not Tae—and so it was she who "called the shots." My dislike for her grows daily.

As much as I'd like to call Quintana and speak my mind, I know there are times when she's a good mother. I've never had kids, so what do I know? She wants the best for Tae, but her life is hard. If she weren't making any effort, it would be one thing, but she has enrolled again at the community college, and I've heard her encourage her daughters to get a good education. She knows it's important. Not the first woman who's allowed men to make her do stupid things—I should know!

Tae's been gone for a couple of days again, and I can't believe just how much the school's not the same place without her. Time drags and there's little to look forward to: opening a box of new books or software or having brief visits with staff, and sometimes, LeAndra. She never visits long and our talks are stilted. Eli and Derek sometimes sneak in after lunch (they never bring me a hall pass) and are always asking me to recommend a good book, though neither get around to finishing one. Mostly, they want me to start up an after-school book club which I've been promising to do for the last year.

At least there are times during the day when I can jot down thoughts in this notebook. I enjoy ruminating and trying to figure out where-to-go-from-here. Come to think of it, it's what I've always done. How have I ever really gotten anywhere in life? Often—too often—I go over my major losses: relationships with men (the longest one lasted three years); jobs (which have also come and gone); friends; plus, both my parents have died. To think at my age to never have been deeply in love! After receiving my B.A. in General Studies, I took so many post-grad courses at various universities that, by now, I should've earned three degrees. Kind of similar to my writing career: I've written countless drafts of poems and stories, but have only one book to my credit (a novel I wrote years ago). I should have had more publications by now…

Enough about me…Most students at Jefferson either live with one parent (rarely both), or with grandparents…sometimes with an aunt. If there are two parents in the household, chances are that one is a step-parent. Also, a majority—possibly all the kids— live in smaller dwellings or apartments. Houses often have grillwork over the doors and windows. Every year there seems to be a few more abandoned houses with weeds instead of lawns, windows covered in plywood and spray painted in gang symbols. Graffiti often covers entire sides of houses. Words like 'pussy' or 'JJ rules' extend several feet in length and height. No matter the word or phrase, the sadness and anger of the house-writer is palpable. Most cars in driveways haven't been driven for years, but sit idle because the owners can't afford to have them towed away. They not only seem to announce, "Once we were drivable," but the more veiled message: "Once our owners' lives were live-able." Those who work hold jobs at McDonald's, carwashes, or Walmart. A lucky few work at two or three part-time jobs; these are the tax payers who are almost able to pay all their bills. So many have given up even looking for real work… Impossible to know how many survive due to drugs, prostitution, or stealing… The lucky ones have family members who help out, but that's rarely a viable arrangement. Also, most kids arrive early to school for the free breakfast. They also qualify for a reduced-priced hot lunch. With any luck, there will be leftover pizza for dinner— soggy or stale, as usual. Naïve of me to think that the president could change the hard economic times, though I'm sure I'm not the only one who was once overly optimistic. The Great Recession is an ongoing Depression in Flint, Michigan.

4/20

Days of rain make the area look so dreary. Trees are scarce. Pot-holed roads, boarded-up houses, businesses… Gang signs and misspelled words are spray painted everywhere. Graffiti born of anger and despair. No, this isn't a dream deferred, but a dream only partly realized, then snubbed out and forgotten so completely that there is now barely any hope left, only people shuffling along, subsisting. I wouldn't be surprised if half the city goes hungry; all are downtrodden in one way or another.

For me, the ugliness is inescapable, overpowering, unavoid-able—unless I'm immersed in reading. Right now I'm between books—hate it when I'm not reading one. During my few years at Jefferson, I've never seen a student so immersed in reading as Tae. And I'm thrilled for her, because I know she'll never be completely without hope—even on her worst days. How I wish I could take her away from all this. Maybe on a vacation to a tropical island. Anywhere but here.

They died in each other's arms, and then my parents' cabin became their tomb for over a week. Both had suffered from insomnia for decades, and in the end they both died overdosing on sleeping pills (two empty bottles were found: one had fallen on the floor and the other was upright on a nightstand). Once they were in their mid-80s, there was talk about selling their home and moving them into an assisted living situation, though neither suffered from a terminal disease. They never did. This was their final act of defiance and togetherness. Their bodies were found five years ago tomorrow. Andrew the Sixth (not the sixth Andrew, but my sixth boyfriend) and I were taking our one and only trip together to the East Coast. Little did I know, they passed away the second day after we'd left home. My last conversation with them had been the day before I left. I don't remember how they worded their final message to me. I wish I did. Something about hoping I'd have a wonderful time, and that they loved me—strange for them because they rarely expressed their feelings, though I always knew. Little did I know that they too would be taking a journey. Good for them that they didn't want to move into some assisted living place, but did they think about how much grief their loss would cause? Not only the way they died, but also at the same time? What a selfish species we are! Yet they gave me their love of reading, their *joie de vivre* (from better days)... If I'd had a child, I would have wanted to pass those qualities along.

4/21

I wake up with a jolt after seeing the image of my parents in their death embrace. My mother had such dazzling blue eyes and my father's dark eyes and wild brows, and his belly laugh, gave him a larger than life presence. One day will I forget their voices? How sad that I have no one to whom I can pass their stories. Caroline is lucky to have her children, Byron and Gwen. And here is that old familiar envy of my sister—just like when I was as a girl. Not that I'd want to be her.

Despite them being of different races and ages, there are similarities between Tae and Caroline: both have long, graceful necks and legs, lovely foreheads, large, wide-set eyes. Also, though they have long feet, they are slender and sure-footed. Both have a confidence I've never had—not even for a day.

Tae told me that her mother signed up for college courses. "My mom is going to become a doctor," she announced with a pride only to be outdone by a mother over her child's accomplishments. Only once have I seen her so excited: last year when she won a school-wide story contest. Does Quintana know how many years of schooling it takes to become a doctor? Will this make Tae now need me more… or less? Tae complains that her mom will be as unavailable (though for a better reason) than when she is sleeping off one of her party highs. Despite my lack of a social life, at least I've felt needed by someone—such a long stretch before Tae, when no one turned to me. The last time was two years ago, when I became a foster parent for a couple of months. I needed Ricky more than he needed me. I needed him to help me get over the raw grief of my parents' deaths, as well as to put Andrew the Sixth in the collection with the others.

I can't go into Walgreen's without buying something for Tae. A few days ago I gave her a notebook and today, a pen. I've been hunting for a good backpack for her, too, since the zipper on hers is broken. Her birthday is coming up, and I hope Quintana lets me take her to a bookstore and out to lunch. She's the sort of young person who needs some spoiling. Am I doing this because I don't have any children?

Do I need to discuss this with a therapist? Hell, no!

4/24

Our book club has swelled to six. I brought cookies and fruit punch. They ate the cookies off my shoulder. I thought the guy who taught me this—years ago in another after-school program—was silly. Now I get it. After much discussion, the club agreed on *The Hunger Games*. The others aren't nearly as well-read or as perceptive as Tae. How could I not pay her special attention? After the others left, we talked about writing, particularly how empty we feel on days we don't write. I admitted how I don't write as much as I used to, and lately only in this journal. During the past couple of months she hasn't gone longer than two days without writing. It was the same for me at her age.

Here's a partial list of books that Tae would like to have our book club discuss. She's read most of them: *The Hunger Games, To Kill a Mockingbird, The Color Purple, The Skin I'm In, The Get Over,* and *Panic.* Good choices, Tae. So many great books!

The following morning Tae came to me in tears. Her mom is going to drop her classes—supposedly because she's been sick, but Tae knows it's really because she's been drinking and getting high. "She's never going be a doctor, Maggie!" I hugged her for a long time. Hardin just walked through the library and smirked at me. Doesn't look good, does it, Boss? Too fucking bad!

4/26

I could tell that Tae didn't want a hug. Her face showed no emotion at all; she was there but not there.

"Was your night as bad as the previous one?"

"Worse," she responded, but didn't say why.

I know she'll talk when she feels up to it. Before she left I clasped both her hands in a hard squeeze. It's now after 11:00 o'clock p.m. All I can see is a frozen disappointment on her face; she feels betrayed by life. If I want any sleep, I'll have to take a pill. A couple weeks ago I spoke to Jocelyn and she told me how I should distance myself because I'm getting too close. Could she be right? I don't think I can stop myself.

Ten years ago I could live with face and figure flaws...my left eye larger than my right, far from beautiful, but I was okay, even somewhat attractive on my better days. Now the face in the mirror or in outdoor photos looks older; the laugh lines are grooved. Who is this person staring back? Yet even on the worst days, I'm not so horrible that I frighten small children. How does Tae see me? Surely, she'd have little to do with me if she were repelled? Vanity, thy name is Maggie!

I dreamed I was chasing Tae down a street, yelling for her to wait for me. When I finally caught up to her, she turned and I was shocked to see Ricky's face. Tae/Ricky began running again, taunting me: "You'll never catch me. I'm the Gingerbread Man!"

4/28

One of the teachers, Jan Irwin, cornered me in the teachers' lounge. She'd heard that I'd been seen with Tae after school and on weekends. "You know, I'd be careful with that if I were you. I mean, it's all well-and-good that you've taken her under your wing, but you never know..."

Thanks for your words of caution, Jan. And now I'll just throw them to the wind!

During nights of restless discontent, I always find myself wondering about Tae. Is she working on one of her stories? Is she getting enough solitude in order to hear herself think? Is she able to shut out the noise of her family or neighborhood? Does she always write at the little desk by her bed? It overlooks a window, and I think there's a single tree at the center of her small backyard, but I don't know for sure. I won't ask if she's been wondering about me. Something tells me that she's not. Young people are pretty self-serving.

4/29

Another weekend without plans: I should be using my two days off for note-taking, but lately I haven't been focusing well. Trying to get into the heads of the last day in the lives of a couple, an elderly couple who die in each other's arms as flames consumes them. They are in failing health and don't want to see the play through its final act…in a nursing home.

Note to self: hot flashes getting worse; welcome to menopause!

5/2

I stopped by Tae's house to drop off the backpack I bought her. It's purple: Tae's favorite color. She seemed pleased to discover that inside it were a couple of new pens and a blank book, a few rolls of Butterscotch Lifesavers (her favorite kind), and a Detroit Tigers baseball cap. Quintana was asleep, even though it was well after 4:00 o'clock p.m. Did this mean I couldn't take her out for dinner at Subway? Tae fidgeted in her usual way, hopping on one foot, then the other. One of her older sisters (I don't know if it was Tyleena or Tasha), sauntered in from the kitchen and suggested that Tae check with Quintana. Tae hadn't wanted to disturb her, but her sister—I think it was Tyleena—had replied: "That crazy woman shouldn't be sleeping now, anyway!" A few minutes later Tae emerged from the darkened bedroom. She had an entire hour before she had to be back to do chores.

Over veggie subs (she was trying to be a vegetarian), she talked about how her early childhood was, at times, a magical one. She'd lived with her mom and sisters on a small farm owned by her grandparents. It wasn't really a farm, but an old farmhouse on a couple of acres. Her Aunt Serafina had lived there, too, for a while. Serafina used to sing romantic songs while her grandfather accompanied her. Her granny would sit at the piano, and soon they'd all be toe-tapping or even dancing to an upbeat melody. But when the others sang and played instruments, Quintana just sat there looking sad. Sometimes, actually quite often, Tae had wished that Serafina had been her mother.

It's wrong to think that mentoring Tae will decrease my own restlessness, my fear that I am observing life instead of living it. I guess I could quit this job and live off my inheritance, but then I'd be lonely. Sure, I could spend the time writing, but I'd always be afraid of writer's block. Then what would I do? What I refuse to do is reflect on my brief career as an author; or my six partnerships; or my parents' deaths. Still, most of it (except for the way I lost both parents) has been better than much of Tae's short life. I wish I could do more for her.

5/4

The night turned strange when Toby (the boy from downstairs) knocked on my door. He's in second grade, but reading at seventh grade level, according to his teacher. In nice weather, we sit together on a park bench next to the building after I get home from school. There is something not quite right about inviting him inside my apartment, yet it bothers me that I can't just invite him in for a milk and cookies. Whenever his mother sees me talking to him, she always calls him home and apologizes for him 'bugging' me. He's been pretty much the only friendly person in the building, except for the tiny, yet mighty, as well as mightily old, Mrs. Innis. Both Mrs. Innis and Toby know everyone in the building.

I'd just finished eating when Toby rapped. He's been dying to see inside, as he always strains his neck to see past me into the living room. I've been fighting the urge to let him check it out; Mrs. Innis has cautioned me against doing so.

"Barnett, are you busy? I got to talk to you!" (He's called me by my last name ever since I'd given him that toy car I found on the deck several months ago. He thinks Barnett is my first name.) We perched together on a park bench and he told me that his fish, Blinky, died the night before. He'd found him floating on the water surface of his fish tank. "Its eyes were all bulged out!"

Toby's large, dark eyes reminded me of Ricky's, the way they hungrily took in the world, though Ricky had been six years older when he'd lived with me. Also, Ricky hardly ever spoke and was much more frightened than intrigued by the world around him.

After Toby returned home to eat dinner, I paced my silent rooms and hadn't known what to do next. He'd messed up my weeknight routine (world news followed by a bath, journal writing, and then reading as long as possible before succumbing to a stupid TV sit com), and then I was at a loss. Turned up a Miles Davis CD, "Bitches Brew," and felt like escaping the routine rather than settling into it. Then it hit me: I'd get dressed up. So first, I applied make-up, coiled my long gray-blond hair, and pinned it to the back of my head. Next, donned a dress only worn once to a friend's daughter's wedding and inspected myself in the full-length mirror. Not bad… Long, but not too long; pale blue scalloped hem with a somewhat fitted bodice. I'd put on about ten pounds, maybe fifteen, during the winter, and so far had had little luck shedding them, as well as another ten pounds from the previous winter. My once smallish waist, now gone, and upper arms, while not exactly fat, are definitely plump. Only my long legs and oval face somewhat redeemed the bulky middle-aged body, which, in better moods, I affectionately see as curvy.

Next, I sip a glass of cheap white California wine (rarely have one following dinner on week days). My phone begins to sing Peggy Lee's "Is That All There Is?" and my heart pounds. Why? It turns out to be Tae. But Tae is whispering. Is something the matter? Tae doesn't want to wake her mother, who had finally passed out on the couch after screaming at everyone and everything.

"You know how she gets, Maggie."

I love that Tae now calls me by name.

She wonders what I've been doing, so I tell her about my evening. I can hear Quintana's voice barking at her in the background. Tae promises to stop by and visit at school the next day.

"Sleep well, Tae," I tell her.

5/5

Today, a teary-eyed Tae: LeAndra is moving next week. Both say they're beside themselves and can't stop blubbering. You rarely see one without the other. Did I mention LeAndra will be living in Detroit with her mother? Reminds me of how bad I felt when Jocelyn first moved away. Just like Jocelyn and me, these two also have a hard time making new friends, even though Tae has many acquaintances. I tried to cheer her up, telling her how Detroit is just an hour away.

Like me, Jocelyn has never had children. Something else in common: she lost her father tragically in a car accident. Jocelyn didn't believe she'd live beyond age forty or ever get married. She was wrong on both counts. At forty, she married a plastic surgeon. Never have I heard her complain about him, but she's always been a little too insistent about her happiness. Her life since her wedding has seemed close to wrinkle-free; at times, I've envied her so much, I didn't think I'd be able to continue our friendship. But then I convinced myself that, despite my many issues, I'd never want to lead such a sheltered existence. Must have been after getting married that she switched from writing poetry to writing New Age books on positive thinking and meditation. As a teen, it was she who'd been the one who got into trouble for possessing drugs and running away from home. My life was always tame by comparison, though I didn't always get along with my parents. Jocelyn has a psychic ability like no other (besides Sulie) and it impressed the fuck out of me when, as a teen, she told me about her experiences of 'knowing things.' She said when I became middle-aged, I'd do something unpredictable and whacky—that I'd have a breakdown... Has she proven to be right? We've always exchanged birthday cards, and Christmas cards with notes in them. Each of the handful of times we've gotten together over the years, it always felt like her life was improving, while mine seemed to plummet from one downward spiral to the next. Maybe it wasn't just envy, but out-and-out jealousy which has prevented me from being better at staying in touch. She's always been amused by my many live-in boy-friends. ("Maggie, you just change partners and keep on dancing!")

5/7

After hearing from Tae two nights in a row, I expected her to call me on the third. She didn't. What's wrong with me? Why does so much depend on an almost fifteen-year-old? I need to get more hobbies, get out more. I found a pack of gum in my purse that I didn't pay for. It must have slipped it into my purse the last time I went to the store. Hopefully, that old bad habit hasn't returned. I know I have it in my power to keep it at bay. Haven't been sleeping well. Hot flashes are worse. Thoughts about my couple for the book keep getting interrupted by thoughts about Tae. Maybe I'm meant to be a mentor, not a writer at this time in my life. Maybe I should throw a Death to the Writer's Ego party. If only I knew others like me.

5/8

Got a call from Quintana. From now on I'm just going to call her Q. The pitch of their voices are so much alike, but the way that they talk is completely different—right down to the words they use. She explained how Tae had been, "kinda low lately." Her other daughters have all been "nasty little bitches," and she, Q, was "tired of all her girls. Tired half to death..."

After ranting for a long time, she told me the point of her call wasn't to "piss and moan," but to make a request. Since I seemed to care so much about Tae, could I "maybe stop by and pick her up, take her wherever the hell you want, for as long as you want." Never has she known such a moody one. "Doesn't help—her being so deep and all..." The way Q saw it, I was adding to Tae's complexity. "Before you came on the scene, Tae wasn't nearly so hard to figure out."

I'm planning to pick up Tae tomorrow morning since there's no school due to parent-teacher conferences. Wish I could pick her up and we could go on a drive somewhere—somewhere far from here.

LeAndra has been gone a week now. Tae has not been as upset as I thought she'd be. I asked why LeAndra hadn't stopped by the library to say goodbye, and Tae said: "Really, Maggie? Don't you know how jealous she was of you because she didn't have a special someone in her life the way I have you?" I'd only clued into my own jealousy after realizing I was getting in bad moods from watching them whisper and giggle. Why would a woman of my age feel this way? I'm a mess. A 'hot mess', as the kids often say.

5/10

This weekend I'm taking Tae to dinner at The Pink Flamingo—a truly elegant restaurant (not many left in the area)… She's excited, but nervous because she's never been to, as she termed it, a "fancy restaurant." She texted me: *Wht if i cn't fnsh all my fd?* And another: *Wht if i knck my plte on flr n spl yr wine?* Evidently, she doesn't mind destroying the language to get her point across in text-talk…

Other places I'd like to take her: The Bower Theater; The Whiting; The Flint Institute of Arts; The Sloan Museum; The Longway Planetarium…She's never seen a movie in 3D either… Not that we have to only go to the Flint area museums, but they're close, so why not? Told her we'll go to a few places every month. She squealed with delight. Since Q's pretty much given me carte blanche, I'll bring her to my apartment as well. Even though my furnishings are fairly basic, my place is nicer than what she's used to; I think she'll especially enjoy the quiet and my roll-top desk.

Another text from her: *At last—i get 2 c the wrld!*

5/12

I heard from Caroline today. I hadn't spoken to my only sibling in a couple of months. She's a successful artist and the owner of an art gallery, married to Lane, an equally successful attorney. Recently retired, he now mostly does pro bono work. They have two successful children: Byron on the East coast, and Gwen on the West. I haven't spoken to either Byron or Gwen since they were kids. They rarely get together as a family and this doesn't seem to bother any of them. Raising kids to their level of independence strikes me as either a sign of successful parenting, or cold-fish parenting. But what do I know?

Her latest art show turned out to be a big success. She held it at a friend's gallery, not her own. Caroline's a multi-media artist, known for her collages of connecting the centuries: Marilyn Monroe juxtaposed with Cleopatra... Also, unlikely pairings of buildings: barns next to sky scrapers. After inviting me to Detroit to see the show, she gave me equal time by asking me how my writing was coming along. She's always chided me for my lack of ambition to publish since publishing my first book. I know she means well, but it's always been irritating beyond words.

The real reason for the call finally came out: Fran, a math teacher and old friend of Caroline's, told her how she'd heard of my spending a great deal of time with a girl from school. Caroline said several staff members had been talking, wondering about the relationship. Can't get over that even in my fifties, my big sister scolds and interferes. I simply tell her how much Tae has enriched my life.

"No one is saying you're doing anything wrong, Sis. Just watch your back. You know how bad the job market is these days, especially in your area."

I hate how she calls me Sis. It has always irked me. Still, since my parents' deaths, the bond has tightened. Maybe someday soon I'll take Tae on a trip to Detroit and introduce them.

5/13

I just returned from Tae's fifteenth birthday party. She's a year older than most students about to complete the eighth grade because she was held back the year she should've started kindergarten. Big mistake since she's so bright...Guess it had been a hard year for Q (which year hadn't been?) and they'd moved to Tae's grandparents' home, located, according to Tae, in the country.

I gave her a silver pen and a pretty rainbow colored scarf—just this side of garish, but she seemed happy with my choice. She made her own cake: chocolate with butter cream frosting. At first she was grumpy because she'd frosted it before it had completely cooled and the frosting tore off clumps of the cake. Q and I both assured her of its tastiness. Thankfully, Q didn't get drunk… Sweet of them to invite me, and a good time would've been had by all, had Tasha not made a scene by bursting into the room wearing a short skirt with a shiny, tight blue shirt, her seventeen-year-old breasts, two cantaloupes, ripe on the vine of her slender torso—ripe to the point of bursting from the shirt. She demanded to know why she hadn't been invited to the party, and why she hadn't had a party on her birthday. Instead of waiting for an answer, she burst into a laughing fit and couldn't sit down because, any minute, her 'new guy' would be there. "I'm the only one getting a date around here!"

No one else spoke while Tasha ranted and paced. Was it because they were accustomed to it? I began to feel uncomfortable. Tae sensed as much, burst into tears and escaped to her room. No one noticed me slip out of the living room and make my way upstairs to her room. I sat on the edge of her bed, waiting for her heavy sobs to subside. When they finally did, I told her it had been a fine party and got her mind off it by telling her about our next outing. In a few days we'll be going to Detroit, maybe to a museum, and to meet my sister. Q readily agreed. Tae smiled through her tears…something she does quite often.

It's just after 2:00 o'clock a.m. If I'd come back home, I wouldn't have been able to sleep, so I went to Pete's Place (a couple of blocks from my apartment in the township, not on the north side near the school) and downed a Gin and Tonic. I wondered how Tae could ever possibly turn into a successful author given the climate of her home. Next to me at the bar was the psychic and private investigator, Sulie Rowen. She wore her characteristic black beret, thin, salt-and-pepper braid (more salt than pepper), trench coat, and had a toothpick dangling from her lips.

"How's your young friend?" she asked me, now, a year since I'd seen her last.

"Did I tell you before about Tae?"

"No, but she's on the tall side, right? Light skinned black girl, right? Laughs to mask the pain, right? Emotional, not physical…"

I nodded. Surely, she'd seen us together, as lately we'd been to many local places.

"You're in deep. Take care. You won't be here in a few months."

"You mean I'll be…I'll be…dead?" I asked, about to fall off the stool.

"No, it's not that. You'll be with her…somewhere else. Did I tell you that I'm moving soon?" A typical remark from Sulie. I shook my head. While I can't say for sure, I don't think I'll miss her. Next, I asked if she could tell me more about my life—either my past or my future.

"Then I'd have to charge!" she exclaimed, laughing hysterically. She bought me two drinks then vanished into the night. While I'm not one to believe in psychics, she'd given me irrefutable evidence. She just knows things. Doubtless, I'll see her again; somehow I know I will.

5/14

Rudely awakened at 8:00 o'clock a.m. by someone knocking on the door. Who could it be so early on a Sunday? I flew to the door without even tying the sash of my bathrobe. There stood Toby, tears running down his cheeks.

"Oh, Barnett, I had a *marenight*! (For some reason he always says nightmare backwards.) "Your apartment was empty and you'd left without saying goodbye."

I tried to console him before sending him back upstairs.

———————

Rainy, dreary looking day… I brought Tae back to the apartment for tea. She had a toothache and wasn't in the best of moods, but there was something she wanted to discuss.

"Have you ever had writer's block?" She swiveled on my office chair.

"All writers do. How long has yours been going on?"

"Two days, and it's been simply dreadful!" she said, dramatically dropping her heavy head in her hands.

Two days are a mere blip in the life of a writer, I told her. I gave her a few suggestions for banishing it: reading poetry, getting in the bathtub fully clothed, smelling flowers. She laughed then began reading the titles on the spines of the books on my shelf: *The Robber Bride, Dubliners, A Room of One's Own...* She took down those that intrigued her and flipped through them.

"How do you write, read, and work a gazillion hours a week at school? Where do you find time for it all?"

"I don't; well, maybe in dribs and drabs, I guess."

She laughed and said I talk funny. She wanted to know if she could come back soon—on a sunnier day—and then we could sit on the deck together and read. Just what I was about to suggest!

5/20

I'm low as a ground slug. I haven't seen Tae outside of school since her birthday. Haven't written in several weeks—not counting journal entries... Just frog-marching through the days... I don't recall putting two pairs of socks in my purse until I got home and saw them there when I was hunting for my brush. Different choices must be made. She visited for a few minutes in the media center. She acted silly, goofy. I asked if something was wrong. She played dumb, but couldn't stand still or meet my eyes. Could she have been high? I wanted to ask, but didn't...

No periods in three months now, and I'm wondering if I'm officially post-menopausal? If so, will these fucking hot flashes continue?

5/21

Tae admitted over our steaming mugs (hot chocolate for her, coffee for me) at Fresh Brew that she'd gotten high the other day. Her braids hid most of her face as she confessed that she'd taken a joint to school and smoked part of it on the playground with her sister, Tasha, during lunch recess. When she visited me yesterday, she must have been high.

"I only took a couple of hits."

"So you had hopes of becoming a writer?" I asked, as I slowly sipped my double espresso.

"Maggie, you've said yourself that artists are free spirits. I was just letting mine out of her cage."

"There are other ways to do it. You definitely have more growing up to do—I hope you're aware of that."

"You sound so white! White and NOT right! Maybe I don't want to hang out with someone as white as you."

What could I say? We drove to her house in total silence. She thanked me for the hot chocolate in a voice much quieter than usual. I want to punish her—teach her a lesson—but who do I think I am?

I don't know why Tae smoking a joint bothers me. I'd smoked my first one by the time I was her age. Maybe I was a little older—closer to sixteen. I never smoked pot regularly, though at times I considered it one of the reasons for losing my ambition, that along with drinking and relationships with men, though it was the men—all except Vince the Fourth—who slowed me down the most.

––––––––––

Tossing and turning, listening to the ringing in my ears, pacing—just to do something, anything in the middle of the night when warm milk doesn't work, nor do the lullabies I sing to myself. Sometimes I lie in bed and recall all the crap I've absconded with from stores over the years (haven't taken so much as a crumb in a long time). Other times, when I go to the toilet, I still check to see if there's blood in the crotch of my panties, though I'm fairly certain there won't be any. Part of me is sad about this now…

5/22

Today I took Tae to Barnes & Noble and bought her a collection of Edgar Allen Poe's stories and poems. We sat in the café and discussed the dangers of social media. We're both pleased neither of us has any interest in wasting time on Facebook or Twitter. She said she doesn't know many people on Facebook, and that Twitter seemed trite.

At her request I told her about my novel. "Pauline is a flight attendant who is kidnapped by one of her passengers shortly after their plane lands. On a cross country trip with her kidnapper, Ray, she wakes every morning blindfolded. Ray had been in Desert Storm in Iraq and ranted about the desert heat and how he wanted to return to the Middle-East to kill Arabs. He believes he is in love with Pauline, but she eventually regains her freedom, and exacts her revenge."

I didn't tell Tae how that happens, hoping that one day she'll want to read it. I also told her how *Pauline's Revenge* had sold a half million copies, though it's now out of print and hard to find. Also, I told her a little about my book tour and about the magazine interviews. I admitted to her that I'd been sure that the door which had opened for me would remain open, and how shocked I'd been when it slammed shut.

Lately, Tae has been hearing from Uncle Tyler. Not exactly her uncle, but he was a close friend of Aunt Serafina. Ever since she can remember, she's been receiving presents from him on birthdays and at Christmastime. Dream catchers he's made from feathers; or bead necklaces; or bead rings… Her sisters have always been jealous. This past Christmas he sent her a photo of himself; a thin, white man with deep-set brown eyes. In the accompanying note, he apologized for being White, and said that he wouldn't blame her if she wanted to stop their correspondence. Tae didn't know why he was making such a fuss about race—it didn't matter to her in the least— but Quintana acted like she knew more about him than she was willing to reveal.

6/1

Yesterday, Tae and I ventured to Detroit. It was Memorial Day, sunny and hot, though the car's AC worked so well that it made our teeth chatter. We both wore our hair coiled and pinned to the back of our heads. Can't get over how fast the drive went! Tae told me how when she can't sleep at night, she makes up stories about Sinbad, the crime fighting dog… Her list of what she wants to write about is now an entire page. How long is my list, she wants to know? Without waiting for an answer and switching the topic, she tells me how she's only once been to Detroit, a long time ago: a picnic on Belle Isle with her mom, Aunt Serafina, and her sisters. It was a pretty good time, but her mom and auntie had argued a lot.

I tried preparing her for Caroline's magnetic, though word-blasting and snide personality. Tae asked if she'd been word-blasting me on the drive; if so, she sure didn't mean to. I laughed, but realized there was no way to prepare her for the experience of meeting my sister.

Tae couldn't get over the Grosse Pointe mansions. Before arriving at Carolyn's house, I drove her through some of the ritzy neighborhoods. Caroline's house, nestled on a street of smaller homes, is modest by comparison. We found her sitting on the kitchen floor taping boxes. She rose briefly to meet Tae, but then went right back to the taping. Caroline's words sped from her mouth like race horses from the gate. Tae and I exchanged knowing smiles. While it was hard to believe that Caroline, of all people, hadn't hired a company to pack for her, it was nearly impossible to believe that her Grosse Pointe world was about to become a thing of the past. She'd sold her gallery and now she and her husband, Lane, were about to become, in her words, "happy hoboes." They plan to travel in the South and Southwest during the winters, and then head back North to their house on Black Lake, just down the road from the location of our parents' former cabin. For a change, I admired her, and envied her more than a little. Then it hit me: we hadn't been to the area since mom and dad died. How could she even think about living there? There's much about her I've never quite understood.

After Caroline changed from her sweaty clothes and into a black slim-fitting dress (her petite figure only marginally different from when she was young), she drove us in her brand new SUV to an upscale Japanese restaurant called The Plum Tree. Tae was clearly impressed, and I felt a little left out as Tae hung on her every word. How my sister loves an audience!

Tae tried sushi for the first time and declared it to be "amazing." She kept calling everything amazing and I bit my tongue to keep from shouting synonyms at her. At least Caroline thought to ask Tae about herself.

Afterward we ambled down a couple of blocks to a gallery on

2nd Avenue, where Caroline's latest artwork was on display. Over a year had passed since I'd last seen her collage series, "The Imprisoned." She'd recently added another series, "Guilty Bystanders," in which individuals are depicted observing crimes as they are being committed. Tae lingered over these the longest and told Caroline they were so powerful that they disorientated her. Caroline thanked her, but I corrected her: "You mean disoriented, right?" Tae nodded admission, but turned away from me and further punished me by giving Caroline her full attention.

Afterward, Caroline chauffeured us through Greek Town and then down Jefferson Avenue. Tae claimed to never having seen buildings as large as the towers at the Renaissance Center. I felt sluggish as we milled through the festival crowd at Hart Plaza and by the Detroit River. Glasses of freshly squeezed lemonade refreshed us. I grinned when Tae spilled hers, and Tae shot me one of her if-looks-could-kill expressions. It made me apologize over and over again. Tae seemed more irritated than ever. Only Caroline seemed unselfconscious in public and equally unaware of the tension that passed between Tae and me.

Caroline snapped several photos of the Ambassador Bridge. Hard to believe it was the same one which had beckoned to me a few years ago... Tae asked why I was staring at it for so long. Caroline knew, but—thankfully—said nothing. (She is, by far, the longest-running bystander in my life. A guilty one?)

Before heading back to Flint, Caroline pulled me aside and hissed at me to be careful about my friendship with Tae—not to let it get 'out of hand,' adding in the next breath, that she could certainly see why I had befriended her.

Tae raved about our time in Detroit almost all the way home. And Caroline had reminded her of her almost-fabulous Aunt Serafina—not just once, but three times: "You know, Maggie, she's larger-than-life, glamorous and chosen to shine. That's how I want to be."

My father was just like Serafina and Caroline, forever imprisoned by his imposing presence.

6/2

Leroy Hardin, a GQ kind of guy who thinks he's more suave than he is, called me into his office for the second time this month to ask me what I thought about my job performance of late. It had to be a trick question, so I wracked my brain: I'd been finishing all required tasks, hadn't missed more than a couple days the entire school year, and got along with most staff and students. Still, I knew he'd been watching me and was displeased with my 'over-attention' to Tae, and my lack of interaction with other students and staff. I sat there mutely as he exclaimed that I needed to reach out, not only to the teachers, but to the entire student body, including parents, and in fact, I should be the go-to person for the entire community.

He further insisted: "You're far too involved with Taezha Riverton. I'd go so far as to say that you're in over your head."

But isn't being intimately involved with others what life should be about? I wanted to scream at him, but didn't. I wanted to quit then and there. Of course, I didn't. Instead, I had this epiphany: I can't return in the fall.

Later, the same evening

Texted Tae an hour ago, but she hasn't responded. No one else matters. I can't believe it's been five years since I had sex. I wonder if I ever will again.

What else do I have besides my job? I'm working on a novel—that's something! A thinly disguised story about my parents: two judges with sharp legal minds but whose judgments about others make them difficult people. A book that's hard to write but feels like it needs to be written. Why? To better understand them and why they decided to leave this world together, selfishly choosing suicide and leaving behind two daughters to come to terms with their act of abdication. But who am I to judge my parents? Who am I to judge anybody?

I could join a yoga or class, or hang out in bookstores more often… I channel surf then click the power off button on the remote. I tiptoe because I don't like to make noise. Except for Toby or Tae, I don't want anyone else to know I'm here.

I furl myself in one of the sheer floor-length living room drapes, then unfurl; am now a bride of silence and slow time. There's no reception, save for the whirling dance of dust motes. I must do something to change my life.

6/3

Despite all my pre-writing rituals, there are few results. Listing the rituals will help me see if I'm missing one, or if one should be added: As soon as I get home from work, I take off shoes, bra, and make-up, then pull the drapes, and play a jazz CD. Following a quick supper, I have a cup of tea and then write for 1 or 2 hours. If the lighting isn't exactly right (not too dim or too bright) I adjust it, as well as music volume (which is always very quiet).

If the subroutines of my routines aren't working for me, I'm careful to amend them: No dessert after one of my Lean Cuisines. I can wear yoga pants but no pajamas, otherwise I won't take my work seriously enough. I must be careful not to re-read the draft about my parents. To work on my book, even if it's a few lines or a paragraph.

It doesn't take long for me to change focus to the miscarriage from Eric the Fifth, the stuntman, or his tragic death from a motorcycle accident (not even stunt related). Miscarried at seven weeks, so at least I wasn't as far along as the time I'd been in my seventh month. That one I'd named: Joel. Sometimes I still dream about him. The umbilical cord got wrapped around his neck. Joel's father, Jason the Second, was incredibly smart, a polyglot (he spoke five languages fluently). After the miscarriage, we resented each other and within a couple months had split-up. Like other relationships, this one didn't make it to year three.

I don't dwell—refuse to dwell—on the men I've lived with. If anyone succeeds at haunting me, it's my parents at odd times, and the three children I almost had (two miscarriages and an abortion when I was six weeks along from Kirk the First). Sometimes, when I can't write, I come up with names for them. Then I think about my time on the bridge and on the ledge. After standing on the ledge for a couple of hours, I gently persuaded myself back inside. But I jumped from the bridge. No one witnessed my near suicide. The guy who pulled me onto his boat hadn't seen me; I told him I was just out for a swim, as I'd almost reached the Detroit-side of the river. Was I a guilty bystander to my own near death? Would I find my portrait one day included in Caroline's "Guilty Bystander" series?

6/4

Tae's problems are many: Q's revolving door-men; a couple of sisters on the wrong road; a faraway best friend; the constant din of TV and rap music; mostly empty kitchen cabinets; cats multiplying and their many unclean litter boxes. Despite obstacles, Tae tells me she worries about me—how tired I seem lately. She says I have this "zombie thing going" at school. I want to tell her how I've curbed my kleptomania, but she doesn't know about it (nor will I ever tell her). Trying to cheer me up, she tells me about the latest letter from her pen pal, Uncle Tyler, and how he's been asking about me lately…

Before Tae falls asleep, she tries to picture as many people as she can, beginning with the ones she knows, then others she's only seen in passing, and finally total strangers. She sees them one at a time, then in groups and crowds. "How is it possible for the mind to picture faces that it's never seen? Do you do that? Does everyone?"

"Insomniacs probably do this more than others, though I've never taken a poll."

She tells me that when she can't sleep, it's usually because she wants to write, but there are things she must do first: wash her hands, and then bring out the food she's hidden under her bed in a shoebox (usually a cookie or a roll but sometimes a piece of fruit I'd given her at lunchtime). Next, she eats it. If she's still not quite ready to write, the following occurs: her arms and shoulders begin to itch; she can't stop swallowing; and then she'll wash her hands again. Then and only then will she retrieve her notebook, pen, flashlight. Lately, she's been writing stories about Sinbad. Together they stop crime in the city before it happens. Together, they have magical powers. She says they're stupid, childish stories, but she simply *must* write them.

When she writes at other times of day, her habits are different. First, she'll take a long shower. She says this drives her sisters crazy since there is only one bathroom. Afterward, she'll don a hat that used to belong to her father—a black derby. Then and only then is she able to write. Also, she can only write with a black pen—never a blue one, or for that matter, any other color.

6/5

Tae was agitated today. Not her usual self. After talking to me for a couple of minutes she excused herself, saying she had to give a book to a kid from class. Normally, she has about ten or fifteen minutes to visit. I couldn't believe how mopey I felt the rest of the day.

I received a text from Tae: *Mom's frnd 2 happy 2 c me.* Then another one: *Maggie HELP! He's creepy!!* I wrote her back, asking if she was in danger. Didn't get a response.

6/6

I didn't get any sleep. I'm angry with Tae. She irritated the hell out of me after apologizing for sending last night's text. She said she was "just being dramatic…you know how I sometimes get, Maggie."

"Is it true, Tae? What happened? In what way was this friend of your mom's too happy to see you? Why was he creepy?"

"I just don't like him. I told you before how he's always grabbing me—rubbing up on me, pinching me. More of the same last night—I guess he was high, too—and the whole thing grossed me out. Don't say anything to my mom, okay?"

I didn't want her to think she couldn't trust me. No point telling her how I paced half the night, almost drove to her house, and was afraid of bursting in on who knew what. Should I confront Q or report this to Protective Services, or is it time for me to back away? If she'd been raped, of course I'd take action!

Some would say that my obsession with Tae is getting out of control. I should take classes. Maybe Tai Chi, meditation, or art history. The community college always offers one in music appreciation. I once had these interests, as well as others. I once had a life. Didn't I?

I can just hear my parents (my judges) remarking: "What's happened to you, Maggie? What's become of your life?" Well, Mom and Dad, it's in shambles. Your tragic deaths didn't help, you know. The fact that you swallowed all those pills, then wrapped your arms around each other in a final embrace. Sometimes I think it would be all too easy to swallow pills, but I can't let you become my trailblazers.

My parents were intelligent, serious, and sometimes somber. As a couple, their gravitas had gravity; they didn't know how to be spontaneous, or how to have fun. Every vacation we took was over-planned and regimented. Since Caroline was so much older, I only recall a couple of family trips with her along. Whenever we went anywhere, my parents were always glancing at their watches. One as bad as the other... Heavy silence during seemingly endless car rides and me longing to be back home.

Although I was an anxious child, I knew the depths of great joy. Sometimes, for no reason, I'd break into fits of giggles. My parents worried something was wrong with me and always asked me what had brought it on. I'd always shrug. There was a moment when I decided no matter how drab the clothes they bought me, or how bland the food, or how serious the dinner-table talk, my free-spirited glee was something they could never take away.

(I should note that Caroline recalls them differently. 'Her' parents were serious only because they'd been in law school when she was a girl. She recalls some of their (almost) wild Saturday evening parties with their friends. Dad would crack jokes and Mother would laugh in a loud, girlish way.)

6/7

Slept a little better, but still worried about Tae. We haven't texted each other since yesterday afternoon. Second time this has happened: put car in parking gear in school lot, turn off engine, and then just sit there feeling as dumb as a cow. First, I'm five minutes early, then five minutes late, and before-I-know-it, fifteen minutes late. Stupidly, I can't get out of the car, go into the school; no way can I force smiles and immerse myself in that world of bells and clocks. Schools as factories in the twenty-first century make little sense to me. Nor does my entire life, for that matter, and now, in the parking lot, I succumb to institutional depression. Self-diagnosis is that I have a particularly bad case; only an injection of truly inspired creativity will be my chance to heal, and sadly, the AMA hasn't come up with the antidote. I could just give my two-week notice and quit.

Tae called me after school wondering what had happened to me. I don't want to transmit my anti-school virus to her, so I told her it was a twenty-four hour bug. "I thought I saw your car in the school parking lot," she said. It's true, you did. Also true that I turned around and headed home. And yes, Tae, thanks for asking. I'm feeling a little better now after talking to you. How grateful I was that you didn't say anything more about Jayvon—I sure wasn't going to ask.

To be able to truly connect with someone, I always thought you needed to tell them everything, or almost everything, about your past and present, as well as your fears, hopes, day dreams and night dreams, nightmares. Yet, if this were true, I wouldn't feel close to Tae, as there's much she doesn't know. I long to tell her every thought I've ever had, as well as everything I've ever done. Maybe someday I will, maybe when she's in her twenties… But how will I possibly be able to wait until then, when the urge right now is so strong? Maybe just by knowing there's much that she isn't ready to hear. How will I be able to remain in her life?

Someday, though, I will tell her about all the men I've lived with. Six different men from age twenty-two until I was forty-six. I'll have to admit that I'm still uncertain why I lived with so many men but married none of them. I guess I've never truly been in love.

Ten years ago I had a job teaching creative writing in a women's prison. Writing, especially the writing of poetry, helped inmates deal with their isolation, as well as their guilty consciences. I worked there for a couple years until one of the inmates, Heidi Atterwall, hung herself in her prison cell. One of the guards found her body. No suicide note, though she left a poem about why she wanted to die. Heidi was the closest I came to having a friend among the inmates. My name was mentioned in the poem, and also words to the effect that I'd given her "the key to her release." The warden asked me what she had meant. I didn't have a clue. A few weeks later I accepted a job as assistant to the director of the media center at Jefferson School. I still dream about Heidi.

Those born beautiful are often objectified, worshipped, preyed upon—not only by sexual predators, but by everyday folks. Net result is that these larger-than-life personalities end up paying for the way they were born. It seems like only the plain and mentally average are left alone—enjoy the freedom of being unseen, undercover. Maybe criminal acts are planned and carried out by those who unknowingly run the world.

Caroline looked much like Tae as a girl, except for the difference in their skin tones. Each has large and wide-set eyes, perfectly arched brows; each is leggy without being too lanky—especially after passing the coltish stage of a pre-teen. By age fourteen, both of them, born lovely, had become stunningly gorgeous. Though neither do anything to seek attention, each simply receives it.

6/8

Tae's been writing Tyler about her life, even the problems with Jayvon. I'm not so sure relying on a man to end this crisis is the right way to go. He wrote her back requesting that she not share his letters with Q. Seems his friendship with Serafina hadn't been exactly condoned by Q, her younger sister. Tae's been so upset that she hasn't been working on a story this week. Still taking long baths, but she now locks the bathroom door.

———————

I dreamed I woke up and had no breasts… Another dream in which my mother is taking Caroline and me on a vacation. Some tropical island and Dad is not coming with us. I ask my mother why not and she just smiles mysteriously. After waking, I discovered my period had started. Strange, after all these months of not having one…

6/9

Q met me at school after students had gone home. I drove us downtown to The Lunch Studio on Saginaw Street. At first she seemed to enjoy being away from her neighborhood and remarked how nice it was to be around students, how she missed being one and who knew if she'd ever be one again? No sooner had we sat down than she wagged an index finger: "Okay, girlfriend, we don't normally do this, so what's on your mind?" Out spilled what I'd heard from Tae. Not that much to tell, but the fact alone that he was feeling her daughter up was something she should know about. Q said, seemingly dumfounded, "She's lying. That girl's just got to have the spotlight!" I tried to disagree but there's no crossing Q. "Jayvon isn't a bad man, Maggie. This time I chose right. I know I did. I'll tell him what to do with those hands of his!" Did I just make things better or worse? I don't care. I had to say something.

6/10

I honestly don't know if I've ever felt this angry. Tae showed up at school with a black eye. She told me Tasha and she were wrestling. She won't rat her mom out, but I know Q hit her after our talk over coffee. I knew it wasn't exactly a beating. Still, Tae knew I felt that what had occurred wasn't right, and she couldn't look me in the eye. I don't think she's angry with me for letting Q know that I know about how Jayvon has been coming on to her. She said something about how she needs to get away from here and hopes she can stay with Uncle Tyler or LeAndra—or both—during the summer.

Today, after work, Toby begged me to take him in—to raise him as my own son. I don't know much about his mother, except that she's not home much. I wish there was more I could do for him.

I heard that there has been a rise in violence at school and in the community. Could be the summer-like weather—emotions rising along with temperatures; no doubt the economy is contributing, too… We had a lockdown at school yesterday and today… Yesterday's was easier because I was alone in the media center. But today, Tae was with me and it lasted almost two hours. We had to lock the doors, turn off lights, and stay as still as possible. We weren't supposed to talk, but since we were in my office, we could whisper. Impossible for us to be together and silent for long!

She told me about a friend of Tasha's who was brutally raped last week (more about that later). How she'd been hearing gunshots for the last couple of weeks, adding how it's nothing new on her street. Then she said the lockdowns don't make her nervous, but being at home does. "Shoot, Maggie, how am I ever supposed to get any writing done?" She's got a point. Turns out that both lockdowns were enforced because strangers—young men in their twenties—were caught walking through the halls. The guy they caught today was carrying a handgun.

6/11

Took Tae to visit Tasha's friend, Kendra, in the hospital. The girl in the hospital bed appeared nothing like the one I recalled seeing only a month earlier. Her face was bruised and swollen, plus a couple of bottom teeth had been knocked out. We gave her a stuffed animal—a kitten—the sort which looks quite real, and also a feel-better-soon card. Kendra, in response, winced and gazed beyond us, at some place neither of us had ever been.

As we rode the elevator to the lobby, Tae remarked how she'd like to write a story about this, maybe how Sinbad, the crime-fighting dog, would "get the bastard" who did this to Kendra.

Will Tae be the next victim in a world teeming with crime? I can't let this happen to her. Not that I can save them all, but why not do my best to rescue her from this bedlam? Anyway, I can at least try. Problem is that I have no idea how to go about it.

I've been drinking too much lately—even on school nights. Not to get drunk, but just inebriated enough to pass out (usually from wine, but on the weekends, vodka & tonic). Never will I tell Tae about this. I know I'll be able to stop when the stress lets up. I've never had a problem doing so in the past... She needs to see me as a strong woman; the right person to catch her if she falls. My pretty Tae, who's lately been so sad, and who is too fucking young to be exposed to all this shit!

6/12

Tyler wrote Tae that "soon wouldn't be soon enough" for a visit: if not this summer, then maybe next. He lives in a somewhat rural area of North Carolina, away from city madness. She told me this on the phone earlier today (Saturday). Then she sounded strange, denied anything was wrong, but in the next breath said she needed a nap—that lately sleep sounded better than anything. I should have asked if Jayvon had been messing with her again. Even though she hasn't quite admitted it, I know he has—it's why she's been sounding so strange. She also has a new nervous giggle after she tells me something. Disconcerting, to say the least.

Would I see things differently if I had my own children? My higher self wants to be Tae's mentor, her anchor, yet my lower self wants her in my life for my own selfish reasons. Last week, she said Q had indicated that she wasn't her daughter in a passing comment, and had asked Tae, "Don't you ever wonder why you don't look much like me?" This, followed by several questions from Tae, but Q clammed up.

The apartment pool just opened. Maybe Tae will want to go for a swim tomorrow.

6/13

One week left of school. What if Tae and I don't get to see much of each other during the summer? Not knowing makes me anxious and depressed. I should have been thinking ahead, making plans. There's enough money in summer savings to pay the bills and keep myself in groceries without touching my inheritance. I could save that for retirement years, but why? I might wind up with health problems, so why not quit my job now and travel the country like Caroline and her husband? Still, I've never been a fan of long distance driving. But what's here for me over the next few months? Internet dating, I guess.

My ad would read something like this: Mid-life female searching for companion who likes to nap and go to bed at 9 p.m.—but couch potatoes need not apply. Or maybe this would be better: Attractive, vivacious female, early 50s (looks like early 40s) seeks bongo player poet to roam with around the world.

But then, what about Tae? Why not take her on a trip? We could fly down to North Carolina to meet Tyler. Can't just leave her to Q and the streets… Not that Q doesn't love her (as much as she can love anyone), but if Tae and I fall out of touch, Tae might become more like Q. Not that Tae would wind up a single parent without a career, but the odds seem against her. Much thinking to do on the matter.

Everything happening in triple time now... The winding up of the school year brings about changes in thinking, an alteration in plans. Anger propels me: took Tae swimming here at the apartment complex pool. Couldn't believe the stares we got, even a few scowls and sneers. Strange part was that we got dirty looks from the black residents, too. (The building, though mostly white, must be somewhere around one-quarter Black and Hispanic.) After many uncomfortable minutes, everyone returned to what they were doing and accepted the situation. Here it is the twenty-first century... If asked, each gawker would deny their fucked-up negative responses. I smiled at them all; sure as hell didn't feel like it—some smiled back, nervously, though most just looked away. She whispered in my ear about how uncomfortable she felt. I thought about leaving, but decided we should stand our ground.

Tae was so pretty in her pale blue and yellow bathing suit with matching flip-flops. She loves to swim and is good at it, thanks to lessons Q had her take for three years in a row. Tae and I could have had a good time had we been the only ones there. Tae writes more stories than poems, but here is a poem that I really like about her friend, LeAndra:

> *Never gonna be the same*
> *this life without you—*
> *my twin, my friend, my life!*
> *All the whisper laughing times*
> *Those crazy together moments:*
> *singing sighing dreaming screaming*
>
> *No one will ever know me like you do*
> *and I won't want them to*
> *There's no one like you*
> *Parting's just sad sorrow and ain't*
> *nothing sweet about it, Mr. Shakespeare*

Sure we'll text and talk when we can
but I know it'll be less and less

My eyes shaded and jaded
and so young old—so old young

Never gonna be the same this life
No one ever like you, twin,
best friend, my life…
Sing, sigh, dream, SCREAM!

6/14

Tae was overwhelmed by her first poetry reading. Larger crowd than most, held at University of Michigan-Flint. Definitely more a performance than a reading: two sisters in black leotards and lavender neon fishnets, wearing various masks. At times they sang, then whispered or shouted their words—actually, they pelted and sprayed them all over us! They voiced their verse rhythmically, near perfectly. Reminded me of Ntozake Shange's play, *For Colored Girls…* Both of us were mesmerized, though maybe since it was Tae's first reading, I think she was even more impressed. She was probably the youngest one in the audience, and me, the oldest. Afterward, we sat by a fountain and spoke of many things. I told her about my job. She cried. Then we hugged and held each other. I told her everything will turn out. But will it?

6/21

I sat next to Q at Tae's eighth grade graduation in a hot, crowded gym. She's not the only entering freshman who's already fifteen (most of the older ones had flunked one of the grades). Tae wore a simple, sleeveless royal blue dress that hit just above her knees. Q had carefully pulled Tae's hair into a ponytail of beautiful black braids that cascaded from the crown of her head. She received several academic awards, along with a special one for 'Outstanding Creative Writer' for one of her stories published in the school newsletter. Her shoelaces were untied. Q and I both worried that she was going to trip on her way up to the stage to receive her certificates. Luckily, she didn't.

Q and I were teary, and even briefly held hands. We each gave her a bouquet of colorful flowers.

Two girls who'd always wanted to become friends with Tae led her to the gym which had been transformed into a dance hall. Knowing we weren't exactly wanted or needed, Q and I went out for pizza (a bit too much after cake and punch). We talked about how lovely and poised Tae was, not in that wannabe model way, but proud (yet not too proud), and naturally beautiful… Turned out Q doesn't mind me giving Tae a small Toshiba laptop as a present. Decided to wait until I see Tae next before giving it to her; can't wait to see her expression when I do!

Q sang the blues about practically every aspect of her life—save Tae—she didn't dare complain about her. Not tonight, at any rate. Then, strangely, she asked how I was doing. I told her about my job situation, without letting her know details. I should have known that she was leading me into a trap. With tears in her large thyroid-diseased eyes, she asked if I could "possibly help out with rent this month." If I couldn't, she'd be "out on the streets in a matter of days." For Tae's sake, I agreed.

Restless pacing due to sleeplessness again. Why did I agree? What was I thinking? Caroline had warned me about this sort of thing, but how can I not protect Tae's interests? I stumbled into the bathroom, sat on the toilet, couldn't go, flushed, paced in the living room. Thought about pouring a glass of wine, but returned to bed, twisted and turned one way, and then the other, sleepless, again, soaking wet from sweat. Finally, I got up to write this.

There is nothing for me here except Tae. Job at school not worth it. Maybe now I'll keep in touch with Tae even if I no longer work there, where I'm either ignored or disliked. My reconnecting with both Kirk the First and Andrew the Sixth—brief and not meant to be. So many stores and restaurants permanently closed in this ghost city. I've just been haunting my past and my future's not meant to be lived out here. That's why my senses have shut down—or almost have—and it's only with Tae that I feel human. The simple but fundamental question: why stay?

Why not take Tae on a road trip?

Not the first time I've had this idea. We could visit Tyler or Jocelyn, be gone for only a few weeks. Less food for Q to buy—surely, that will sweeten the pot for Q. Tyler's would be the better destination, though I doubt Q would agree. We wouldn't want to disrupt Jocelyn's country club Floridian life (though part of me might enjoy doing so). But what would a trip do to my relationship with Tae? Maybe put too much of a strain on it. How many friendships are able to withstand the craziness of travel?

Even though I've lived in various cities—New York, Chicago, LA—I've never driven for long periods of time. It would take me about a week to get to North Carolina. Three hours a day sounds like plenty. Maybe we could see other places along the way.

6/23

I gave Tae the laptop yesterday. Never have I heard her squeal in such delight, though she quickly composed herself, and claimed she's still going to write rough drafts in longhand. I was worried that her sisters would be jealous, but they acted like they could not care less.

School's out at last! This year I'm more excited than most others since I won't be back in the fall (not counting the graduating seniors). If things work out at Tyler's, maybe Tae could go to school down there. I could buy a small house nearby and even homeschool her. Endless options and possibilities... I won't, of course, say anything to Tae or to Q quite yet. At last, I'm out of my middle-aged rut! Why didn't I realize before that I could leave at any time? I'm such a dope! First: how to bring up the small matter of discussing the trip with Q? My financial help should give me some leverage—she'll have a harder time turning me down. What at first was a worry has now become a ticket—two tickets—out of here! Or so I hope… Will it take much to convince Tae to go? Something tells me it won't.

Stopped by to see Q. Luckily, none of her daughters were home. (Tae spent the night at one of her new friend's house—one of the girl's from graduation; I can't recall her name.) We drank coffee together on her large screened-in back porch. It tasted much better outside than it had in her living room a few months ago. "Hot out for so early," I remarked, fanning myself. She didn't agree or disagree.

"You want to take my baby girl where?"

"On a road trip…Maybe visit my old friend, Jocelyn, or go see her uncle. Just for a few weeks."

No argument, but no blessing from her either. Hope broke from me like a pregnant woman's water. Then she told me she'd have to sleep on it, especially if we were going to wind up at Tyler's house.

6/27

Tae came over and we discussed how writers need a change of scenery now and then. I could tell that Q hadn't yet mentioned my proposal. We talked about Tyler, and I told her how I had seen a red minivan in great shape that I was thinking about buying, then switched gear: "How would you like to *not* spend the entire summer in Flint?"

"Really? You mean we could take a trip somewhere?"

I've never seen her eyes so large. I informed her that I'd asked Q but was still waiting for an answer. Hope she won't keep us waiting forever...

6/28

Tae was on the phone when I stopped by this morning. Q gave me permission to take Tae on road trip! She was about to give me stipulations when Tae entered the room… Apparently, Q had already told her, but Tae wasn't smiling. My stomach flip-flopped. Looking perplexed, she told me she'd just received an invitation to spend part of the summer at LeAndra's house in Detroit. She asked Q if she could do both. This made perfect sense to me, but Q's response:

"You're too young to be gone the whole summer! One or the other, Little Miss Popular!" Again, bubbles burst; flowers droop and wither in an instant; and worst of all, some demon has sucked all color from life in one deep inhalation. I pointed at my watch, told Tae to think about it, and made some excuse about errands I had to run, and that I'd pick her up tomorrow for our bookstore date.

6/29

I'm writing hurriedly in bookstore café. Tae's seated across from me, working on a poem. It turns out that LeAndra had to cancel the summer plan because her mother is moving them (LeAndra and her younger brother, Lamott) to California. Tae's been teary-eyed ever since she found out last night.

"How can her mom be so mean and move again so soon?"

"These days, people move where they can find work, Tae. I'm sure she wouldn't move if she didn't have to…"

So we began to discuss our plan again. The more we talked about it, the more excited we both became. Doesn't matter that I'm 'Second Hand Rose.' I remain upbeat, even though Q's now reconsidering her decision. Could be she doesn't want her baby going off with me, but I recognize her words for what they are: a woman who doesn't have much control over her own life, and is therefore always trying to control others. Mainly, Tae really wants to go. Of course, I'd never take her against her will.

I asked about one of her poems and she was most secretive. "What's it called?"

"'Poem'," she said. "It's about reading a poem that's difficult to understand. Also, it's written by Anonymous."

"No, it's not. It's written by Taezha Riverton. Someone who—if she so desires—will one day be ranked as one of the nation's foremost writers!" I told her how keeping a journal will help her writing, just as much as reading or doing other forms of writing. Before we leave I'll buy her one of those hard-covered blank books. It'll help her to believe in the importance of her own thoughts. She can take it with us on the trip.

The road trip of a mentor and her muse...

———————

Q isn't Tae's real mother. This she confided while Tae was out of ear-shot and bickering with her sisters. She added how she can't tell me about Tae's real mother just now, but will someday. Also, under no circumstances is Tae to know this; not yet, anyway. She said she'll tell her at some point—that is, if Tae doesn't find out from someone else. Tae's been through so much over the past couple of years, the time has just never been right, she told me. Her real daughters have always known without knowing, and have always teased Tae, telling her she was adopted. "I raised her mostly myself, so she might as well be another one of my brood," Q whispered. Just then, Tae entered the room. No chance for further discussion. I don't think she heard what Q said.

6/30

I bought the red minivan. Just about ready for life on the road! Sense of exhilaration almost overwhelming. What's about to happen is such a wild card.

From the Highway

goodbye hand-me-down, run-down, sick-a-downtown life
low-life… *'wuz-up?'* kinda-living ain't my kind of living
let me tell you what's up: **i am!** and i'll never look back
so stand back, Jack, out-a-my-way, Ray
cuz now i'm on the highway
maybe I'll visit on a holiday
can't take you with me and i ain't even sorry
i'm gonna live life my way—seeing places, lots a places…
ain't you just a little amused i'm a white lady's muse?

—Taezha Riverton

Chapter 3

Maggie lies on the hard motel bed listening to Tae softly snore. Whenever she closes her eyes, they spring open. A familiar panic grabs hold—one she hasn't experienced in a few years. No sooner does the snoring cease before she can hear her own pulse beating in her ears. Not her usual tinnitus. Could something be wrong with her heart? She can't lie here any longer. Will it disturb Tae if she turns on the light? Strange to have someone else in the room, but since it's Tae in the other bed, she begins to feel better.

She must have misunderstood Quintana. Surely, she had simply been pulling Maggie's chains back in Flint, just before she and Tae left town. Hadn't she, on the previous day, given Maggie, if not her blessing, then at least her permission? Okay, maybe driving off with Tae had been somewhat sneaky, even a little underhanded. Still…

She makes her way blindly to the bathroom, almost enjoying the glare and the icy cold that penetrates her feet from the motel room floor. Then she sits on the toilet for several minutes, straining to pee, knowing that she will return to bed only to have to get up a short time later to try once again.

Had her parents been alive, she wouldn't have done this. Had anyone told her she would wind up doing this at this point in her life, she would have looked them squarely in the face and called them nuts. Still, how could she have absconded with Tae? Who is *she* to think she can change someone's life? Who is *she* to intrude—to judge—to alter someone's life so radically? Even if the trip lasts only a week or so, she is little better than her self-righteous parents were when they criticized others. But it's far too late to worry about the ethics of her actions. What's done is done. All she can do now is proceed as cautiously as possible. After all, another life is in her hands.

Chapter 4

After choosing French Toast and orange juice from the breakfast menu, Tae waits as patiently as possible for Maggie to make up her mind. It's taking forever. Tae bites her tongue and plays with her braids. Tae's left eye begins to twitch. It's hard for her to sit still.

This person, whom she thought she'd known for a couple of years, now strikes her as strange. Even though they've gone places together, it's weird, definitely weird, to be on a road trip with her. This morning, walking to the restaurant from the parking lot, Maggie fired questions at her: "How did you sleep?" "How do you feel about the trip so far?" "Excited?" "A little nervous?"

Is this how white people talk to their kids while on vacation? Maggie had barely given her a chance to answer. No one ever asked her questions at home—especially not in the morning. Not that she minded really, it's just that Maggie is a little too chirpy, too wide awake, even though Tae's been up a lot longer. At least two hours longer. Maggie had said that she was mad at herself for 'sleeping in' as she called it. Still, it was only 8:00 o'clock, way earlier than Tae usually awoke during summer.

Early Risers' Diner isn't crowded. Not yet, anyway. Yesterday, when they stopped for lunch, several customers had given them looks— stares almost—just as they're doing now. Later, she'll ask Maggie about it, though she's pretty sure it's because they are of different races; plus, it's obvious that there's a big gap in age. Customers must be trying to figure out their relationship. Mother and daughter isn't likely, so they're probably wondering if they are teacher and student. Maybe they think Maggie is her parole officer, and she is hauling Tae off to 'juvie.'

"Sorry I'm taking so long. You know I usually don't." Maggie must have noticed her squirming in her seat. She tries to sit still.

"What do you think of the rooster theme in here? There's so much orange in the wallpaper. A bit 1970s, I'd say."

Tae wants to scream: "QUIT WITH THE QUESTIONS AND MAKE UP YOUR MIND!" but instead says, "Definitely 'old school,' but I wouldn't know which decade since I wasn't around then." She holds out her cup to the waitress, who is wearing too much orange lipstick.

Finally, Maggie orders. After waffling about waffles, she settles for French Toast. Tae dumps three packets of sugar into her coffee and slurps some so she can add extra cream without the cup overflowing. The waitress has so far given her ten containers of cream. Maggie says something about the apostrophe on the menu being incorrect.

"Look, Tae, it reads 'Early Riser's Diner'. As if only one person could dine here at a time!"

They laugh about this, though Tae is annoyed that Maggie was first to see the mistake.

"How far do you think we'll go today?" she asks, beating Maggie at her own game. It's chilly in the large room—too chilly. The air conditioning must be turned on full blast, probably to get customers to order more food, eat quickly then leave so that new customers can take their seats. Waitresses must make good tips here. She'd forgotten her hoodie in the red minivan. At least the coffee is beginning to take effect. Maggie looks a little thrown off by Tae's question.

"I'm not sure. Maybe somewhere around Hocking Hills—I think that's what they call that pretty area in southeastern Ohio."

"Can we try to call Uncle Tyler again before the end of the day?"

"Anytime is fine by me, sweetie."

Sweetie? The word sounds foreign. Hearing it now makes her feel like a little kid. Maggie's been acting different somehow since they began the trip. Should Tae let her know?

"Is something wrong, Tae?"

Tae shakes her head, snapping her braids in the air. She mentions the stares they've been receiving. Had Maggie noticed them, too? Maggie looks around but doesn't comment.

Breakfast finally arrives. She has never felt so hungry in her entire life, and Maggie claims to feel the same. Maybe the food will lift the mood, or if not, then at least make them drowsy. On her way back from the restroom, she catches Maggie staring at a cute boy who is maybe a year or so younger than herself.

Chapter 5

Maggie stands inside the doorway of their suite at Knollwood Lodge with her hands on her hips. Every light in the suite is turned on, and Tae can see that Maggie is not pleased.

"Why didn't you tell me you were going to be out so late? Better question: why were you out so late?"

"I came back a while ago and you were asleep. Sorry, Maggie."

Tae's left eye begins to twitch. She wonders if Maggie notices it.

"I've been worried sick. Not because I think there's anything to be afraid of here, but crazy people are everywhere. Probably not a good idea to go out at night without me… You think you're old enough, but you're not. No such thing as being safe if you're out at night alone." Maggie paces as she scolds, holding a red coffee stir like a cigarette. She inhales deeply, and then twirls it between her fingers.

Tae decides not to say anything more and patiently waits for Maggie to run out of steam. She desires nothing more than sleep.

Maggie confides: "Know what I was really worried about? That maybe you'd decided to go back to Flint. Sounds silly, I know, but I was beginning to have a little pity party about what boring company I must be. Honestly, I don't know why I've been snoozing so much. Maybe stress… I think staying here a few more days might do me some good. What do you think?"

———

The next morning, low lying fog blankets the fields and ravines.

The trail leading to the first cave is too narrow for them to walk side by side, so Tae leads the way and is surprised that Maggie does not object. Silence is thankfully interrupted by a birdsong symphony. She can identify robins, bluebirds and sparrows, but none of the others. Does Maggie know the little yellow one that just flew overhead? What about the black ones with orange wings? If so, she isn't saying. Onward they march. Tae is aware that she can disturb the silence anytime, and that, if she talks long enough, Maggie will eventually join in, but she is beginning to enjoy the sense that she is all alone, even though she's not.

Something is preoccupying Maggie. Likely there's much to think about at her age. What has she seen in her lifetime? How many friends and boyfriends have there been? Why hasn't she ever married? Why hasn't she ever had children? Not all women want them, of course. Maybe Tae will never want any either, especially after being raised in a big family. Maggie's book, *Pauline's Revenge*, almost made her famous. Tae feels bad she hasn't read it, but she doubts that that is what is bothering Maggie. Now is not the right time to ask. Later, she'll find a way. Maybe once they're comfortably situated back at the lodge.

They don't pass anyone else on the trail. If others are behind them, no voices can be heard due to the breeze blowing through the upper branches of the trees. According to the signpost at the trailhead, it is two miles to the cave. Maybe by then the mood will have changed; Tae certainly hopes so.

She can feel Maggie's eyes burrowing into her, yet when Tae turns around, Maggie quickly looks away. Come to think of it, this has happened a couple times before. Something about the way Maggie has been watching her lately makes Tae want to take a shower. And for the first time, Tae doesn't feel comfortable being alone with her. Yet maybe Maggie is simply lost in thought and unaware that's she been staring so intensely. Like Tae, she is a deep thinker, so she's probably just lost in her thoughts. But what are her thoughts? Suddenly, Tae feels guilty of a crime that neither has actually committed.

"There it is!" shouts Maggie, pointing at an immense boulder. "The only way to enter the cave is to inch along behind that boulder. Be sure to suck in your breath so you can make yourself as skinny as possible. But wait! Let me get a photo of it. Caves are also doors, wouldn't you agree?" Maggie snaps several pictures of the cave entrance.

As they inch along, little light filters through, except at one end where the sun streams in like a weak beam from a flashlight. Tae is able to make out a large, hairy spider. Creepy! She shrieks and grabs Maggie's hand. It feels as if they can't go forward or backward, but are stuck within a moment in time, bewitched as much by the place, as by the spider. Maybe they are actually caught by a magic web. Standing still and silent, something passes from girl to woman, then back again. A current bonds and transfixes them. Does Maggie feel it? It's almost as if time itself has been suspended. A bird on a nearby tree branch calls out. Tae imagines a chrysalis which bursts open to reveal two human females. The light grows brighter and both blink madly in the sunlight. Neither has yet found her voice. The scene is primordial. Both are dazed by the experience. The startling moment is not mentioned—at least not on this day.

Everything in due time.

⸻

During the ride back to the lodge, Maggie wonders aloud if Tae is disappointed by what she has seen. Neither has ever been anywhere quite like this, though it isn't exactly the place alone which they find amazing. Hocking Hills, Tae confirms, is as close to Heaven as she's ever been in this life. Never has she been surrounded by so much beauty, both in nature and in the rustic beauty of the lodge. Maggie, like a fairy godmother, had performed some lovely magic and turned Tae's old life inside out. First thing Tae did once they'd unpacked their bags was to jump on her new bed, feeling even more crazy joy than she had at the first motel. Her plan is to jump on the bed of every place they stay during the trip. No reason to tell Maggie, just in case she'd scold her about doing such a thing. But that seems unlikely. Tae had even caught her smiling before looking away. Maybe one day she'll even join in the fun.

Over dinner, Tae confides how few trips she's ever taken, not counting the visits to see Serafina in New York City. She has experienced only three excursions: to Cedar Point Amusement Park in Ohio on her tenth birthday; to a family reunion at a swampy, bug infested, river-side park in Mississippi; and a night at a local Holiday Inn for one of Tasha's birthdays. None of those times had been much fun, unlike her visits with Auntie Serafina. Once they rode the train together all the way to New York from Michigan. That had been the best time ever, because her aunt was one of those people who was simply fun to be around. The only other trip she'd taken was to Disneyworld when she was so young she could now hardly recall it, Tae informs her. Maggie herself had been there once, but she doesn't feel like talking about it. Maybe another time. Tae feels chilled until she notices the roaring fire in the stone fireplace. So far she's counted three: this one, the one in the lobby, as well as one in their suite. One wall of the restaurant is made of triangular glass and has a high ceiling. The glass must be a couple hundred feet high. What she doesn't much care for in the lobby are all the animal heads: three deer, two brown bears, and a buffalo.

She keeps her opinion to herself as she bites into a piece of roast chicken, followed by a taste of garlic mashed potatoes and then a sip of water with a slice of lime in it—her new favorite drink. This is the first time she has eaten meat in a couple of months—so much for her vegetarian diet. Maggie dines on eggplant parmesan and a salad.

"Wouldn't you agree, Maggie, that the ambiance here is not quite as spectacular as the Pink Flamingo, but very pleasing, all the same?"

Maggie acts like she hasn't heard her, so instead of repeating her question, Tae adds: "*Ambiance*: Word of the day!"

Maggie nods and gives her a half-smile. She must be bored, tired, or depressed. Whatever…It has become almost impossible to read this woman.

"Maggie, forgive me for saying so, but you seem out-of-sorts. Between you and me, you're not usually the moody one."

"I know I've been rather quiet. My tinnitus—the condition I

have that makes my ears ring—has been bad today. This is a lovely place, Tae, but I've been worried that you might wake up one day and wonder why you're here with me. And I'm a little worried that even though you wanted to go, taking you on this trip could land me in hot water, legally. If your mom says it's time to head home, I think we had better heed her words."

"Well, she's not about to! You know her: her hard times got harder awhile back, and now there's one less mouth to feed." She'd successfully broken the ice of Maggie's bad mood.

Their room—or rooms—is called The Lavinia Suite. Who precisely Lavinia was, they aren't sure, though it isn't long before they begin making up stories about her: She's the mistress of the man who built the lodge. Perhaps she was the true builder of the lodge—one of those incredible yet understated females of the nineteenth century that *his*-story just cast aside.

The suite is perfect. There is a bedroom with a bay window overlooking Loon Lake, a small kitchen and living room full of rockers and braided rugs. The best part (according to Tae) is a spiral staircase leading to a turret with a rolltop desk and a 'fainting couch' covered in burgundy satin upholstery. Yes, it was here, no doubt, that the lovely Lavinia was kissed by the rugged Jacob LaForge, a lumberjack, who, once upon a time, had been a sea captain. Thinking about it nearly causes Tae to fall into a swoon on the couch.

Also, there's a balcony off the living room! (Did Tae just squeal in delight? She did...)

Is it the newness which makes it hard to sit still? She can't wait to take a pedal boat out on the lake, or to enjoy the nightly campfire, or to sit on one of the wooden swings at the lakefront. It's like riding a bike in water, Maggie says, but easier. Maggie seems content to just relax inside their suite. This takes Tae by surprise: usually Maggie speaks and acts like a younger woman; it's hard to remember that she's not.

After dinner, Tae calls Tyler. He answers on the second ring and at first sounds happy to hear from Tae. Will it be okay if they show up in a few days? Maybe three? "Sure...I mean, it's great that you're on your way," he says, "but I'm a little surprised that you'll be here so soon." Turns out he has "some business to attend to"—doesn't say what exactly, so Tae isn't about to ask. He continues, laughing nervously: "If you could plan on getting here in about a week, that would be better, and I'll be a little more ready for the both of you!"

Later, when Tae tells Maggie about the conversation, she confides that she is uncertain whether they are really all that welcome. The call puts an end to Tae picturing Tyler welcoming them with a wide, winning smile and open arms. Come to think of it, it's not like he'd actually ever invited Tae, as well as some white woman; though he himself is white, he doesn't sound it. Because of his soft Southern accent, she has always thought of him as a shade or two darker, even though in the pictures she's seen (one in her possession and one at home) he is nearly as white as Maggie. Maybe now that he has shown a coolness, which she has always somehow associated with the British, she'll at last realize his whiteness. Tears first trickle then flow down her light brown cheeks. She feels foolish. Once again she has been tricked. Her expectations were too high. It had been such a good day until now.

Maggie sees her slap-wipe the now streaming tears and throws her arms around her. For a second Tae puts her head on her friend's shoulder, but pulls away and plops down on a soft cushioned chair in their suite, shaking her head. She tells Maggie about the call, about Tyler's guarded friendliness, as well as her own response.

"Do you still want to visit him?" asks Maggie.

"What if he's not what I thought? What then?" Tae asks, covering her eyes with her hands.

"You probably just caught him off guard. Remember, all he knew was that sometime this summer, you and I would be at his door. We never told him exactly when."

Maggie then expresses how there had been many times in her own life that she'd anticipated someone being as excited to see her as she was them, only to find that feelings weren't the same; in some instances, not even close. That sting of realization has never been something she has learned how to avoid. So typical of Maggie, Tae thinks, to say how she has felt the same about something as Tae feels now. How would she know, really? Or is Maggie just trying to show empathy? More likely, in the room, just now, is that sappy, flowery-dressed friend, *sympathy.*

"So maybe we'll just take a little longer getting there, and spend a little less time with Tyler than we first thought. How does that sound?"

Some problems Maggie solves so quickly, so effortlessly. Tae can't help but like that about her. Maggie often makes better sense of the world than Tae does, but then again, she's older, so shouldn't she be wiser? It really doesn't matter when they got to Tyler's house, she supposes, despite the fact that there are mysteries to be solved.

Maggie decides to stay in the room and rest, so Tae ventures down to the lake alone. An almost full moon shines on the nearly perfect oval of Loon Lake. She hardly needs her flashlight, what with the moonlight and the enormous bonfire on the beach. Several guests have gathered in what appears to Tae to be a nightly ritual. She decides not to join them—mostly couples, and only one kid, as far as she can tell.

She keeps walking until she reaches the last of several wooden swings along the lakeshore. The dancing light of fireflies adds more magic to a special night. At first, she swings slowly back and forth, listening intently to the gentle lapping of water against the sandy shore. The water itself is inky black, and when it caresses the shore, it creates a ribbon of froth. Is the bonfire crowd watching her? Not wanting to draw too much attention, she packs the flashlight inside her bag with the other few items she'd thrown together before leaving the room: a towel (in case she decided to go for a swim), a notebook, a pen, and a baseball cap she never wears. Inside the notebook is a photo of Tyler. He is a stranger. She hurriedly puts it back in the inside pocket of the notebook, and then the notebook back inside the bag.

One question on Tae's mind lately: if she had had darker skin, would Maggie still have taken her on this trip? Maggie would no doubt deny it, so maybe it's a pointless question. Not always easy to confide in her. It used to be, but this trip seems to be changing all that. There are times when Maggie makes her feel like she's in the way. Not always, of course. What's curious is that Maggie would not have taken this trip had it not been for Tae. Sometimes Maggie treats her like she's a friend, but then an hour or two later, like she's just a stupid kid. And why is it so important to constantly try to act grown up around Maggie? Tae isn't quite ready to be a grown-up yet, so why does she want to impress Maggie with her maturity? Isn't there some way she could skip the teen years altogether? Not that she wants to be anywhere close to Maggie's age. Ageing bodies can be pretty gross: all that sagging skin and the wrinkles…way worse than zits! Does Maggie wish she were younger, maybe Tae's age? Maggie must have been pretty good-looking in her prime, though her shoulders probably slouched. Still, she must have been pretty with her blond hair, almost aqua-colored eyes, long fingers, and curvy figure. Why so many women—especially white women—have a problem with curves, she doesn't quite understand.

She peels off her shorts and prances into the water. Was there ever a time she hasn't enjoyed being in water? Once she'd asked her mom for a pool and had been told there was barely enough money to buy food, so no way could they afford one. It was the first time Tae had realized that her family was poor. She must have been six or seven, and no doubt thought her mom was just being mean. It still depressed her and even made her angry to think that most people had more than they did…

Maggie had once explained that while her family was fairly well-off, and she'd never gone hungry, she and her sister had often been left with sitters or on their own for long periods of time. Their parents had rarely been affectionate. Tae couldn't complain about her mom being distant; she was always in Tae's face, but usually it was when she was scolding her or bossing her about. But Tae knew—mostly she knew—she was loved, and that was her mom's way of showing it.

She wades out to her waist and a wave—not an actual one, but a wave of missing her mama—almost knocks her over. First time since Tae had been gone that she truly missed her. She runs back to the beach, shivering. Why does it so often feel like Quintana isn't her real mother? She's almost certain that Quintana loves her sisters more than she loves her.

Has Maggie begun to miss her yet? Silly, that she's worried about it, but Tae doesn't want to upset her. Maybe she should go back to the lodge. If only she didn't have to walk past the party at the bonfire.

There are fewer there than earlier. Still, she keeps her gaze down, feels once again like she doesn't belong. She doesn't know how long she spent, first on the swing and then in the water, but afterward, she feels more content than usual. Tomorrow she'll return, maybe right after breakfast.

She can't wait to tell Maggie about her time at the lake, but Maggie is already asleep when Tae returns. Snoring rather loudly, too… It's only 10:30 and Tae herself doesn't feel at all sleepy. Why not go back outside? This time she could walk the trail that goes around the lake.

She removes the flashlight from her bag, creeps back outside as quietly as possible. It's only when she reaches the lobby that she realizes that she has left her room key on the desk inside the suite. No way would Maggie wake up pleased to have to answer the door. In fact, she'll either be annoyed with her now or later, so what does it matter if Tae stays out a little longer? If she disturbs her now, Maggie probably won't allow her to go out again.

There is only one couple still at the bonfire. A pretty woman with long dark hair and a guy with braided dreads. She has never seen a white person with dreads. It looks, if not exactly weird, not quite right either. It dawns on her that she hasn't seen a single person of color since they arrived here. The couple is busy kissing and doesn't see her walk past.

Will she ever have a boyfriend? Only one boy has ever liked her— at least that she's known about: Aaron in sixth grade. She became aware of his attraction not long after returning home from one of her visits with Aunt Serafina. They had kissed only twice, but often held hands on the way home from school.

She again sits on the swing that she's begun to think of as her own. This time, lost in memories, she notices less. How do older people manage to deal with so many? That is, the ones who are still capable of remembering, she laughs. Seems like all the memories would be crushed beneath their accumulated weight. She is only fifteen and has already collected so many. Maybe that's why people become forgetful as they age—they have to let go of some of the cargo so that they don't drown. Maggie has told her some things about her past, but Tae knows there's more, way more, that has happened to her. Maybe that's why Maggie needs to sleep so much lately—just to get away from her memories. Who could blame her?

Her visits with Aunt Serafina weren't the only times that Tae was away from home, though all her best recollections are from her times in New York with her auntie between the ages of eight and ten. She hadn't begun school until she was six. It was before she was eight—maybe when she was still seven—that things had been crazier than usual at home due to her mom's drinking, smoking, and throwing all night parties. Back then, Tae hadn't needed the house to be quiet so she could write, of course, plus she never minded the attention she received from adults. In those days she thought her family saw her as a comedian because she so often made them laugh.

One day, an unfriendly looking couple came to the door. They didn't sit down like grownups do when they stop by for a visit. She thought they were mad at her mom. In turn, it made Tae so angry at them, that when her mom was out of the room, she shouted at them to "get out of my house!" Instead, they dragged her kicking and screaming to their car. She screamed for help, but no one came to her rescue. Didn't Quintana realize she was being kidnapped? The image of Quintana following them with a suitcase of Tae's clothes, still causes Tae to feel like she's going to vomit. Even though Quintana had kissed her and said it was going to be "for just a little while." The little while turned into six long months. This is why she so far hasn't read Maggie's novel: she knew it was about a kidnapping. And it's also why she sometimes feels like something's not exactly right about this trip (not that Maggie had forced her into the car or anything like that).

For a time Tae lived with an elderly and plump white lady—Ruth Tilders. She still hasn't told Maggie about this. Mrs. Tilders lived in a tidy little house with a white picket fence. She had twenty cats that lived in a back room, and Mrs. Tilders never allowed any of them into the rest of the house. The cat room was the largest, with windows on all sides. Tae's bedroom was upstairs in a converted attic. She felt important at first, being allowed to sleep there. Mrs. Tilders didn't have a husband; she was a *widow*. (A strange and interesting word, Tae had thought at the time, and she hoped to someday become one.) There were more framed pictures of her husband than there were cats. Mrs. Tilders dusted while she spoke to him, often doing so several times a day. It was *he* who supposedly said that Tae needed to clean the ten litter boxes in the basement every day; *he* who commanded Tae to scrub herself for an hour in the tub every night; *he* who insisted that his wife put her in the corner when she spoke out of turn. When Tae misbehaved and used slang, it was supposedly Mr. Tilders who had his wife make Tae stand with her face in the corner.

Mrs. Tilders sent Tae to an all-white school. Except for two stuck-up girls who pulled her braid and one boy who stuck his tongue out at her, the other kids were okay. She was something of a celebrity and hated to return to the house to clean up cat poop and spend evenings in the corner. The teacher, Mrs. Jennings, never believed her when she complained that Mrs. Tilders was very strange.

Every night, she'd cry because she missed her mom and sisters. Then one night it occurred to her that despite the fact that life was so messed up, it was in fact *her* messed up life, which must have been around the same time that she began to have doubts about Quintana being her real mother. Maybe she was a relative, but no way could she possibly be her mom. One day, Tae resolved, she would get to the bottom of it.

When she finally returned home she understood what words and terms were slang or ghetto, and she always took care to speak politely and carefully. More than one teacher would tell her how good she was at speaking Standard English. (As if it were an award-worthy accomplishment!)

One day she'll tell all this to Maggie, but she doesn't know when. Right now her plan is to come up with a poem or a story idea on her walk around the lake. Earlier, she realized that neither her fantasy story "Park Isle", nor the murder mystery she'd been working on in

Flint, held much appeal. At home she used to pace in the basement when she brainstormed, since it was too dangerous to walk alone in her neighborhood.

The moon and the fireflies have now vanished. The only light comes from her flashlight and the lights in the distance from the lodge. Now the paved path has turned to dirt and there are all sorts of branches and vines which seem to be groping at her as she passes. Can plants feel? Do they have a sense of touch? Halfway around the lake she notices how quiet it is, save the hoot of an owl and a few crickets. She breaks into a jog, but begins to feel a familiar panic, like she had felt whenever she had to walk down her street in the dark. Unsafe and vulnerable: another possible victim of the night. Aware, of course, that by day it would appear totally different, and the danger would have diminished with the dawn.

Chapter 6

When Sulie first met Maggie at Pete's Place, it seemed as if she some-how knew everything about her. For example, she knew that Maggie had lived with several men (though not exactly how many); that she had a sister; that her parents were dead, and that she disliked her job. Most importantly, she knew that Maggie fancied herself as a writer. She was aware that Maggie had written a book and now had a bad case of writer's block. Plus, she knew that Maggie wanted to be an author with a capitol A.

"Maggie, it's not the author that is important; it's the book!"

One of Sulie's goals was to create a book museum. A few years ago she had a nightmare that one day all books would be gone except for those lost cloistered in attics…E-books had become so popular that all the hard and soft cover books were now gone, as were all the bookstores. In fact, she'd had several dreams about worlds without books. People walking the streets: bored, hungry; because although there was enough to eat, they were ravenous for written words.

A former client had bequeathed a building to Sulie in his will—a once vital factory in the middle of Oregon. At first she thought about having it torn down, but then she had an epiphany: she would create her book museum! Not a library, but a museum with an adjoining store that specialized in rare and banned books. She knew she wouldn't be able to do this alone, so who better to recruit than ignored writers?

Maggie was one of the first who came to mind. "How about coming out West with me, Maggie, and helping me with the museum?"

Maggie was contemplative. "That *would* give me more time to make an honest start on my next novel," she said.

She had known before Caroline called her that Maggie had left Michigan. Just as she knew a great many things, it had come to her the same morning that she'd heard from the older sister... And it wasn't good—Maggie leaving and taking the girl, Taezha, with her. Once Sulie was able to locate her, she would send the girl home, provided that she could get Caroline to persuade Quintana not to press charges (though she wasn't sure Quintana was even thinking along those lines, or that she even wanted the girl back). But there was also a condition that Maggie must meet: to agree to move out West with her. Caroline told her that Maggie had said something about Hocking Hills, so Sulie left that very afternoon. Caroline had no idea how much Sulie knew about her sister (and Sulie wasn't about to tell her either).

While it wasn't unusual for her to travel out of state for her job, Sulie wondered if tracking Maggie throughout the Southeast would prove to be the longest pursuit of her career as a private investigator. Her cases mostly involved jealous wives or husbands who wanted proof that their spouses were cheating, though it wasn't unheard of for her to find missing children or Alzheimer's patients. She was known locally as having found more missing persons than most investigators—no doubt due to her strong psychic abilities. Most of the missing she found alive. And the very best part of her job was reuniting them with loved ones.

Chapter 7

Again, reality proves to be different from her expectations when Tae tries to recreate the previous evening at Loon Lake. She had been hoping to write in her journal, or maybe work on a story, but she decides that this might not be the best time. To her chagrin, it looks like most of the guests are sunbathing at the small beach. Plus, an elderly man is sitting on her swing, so she'll have to figure out another place to hang out. Two girls about her own age smile and wave as she walks past them on the cement pathway that leads to the woods. For Tae, it is starting to feel like it did at home when she hadn't written in a few days: borderline crazy, because her thoughts are overflowing and so out of control that she can't make sense of anything.

The shade from Oaks and Pines brings relief from the intense sun. The mosquitoes, however, are out in force. They like her arms (slap!) and her legs a little too much. Slap again. Squish. At least she hasn't seen other people, so she can pretend that she is in an unspoiled place. After walking a little further, she trips on a rock right at the place where the pathway branches in different directions.

From her viewpoint on the ground she surveys the area, while rubbing her ankle. A stabbing pain shoots up her leg when she tries to walk. She'll make it back to the lodge only if she favors her injured ankle. She tests the leg, hobbling a bit before returning to her normal stride. How many times during her short life has she tripped over her big feet? Way too many! Maggie always calls her graceful, but she knows she's not.

Halfway back to the lodge, she sits upon a wooden bench

overlooking the water. The bugs don't seem as bad as before. She rests her ankle and tries to think clearly. She opens her notebook. Maybe this is the place where she'll at last be able to write. Yet thoughts of Maggie intrude. Before leaving Flint, she hadn't realized how peculiar Maggie could be. Even after hearing that she'd once written a novel—even after finding out about her parents' tragic suicides—it hadn't occurred to Tae that there might be many versions of Maggie—younger ones who had sometimes spun out of control. Just as she's about to put pen to paper, the sound of rustling in the woods reaches her ears. She notices a strong odor. She's never smelled a skunk before, and having no interest in being sprayed by one now, she stealthily removes herself from the bench and gingerly makes her way back to the lodge.

———————

She takes bottled water from the mini fridge and gets halfway up the spiral staircase to the turret of their suite and comes across Maggie sitting at the table, writing. Tae feels bad at having disturbed her, and without saying anything, turns and heads back down the stairs.

"Wait, Tae! Do you want to work up here? I can find somewhere else."

"Just here to get water," Tae says, and races down the stairs.

Why does Maggie always call writing work? Shouldn't it be fun? If Tae ever perceives it as work, then she'll no longer want to do it. Sad to think that Maggie is working in the tower room, which strikes Tae as a good place for a little romance. If Tae were older, and if she lived here, she'd bring a cute guy up to the turret for a romantic encounter. On a day when she knew Maggie would be out, of course.

The swing by the water is hers again, and there are now only a few sunbathers lying on chaises. She realizes, once more, how much she enjoys *solitude* (word of the day)—something that she has in common with Maggie. Is this what makes them writers?

She sits sideways on the swing. What bliss to not hear the constant chatter of her sisters and her mama, the TV, the sounds of sirens, car stereos blaring music, honking horns, and gunfire… For an hour she writes about how she needs solitude in her life.

Maggie joins her on the swing only minutes after Tae has closed her notebook. She tells Maggie how fantastic it felt to write, even though it was just an entry in her journal. Maggie smiles, and responds that any sort of writing involves a microscopic look at circumstances, and sometimes seeing that deeply can hurt.

"Why?"

"Well, I can't get into all the details of my past just now, but I'll tell you a little about my relationships with men. Maybe you wouldn't guess it now, but when I was younger, it was almost as easy for me to get a marriage proposal as it was a date. Have I told you before that I've lived with six different men?"

"Six?" Suddenly, it's hard for Tae to swallow, and harder still to breathe deeply. Who exactly is this person? Because Tae is curious, Maggie begins to tell her about them. Eric the Fifth was a stuntman in L.A. He was killed during a driving stunt after they'd been living together only a few months. Such a rough time…First, her agent had tried selling her book rights to Hollywood and nothing had come of it…then Eric's untimely death. They'd had such fun together, too. He got her to take risks: once she'd sky jumped, another time she flew his small biplane. They laughed a lot, probably drank too much. It wasn't long after his death that she moved back to Detroit. At forty she'd already lived with five men, and by forty-six, she'd left Andrew the Sixth. With the exception of Eric, she'd always been the one to call it quits: forever restless and more than ready to move on and in with another. By age forty-six, she'd given up on finding true love. She felt better being on her own, or at least she had until she lost her parents.

"What cities have you lived in?" Tae wanted to know.

"Detroit, New York, San Francisco, L.A., Chicago, and finally, Flint, the smallest."

"What were the names of the men you lived with?"

"From first to last: Kirk, Jason, Todd, Vince, Eric, and Andrew."

"Did they support your writing career?"

"Vince the Fourth, my Chicago guy, certainly did," Maggie said.

"He was—and continues to be—the editor of a poetry magazine and half owner of an art gallery. A good man… I stayed with him about a year before he confided he was gay."

Tae tried to hide her shock.

"Actually, I'd realized it shortly after we moved in together, so it came as no shock to me. We're still friends, just like with Andrew the Sixth. Andrew had been jealous, not of me, but the time I devoted to writing. Same thing with Todd the Third… It was at thirty that I'd written *Pauline's Revenge*. I had worked on it so much that there had been little time for Todd, or anyone else. Eventually he gave me an ultimatum: I chose to finish my book."

"Don't you envy those long, death-till-you-part marriages?"

"Do they still exist?"

If there's one thing Tae believes in strongly, it's love. And she knows, without a doubt, that someday she'll find it. Tae's sorry that Maggie hasn't, but Tae knows with great certainty that one day she will.

Dinners at the lodge are delicious, but it's not just the food… Maggie and Tae take their time changing from beach or hiking clothes to sundresses or skirts; spritzing themselves with body sprays; applying lip gloss while standing next to each other at the bathroom mirror. Dinner is served between 7:00 and 8:00 p.m. They are careful not to be late.

Some choose to dine on the balcony, but the day's heat usually lingers, so most prefer eating inside beneath the knotty pine beams of the dining room ceiling. The two female writers enjoy both settings. Tonight they've chosen to dine inside. With white linen tablecloths and a picture window running the length of an entire wall, it has what Maggie terms casual elegance. Maggie doesn't always seem herself during dinner, the way she does when they're enjoying the grounds, or in the privacy of their suite. Instead, she often glances around to see if they're being watched. This seems especially true tonight. It causes Tae to fidget, but still she manages to enjoy the meal. She can still taste the leftover pizza or cereal she so often ate for dinner in the past. An after-taste she's sure will last the rest of her life; maybe for the best so she won't be shocked when she must return home.

Tonight, synchronicity is playing its game, and only a couple of hours after going into great detail about her long-term relationships, Maggie hears from Andrew the Sixth. She takes her cell phone out onto the balcony of their suite; meanwhile, Tae eavesdrops from her bedroom.

"I told you, Andy, that I was thinking of taking a road trip this summer. Don't act so shocked…She's fifteen. I've mentioned it before… Of course I know she's a minor. It's just a vacation, a road trip. Her mom knows, and she is okay with it. We're on our way to see her uncle in North Carolina…. You know I sometimes do things on a whim."

The following day, Tae learns that Andrew the Sixth had been married to someone else when he moved in with Maggie. Maggie says that Andrew has always been a sort of witness to her life. Still, there were other problems: he is an habitual pot smoker. She'd first met him at a bookstore where he hosted poetry readings. He wrote some of the finest poetry Maggie has ever read—love poems to the memory of his wife, before she developed Alzheimer's.

"You see, Tae, circumstances are never black and white. While cheating is wrong, it's not like his wife was much of a companion anymore. I left him more because of his constant pot smoking habit, not because he was married to someone else."

Later that evening, Maggie's phone rings again. It's Caroline, checking up on her. They're having a shouting match, and Tae doesn't have to listen very intently to realize that it has to do with Maggie taking Tae on this trip. Tae can't help but wonder why it's such a big deal to the adults: do they think that Maggie has kidnapped her? True, her mom wasn't exactly happy about it, but she's never happy about much in life.

The dream had been so real: She was in bed with a man who looked like her photo of Uncle Tyler. First gently, but insistently, he began prying her thighs apart. Then, with force. Why would she dream such a thing? He is the one good man she knows, at least from afar. In the dream, Tae was sleepy, so sleepy that she allows him to take advantage of her. Then the person changes from Uncle Tyler to Jayvon. He is wearing the same red do-rag and gold earring as always. She tries to scream, but she can't breathe. "All these gifts I gave you—don't you owe me something in return?" Then, it's Uncle Tyler again; and then Mama is there smiling down at her. How can she smile? And then it isn't Mama but Maggie, the real Maggie, asking if she's okay. Tae is awake now, twisted up in the sheets, dripping with sweat. She finds her voice: "If Mama's calling, tell her I'm too busy to talk…"

Telling Maggie about the nightmare doesn't vanquish it from her mind. Instead, its effects persist into the next day. And it doesn't help that it rains the entire day. She feels confined, trapped. Maggie senses this; they're both in bad moods. Tae wonders aloud about the point of seeing Uncle Tyler.

Tae's phone rings. Not Mama calling, but Tyleena.

"Mama told me to call and tell you it's time to come home. Mama's sick."

"She's always got something wrong with her," says Tae after a long silence.

"Her cough's worse this past week."

"Tell her to stop smoking and doping!"

"This isn't from Mama, but me: Tell your white mama that if she wants to help, she can damn well send you to college. And your three sisters, too!"

"Tell Mama to call me herself next time!" Tae screams into the phone.

"Well, this is from Mama: *'If that white bitch don't bring you back, we'll get a lawyer.'* And this is from me: Girl, you're a minor! Hear me: MI-NOR!"

At last the afternoon rain turned to a fine mist. Bad moods diminish. Tae's clothes are scattered on the back of a chair, and on the floor. Once again, Maggie accuses her of being disorganized. If Tae can learn to be a little less careless, she might be less likely to lose things.

"Maggie, you're like an auntie, but you're not my mom, remember?" Tae says, addressing Maggie's face in a large mirror on the wall.

"Yes, but I am the adult here. Right?" Maggie's reflection responds.

"That's sometimes dubious," Tae says, turning to face her.

"Excuse me?" Maggie's taken aback by Tae's sassiness.

To break the mood they decide to go to a nearby town where there are a few gift stores and coffee shops. At first it's fun. Maggie snaps pictures of almost every store door in town. She buys ankle bracelets for them both, purchases a scarf for herself, and also a gift for Tae—an abalone ring. The ring is instantly Tae's favorite. There's so much to see and do, but while they are browsing in a second gift store, this one pricier than the last one, Maggie tries to hurry Tae along. Is it her imagination or is Maggie getting bossier by the day? Or is it because this place is so expensive? Maggie nudges Tae and points to a short woman wearing sunglasses and a black beret in the back of the store. "That's Sulie. We have to leave."

Chapter 8

Tyler rocks slowly back and forth on the creaky glider on his wrap-around verandah near Monroe, North Carolina. The sun balances on the tips of Norfolk pines on the western edge of his forty acre homestead. Kip lies curled up at his feet, and Miss Sophie's snuggled up against him, purring away. He doesn't feel nearly ready for the upcoming visit. While he knows he shouldn't view his own daughter as a visitor, how can he help but do so? True, he's gotten to know her through letters. She seems like a sweet girl, and from the photos she's sent, more than a little like her mama. How long will he have to keep up the uncle routine? It was easy enough to do in letters, but sooner or later she will have to know the truth. Smart as she is, maybe she's already figured it out. He doesn't know why he ever agreed with Quintana about keeping it secret in the first place... Sweet Jesus! He is so tired of accommodating that woman. She has never stopped blaming him, and for her to allow Taezha to come for a visit surprises him, but he won't question it. He's heard a little about Maggie from Taezha, but he has no idea what to expect. Taezha has written that Maggie is 'nice' and 'interesting.' Still, he doesn't have the guestroom ready. So much dust on unused surfaces. Maybe he should hire someone to help him clean the rooms. With any luck, they won't arrive for another week or two.

After the last of his livestock—a cantankerous nanny-goat named Zinny—was sold, Tyler retreated to the pole barn to work on one of his wooden birdman statues. The wings were giving him fits. He hadn't slept or eaten for twenty-four hours.

First time ever that he'd lost a job…Worked at the hardware store in town for years, and while he'd never made enough money to make ends meet, the job had paid enough so he could keep his house and his land… The occasional music gig or freelance carpentry job simply will not pay the bills.

Now, with Taezha and Maggie soon to be on his doorstep, he feels embarrassed and out-of-sorts. A tough decision to sell his horse, his pig, his goat, and also one of his two John Deere tractors, but he'd had little choice.

Yesterday, it occurred to him to step up his birdman creations and maybe try to sell them, too. He knows he should take a break since his back has been acting up. And he will, in an hour or so. Maybe sit on the porch and play his harmonica, and get Kip to howl and sing the way dogs do. A small but necessary amusement for Tyler in an otherwise bad patch of days…

He'd lived in this house almost continually since he was ten years old—the exception being a two-year stint in the Navy. From the fifth grade through the seventh, he'd resided here with his dad and grandmother, Nana. Nana doted on both her son (Neil) and her grandson, and she would have defended both to the death if she'd had to, but luckily it had never come to that. After Grandpa James was out of her life, she'd turned all her attention to Neil. Neil lived the simple life of a farmer. Forty acres, minus the mule, though at one time they'd had a few cows, horses, pigs and chickens. Neil was a man of few words, unlike Tyler's Grandpa James. After supper every night, tired from the day's work, Neil would sit on a step of the wrap-around porch and play his harmonica. Tyler joined him most evenings. He knew better than to interrupt, even though there were always a half dozen things he wanted to tell his dad. On Tyler's eleventh birthday, Neil gave his son two presents: a harmonica and a saw. Neil taught him much about both instrument and tool during the following year. A few weeks following Tyler's twelfth birthday, Nana found Neil on the ground outside the barn. By the time the ambulance arrived, Neil was dead.

Tyler had lost both parents within two years. A Godsend that he still had Nana. Those who lose their parents early in their lives—when still a child—come to view anyone else who matters as temporary. Not Tyler. The type of security Nana provided made him almost take for granted that she wouldn't always be there. It also made him content with his small world of few relationships. Nana struggled with the farm for a couple years, but gradually sold the animals, keeping only the chickens and vegetable garden (its size greatly reduced). It was only after she was gone that Tyler had bought a few barnyard animals, thinking their company would make up for the loss somehow. Kept him busy for a time, but he wasn't a farmer. Instead, Tyler became a furniture repairman and carpenter, not to mention a Blues harmonica player of some repute.

Chapter 9

Sulie has lived alone for the past twenty years, and she is sure she will continue to do so for the next twenty, as well as the twenty after that, if she's a lucky puppy and lives that long. She's dated here and there, but no one has ever proposed to her, nor has she asked for anyone's hand in matrimony. An only child from old-money in Grosse Pointe, Michigan, her parents kicked her out at age twenty for smoking pot and for proclaiming to be an anarchist…maybe also for bad table manners and being an atheist. She's never known for sure, as they didn't offer an explanation. During her twenty years under their roof, it never felt to her like they were her parents. And they probably weren't, as neither spoke French, and she did. Or she once did.

Five years ago, she'd been in a car chase and slammed into a brick wall; the air bag hadn't deployed, and her head went right through the windshield. Afterward, she couldn't remember any of the French she'd known, but had never formally learned.

It was then that she discovered she had psychic abilities, though she's either spot on or terribly off, regarding what comes to her. That's why there could be someone on her tail, just like she's now on Maggie's tail. Sulie owes money to folks who claim her fifty-dollar readings are bullshit. And they're right: there's no proving to them that others have been amazed by what she has gleaned in her crystal ball skull.

She is keenly aware that she has caused Maggie anxiety in the gift store, yet she is unsure about what her next move will be. Keep a safe distance, but don't let Maggie get too far from view. Not much else she can do… She had done a fine job lying low in the parking lot at the lodge, but now she has blown her cover in the gift store. Does Maggie know that she's on her tail? Sulie can't help growing restless with all the waiting inside the car. Maybe she should trade in the yellow VW and get something larger. Something less eye-catching. Anyway, she can notify Caroline that their suspect and her victim have now been spotted.

Will Maggie later say that her mind was already made up to continue the road trip *before* seeing Sulie Rowen in the gift store? If she does, she'll be re-writing history…

She'd first met Sulie shortly after getting out into the world again, following her parents' deaths. Both Andrew the Sixth and Jocelyn, too, had been encouraging her to *get back in the swim.* So after school, one high-stress day, she took herself on a solo date to Pete's Place. On the bar stool next to her sat a little woman wearing a black beret, a beige trench coat tied at the waist, and scruffy walking shoes. She had a long thin salt and pepper braid. After giving Maggie several sidelong glances, Sulie introduced herself, and it felt as if they'd known each other forever. Sulie especially seemed to know her.

"You're a writer, aren't you?" Sulie asked.

"Ah, you've read my book? It was published ages ago." Maggie felt honored to be remembered, as it had been years since someone had remarked about her book. Ten years ago, however, Maggie Barnett, though hardly a household name, was an author known to many fiction readers nationwide.

"Actually, I haven't read it. And I don't know you. But you have the look…" Sulie laughed, and it wasn't the laugh itself so much, but the way that it came on in a sudden burst, and the even quicker way her larynx sliced it off in mid-trill that made Maggie deeply curious about this strange person.

Maggie had been dressed simply in black pants, a long white shirt, long loose ponytail; she'd put on a touch of lipstick in the car—beside that, no makeup. Her mood had been initially subdued after a long work day. Now, though clueless how to respond—not flustered, necessarily, she felt engaged and amused.

"And you're still hoping for a following, right? Thinking about publishing again, I'll bet. I used to be a writer, but I quit. Gave it up like a bad habit."

Had Maggie's parents hired this woman? Had one of them managed to contact her from beyond the grave?

Something told Maggie that it was best not to disagree, so she nodded as Sulie postulated that the number of writers in America would soon—if they didn't already—out-number readers. She knew, too, that Maggie had been involved in several relationships, that she didn't have children, and that she had lived in several cities, as well as the fact that her parents had died tragically and were together when they died. For her part, Maggie had known exactly what Sulie's voice would sound like (low and raspy). Also, she felt as if she'd known Sulie her entire life, though unlike Sulie, Maggie didn't know any details about her.

Two vodka & tonics later, Maggie excused herself to the restroom and snuck out the back door.

She shouldn't have felt so relieved (or so confident) about her stealthy get-away. Less than a week later, she passed Sulie on the street, then another time encountered her at a gas station, as well as in the frozen food aisle of a grocery store, not to mention at a jazz concert. Then Maggie had run into her again at Pete's Place, and Sulie seemed to know all about her relationship with Tae.

How did this woman know so much about her? Why was she stalking her? And here she was again, in Hocking Hills, far from the flatter terrain of Flint. It had to be more than a simple coincidence. Had she been following Maggie ever since they'd first met at the bar? Or had Maggie only noticed her on occasions when Sulie actually wanted Maggie to see her? Maggie wondered whether or not she should tell Tae about Sulie. Senseless to worry Tae, as it might make her change her mind about the journey.

Chapter 10

Little does Tae know, but this is their last day at the lodge. Telling her won't be easy, though it's not like she dreads Tae's reaction. She quietly takes photos of the Lavinia Suite doors, of which there are five. Next, taking advantage of the nearly empty hallways (most guests are probably still asleep, as the sun isn't even up yet), she slips out of the suite and descends the grand staircase and makes her way to the various doors on the first floor. She snaps two or three shots of each door: the massive wood doors at the main entranceway; the glass doors leading to the dining rooms; the library doors; the large double doors leading to the kitchen. She even remembers to take shots of the smaller doors leading to the verandah.

Most of the day is spent on their own. She still hasn't told Tae. Why deflate her mood before she absolutely has to? They've been here for almost two weeks—it's time to move on. She finally informs her shortly before they go to dinner. Tears well in Tae's large brown eyes and trickle down her cheeks. "Guess this means you've been having a pretty good time here…" Tae nods as Maggie daubs the girl's wet cheeks with a tissue, hugs her and promises that they'll have a memorable night.

This is the perfect time to give her some better news: Tae has won a short story contest! At first, Tae's annoyed because Maggie had submitted her story, "The Long Wait," without saying anything to her, but once the news sets in, she dances around the suite then yanks Maggie up from her chair. They spin until both almost fall. Neither can stop laughing and all seems right with the crazy world—for the moment, anyway.

"To celebrate, we must have a champagne toast before dinner!"

They both wear their finest sundresses to the dining room. Maggie's is mid-calf, black with teal blue flecks and shows off her still-smallish waist. Tae's dress comes to just above the knee. It's purple and yellow paisley with a halter that ties behind the neck. Maggie recalls wearing a similar style when she was Tae's age. No way could she get away with wearing one now. Tae is wearing patchouli, but her too-generous sprinkle on her skin overpowers Maggie's La Poeme (a perfume she's worn for years). She'll have to mention how a little goes a long way.

Most of the guests are friendly. They nod and smile at Maggie and Tae. A few even compliment their dresses. An elderly woman, Mrs. Hattie Simpson, asks if they have enjoyed their stay and divulges that she and her daughter have been summering here for years. Tae later asks Maggie if summering means that they stay all summer long; Maggie doesn't think so, but isn't exactly sure. They agree that most of the guests must be very wealthy.

They dine on seafood bisque, mixed green salads, followed by *Coque au Vin*. Maggie orders a split of champagne and pours a little in an extra glass for Tae. "Try not to sip it when the waiter is looking our way," Maggie whispers. They make a game of it for a little while. Maggie proposes two toasts. They first clink glasses to good fortune for the rest of their travels, followed by Maggie raising her glass to Tae, due to the e-mail she received that afternoon revealing that Taezha Riverton had taken first place in a national short story contest for young adults. Maggie had submitted one of Tae's stories months ago as an attachment to her own email. Not only is her story to be published, but she will be awarded $500 dollars in Washington, D.C.

"They're going to fly me there all by myself?" Tae wonders, sounding overwhelmed. She looks relieved after hearing that Maggie will be happy to accompany her, that is, until Maggie adds how the letter also claimed that she would have to read her story, or at least part of it, aloud. Tae is suddenly feeling overly warm and her stomach is in a knot. Maggie reassures her by telling her that the judges won't force her to read it. Maybe if Tae practices reading it aloud, she'll even change her mind, and when the time comes, she might even look forward to reading it.

"Tae, it's not like they're asking you to memorize it."

Real life had bled from Tae's heart and pen onto the pages of "The Long Wait." Talaya, a girl from a poor family, was taken to New York City by her jazz singer aunt, Josefina. At first, the tale focused on a young girl's reaction to seeing the sights of New York, including the Statue of Liberty, Times Square, and Central Park. Then it diverged to what Tae had actually seen. One night, Josefina didn't return from a bar where she'd had a month-long singing gig. Talaya, left with a well-stocked kitchen and a thick envelope of cash, became not only a sleuth, hot on the trail of her aunt's probable murder, but had also implemented her plan to become the 'new' Josefina. In fact, Talaya hadn't believed her aunt was dead until she'd heard about a body believed to have been Josefina Jenkins, a once popular jazz artist.

Aunt Serafina hadn't died when Tae was visiting her, but six months later. It was shortly before Tae and Maggie met at school over two years ago. On an icy night, Serafina's car had plunged into the Hudson River. The autopsy report showed alcohol in her blood, but not enough to cause her to drive off a bridge; examination of the car had revealed that the brake line had been cut. Only a few suspects were questioned, and the case remained unsolved.

Quintana had divulged this information to Maggie shortly before the trip and told her that under no circumstances was she to let Tae know the truth about her aunt's death.

Following dinner, the two walk along the sandy beach. The sun is about to set and the sky is awash with lavender. The squeals of children, not unlike seals, carry on the air above the incoming surf. Tae chooses this moment to tell Maggie about her time at Ruth Tilders' house.

"How awful!" declares Maggie.

Only six at the time, Tae nevertheless realized that Ruth was off her rocker. "You know, Maggie: bonkers, crazy, mental." Looking back on that time, Tae finds it somewhat surprising that she is able to trust

Quintana. But she does. "I love my mom." Maggie doesn't doubt it.

After some discussion about how far to drive the following day, Maggie suggests that Tae call home. Quintana should know that they are getting closer to Uncle Tyler's place, and also that one of Tae's stories has won an important contest.

Quintana answers on the first ring. She doesn't recognize her own daughter's voice.

"It's me, Mom. Tae."

"Hello, baby girl!"

Maggie finds it curious that Tae doesn't immediately tell her about the contest. Tae eye-rolls the chatty voice on the phone. She can no longer stand it and blurts out: "Listen, Mom, I got some great news: I won a writing contest! There's even going to be an award ceremony for the winners in Washington, D.C."

"No way are you going to D.C.!"

"What do you mean? It's not for a few months." Tae gives Maggie a 'please rescue me' look.

"I'd say you been gallivanting around plenty!"

"Aren't you at least happy I won a contest?" More than being upset with Quintana, she doesn't like the fact that Maggie is just standing there, listening. She makes her feelings clear to Maggie by stomping into the adjoining room.

"I'll be happy when you get your black ass home where it belongs! Put Maggie on the line."

Maggie knows better than to argue with her. Is it her imagination or hadn't Quintana once thought that visiting Tyler was a good idea? So why would she change her mind now?

Chapter 11

The next day Tae mentions how Quintana had brought up Jayvon on the phone the previous night. Suppressed anger now returns. Maggie, not knowing what to say, says nothing. Tae pounds her fist on the dashboard as they drive southeast. *Take a breath, Tae; breathe deeply…* When she's calm enough to speak, she confides how Jayvon is the creep who got her mom to take crystal meth a couple of years ago (luckily she didn't get hooked). Her mom's known him on and off for years. "No way I'll ever return to Flint. That part of my life is over!" she tells Maggie.

Maggie's anger is taking hold of her now, but there is little point in displaying it, as it would only make it more difficult for Tae. Driving them ever further away from Michigan is the best that Maggie can do. She can't get over Quintana's lack of support for Tae's writing talent. *Damn her!* She realizes that her anger is not solely toward Quintana, but over the lack of support that she herself experienced while growing up. Her parents had cared *only* about her academic success. While her ability to express herself through the written word was fine, they were mystified as to why she felt compelled to write poetry or stories, as neither cared much for contemporary literature. She recalled her mother saying, more than once, how writing was a waste of time. And Caroline had supported and adopted her parents' viewpoint. Had it not been for a storyteller grandmother and a couple encouraging teachers, Maggie doubts that at Tae's age she ever would have taken pen in hand.

This she explains as they wend their way through the last stretch of rolling roads in southeastern Ohio. Soon they'll be passing through Athens, where they plan to get out and stretch. Maybe there, too, they'd pick up lunch at a drive-through and eat at a park before venturing into West Virginia.

"What if I'm a fake, Maggie, and not really a writer after all?"

"A writer isn't always writing, Tae. A writer observes, listens, takes in as much as possible then filters material. It's important to observe the bigger world, as well as the inner one. It's only later, when images and perceptions have been transformed into language that the writer can select what is to be written about. It's like bringing up buried treasure from the deep. Some days there are precious gems, while others yield wooden planks from a shipwreck, though at times, even those wooden planks can be gems. Guess I'd better quit with the analogy before I 'wreck' it, no pun intended!"

They laugh together and feel relaxed. "Isn't it great, this lightness of being?" It is apparent that Tae knows what she means without having to explain herself. Suddenly, they come to a dead stop, almost slamming into the pickup truck in front of them. There's a traffic jam stretching for what looks like several miles, no doubt due to an accident ahead.

When they finally pick up speed, Maggie has an anxiety attack: the all-too familiar tingling in her fingers, plus that inability to take a deep breath. Last time she had one was on the drive to Hocking Hills. All this driving should make her immune, so why is it so hard to catch her breath now? Maybe the trigger is all her prattling about the places she's been during her life; that catalog is making her feel old, plus she's finding it harder to multi-task these days.

Then Tae says something that really puts her on edge: "Uh, Maggie, I think I left my phone charger at the lodge."

"You did what?"

"Left my charger…"

"We can't turn around now! It's not worth getting stuck in traffic again. I asked you twice if you had everything."

"I thought I did…"

Maggie begins to wordlessly growl and swallows hard.

Tae doesn't respond, and remains quiet for the next several minutes. How Maggie hates silence, especially when she cares about the other person. Normally, conversation is so easy between them, so effortless—it's one of the things she loves about being with Tae, unlike some of her former boyfriends. Not that Tae is like a spouse. Similar only in that they share an emotional intimacy, in the same way it would be if Maggie had a daughter.

"Did you notice the person behind us?" Maggie asks. Tae swivels her head to see behind. "Don't be so obvious! Try not to let her see you."

Tae slides down in her seat—probably not fast enough. She covers her face with her braids.

"Do you see who I see? It's Sulie, the woman in the gift shop yesterday."

"It can't be," states Tae, matter-of-factly. "She's driving a VW Bug. A yellow one… I don't think that's what the person we saw yesterday was driving."

Maggie knows it is Sulie but says nothing more about the woman she thought had been Sulie, but the VW Beetle remains behind them as they approach the entrance to the State Park. Why is she following them? Maybe Quintana or someone from the school has hired her? But no, Quintana didn't have the money to hire a P.I., nor would she go to such lengths even if she did.

The park is a perfect place for a picnic. Maggie can't believe how stiff her joints feel as she gets out of the car after the long drive. All the picnic tables are in the shade, so they arbitrarily choose one.

"It's hillier than I expected, though not as picturesque and charming…"

"Maggie, nobody says 'charming' anymore!"

"Let's settle in and enjoy our picnic."

They devour every last French fry and sip every last drop of their milkshakes. Mosquitoes and flies are as ravenous as they were when they first sat down. Maggie says it would probably do them both good to take a hike, but they concur that neither is feeling exactly energetic. While Maggie is at first the more motivated of the two, heat becomes an issue for her after the first mile of searching for songbirds and Indian mounds. Plus, her left knee begins to bother her. She doesn't mention it to Tae.

Maggie lets Tae get ahead of her after the first mile. She is amazed at the girl's energy, which is so much greater than her own. No doubt menopause is to blame for some of her sluggishness and foggy thinking. Maybe she'll give some thought to taking a hormone supplement.

It isn't that she's envious of Tae's energy, her beauty, or her brains. Mostly, she envies her because she's inspired by her little muse. Maggie can't help but watch her, as she hikes the trail without a care. More than other qualities, it is her unselfconsciousness that Maggie enjoys, although it's obvious that Tae isn't always comfortable in her body. It's like she can't get enough of watching the girl. It occurs to her that with the exception of sleeping and driving she has been watching Tae almost every waking moment since the beginning of the trip. Had Maggie realized it before now, she would have turned the car around and headed back to Flint. But while she's strangely attracted, Maggie surely knows she has the presence of mind to never cross the line... Are the sexually depraved really all that monstrous, or are they just a little less able to see the boundaries between appropriate and inappropriate?

Maggie's pedometer logs the hike at three miles. Tae tells her she could easily go another three, but knows better than to push too hard, and it's mid-afternoon by the time they're on the road again.

Chapter 12

A few hours down Highway 50, Maggie stops at the Econo Lodge Motel on the outskirts of Morgantown, West Virginia. Like Athens, Morgantown is a college town, the home of West Virginia University. Tae appears to be disappointed by the roadside motel. "We can't always stay at four-star hotels," Maggie explains. She tells Tae how most of her life she hasn't made enough money for vacations like this one, but promises that tomorrow they will visit the part of the campus that runs along the Monongahela River.

And how to explain what happened that night in the motel room while Tae was taking a bath… They were both tired from the drive even though it was not a particularly long distance. Maggie had had another call from Andrew the Sixth, who'd tried, more persistently than the last time they'd spoken, to persuade her to return to Michigan. She did with him what she did with all her former lovers who still showed interest: she strung them along, but made no promises. She hated the finality of goodbyes. Unlike some of the others, she and Andrew had remained friends—better friends, in fact, than they'd ever been lovers.

So after listening to him lecture her for almost an hour, she cut him off in mid-sentence as she suddenly that Tae had been in the bathroom the entire time. Usually her baths didn't last more than twenty minutes.

Maggie had stood outside the door and listened. No splashing of water. No quiet singing. No sound. What if she's drowned in the tub? Maggie rapped, first gently, then pounded as if she's about to break down the door.

"What?"

"You okay in there?"

"Yep… You okay *out* there?"

"I was worried. You've been in there a long time."

Maggie turned the door knob and pushed open the door a crack, as if she still didn't believe that Tae was all right. Tae sat up, startled, and cupped her small breasts so Maggie could not see them. Her braids were coiled on top of her head to reveal her slender shoulders.

Yes, it is awkward. And Maggie feels…something else… What? It's not exactly sexual; it's even more primal. She fights the urge to enter. She might want to embrace her, but she knows it's not right.

"Would you like for me to wash your back?" Maggie tentatively asks, fearing rejection. She feels her cheeks burning.

Tae accidentally rubs soap into a twitching eye and blinks rapidly.

There is nothing wrong with what Maggie is feeling. Nothing wrong… And she is relieved that Tae does not pick up on her emotions, so complex and so confusing. Or does she? Maggie rubs a bar of soap up and down Tae's long, lean back. Then she soaks a fresh washcloth in the warm water. She doesn't ring it out before drawing it over Tae's smooth, pecan-colored skin. And how close she comes to asking the girl if she can take a picture—nothing sexual—but her lean back is so lovely, her skin so smooth… In the end, she decides against it: a fine line not to be crossed, at least not now… Besides, Maggie is not a good photographer, so the picture would likely not do justice to the girl's beauty.

"Everything will be better once we get to Uncle Tyler's," she tells Tae before turning off the bedside light.

But Tae is not so sure.

Maggie dreams she's lying between her parents in their bed. Their bodies are turned sideways facing away from her. She can't figure out why she's cold since she's flanked on both sides. Lying as still as possible, she is afraid that if she moves, it will cause one of them to awaken and realize that she's there. They might tell her to return to her own bed. "You're too big to be in bed with us!" How often had they actually told her that as a girl? But this doesn't happen because she realizes she's lying between two dead parents and she has no idea how to get out of the bed.

From Maggie's Journal

Detroit, mid 1960s

Caroline had a graduation party in the family room of our basement. I wasn't allowed to attend since I was too young—a few months before I'd even started kindergarten, but at least Mom let me greet Caroline's friends when they arrived. How I loathed being viewed as a little kid—Caroline's skinny little sister. Not about to let it stop me, I snuck downstairs and spied on them as they laughed and danced to loud music playing on a record player. Hating to be invisible, I joined them and played my role of 'silly little sister' just to get a few laughs, especially from some of the cute teenage boys. The nicest was Bill Binder. I don't know whether it was his smile I first saw, or the fact that his skin was as dark as coal, but I loved that he had noticed me, while no one else had.

He was the only 'Negro' there. I studied him from across the room then slowly approached and asked if he "felt all alone." He had a stethoscope around his neck, exactly like the one my doctor used. I asked him if he would listen to my heart. After he'd carefully listened to it, he told me that mine beat a little faster than normal, but that was okay because even though I was a little girl, he could tell I was "more caring than a lot of other white folks." His words—true or not—stayed with me always. Years later Caroline told me that he had, in fact, become a doctor.

The '67 riots changed everything. I was still in grade school when I watched downtown Detroit burning on our black & white TV (I was jealous of friends who had color sets). Kids on my block usually got together after dinner to play flashlight tag, but now we huddled around walkie-talkies to hear the latest. Due to a curfew, we couldn't stay outside for long on those hot summer nights: all children had to be off the streets by 7:00 p.m. Caroline said some of the riots were only about a mile away. The choppy static on the walkie-talkies confirmed she was right: looting was taking place just over on Grand River and Greenfield. Downtown was becoming uptown; home wasn't home anymore. Adults talked about a second civil war ready to break out. Who could blame all the downtrodden Negroes who had no jobs? They, too, deserved a piece of the American Dream. Caroline pointed out how our family had two cars, a window air conditioner, and every summer we could go away on vacations for a week. Some of the 'bussers' (kids who were bussed to my school) told me they never went to northern Michigan for vacations; vacations to them just meant being out of school for the summer, and on occasion going 'down South' to visit relatives.

Luckily, the riots ended and the curfew lifted. Although a lot of damage had been done, the entire city didn't burn to the ground, as many had feared, but nothing would ever be the same. Kids in my neighborhood talked about how their parents were installing dead bolt locks and burglar alarms. Dutch Elm disease hit the lovely vista of trees on the neighborhood streets and buzz-saws drowned out the cicadas. They sawed away my idyllic childhood and I was jolted awake from a sweet slumber to which I was never again able to return. The following summer for-sale signs had taken the place of trees. Then in 1968, Martin Luther King was assassinated a few months before Robert Kennedy. Giants were felled. The Vietnam War—despite the protests—was still going strong, though technically it still wasn't called a war. The world had turned upside down in a year. I wanted to go to Woodstock, but was too young. Caroline went with friends and had a 'freaky' time, whatever that meant. It seemed like the hippies were the only happy people on the planet (maybe because they were stoned).

Chapter 13

It's only 8:00 a.m., so there is no reason to wake up and start the day. Squeezing her eyelids shut does little to return Tae to slumber. Maggie is out getting fresh fruit and muffins for breakfast. They plan to enjoy it on the terrace, as it's the only nice part of this motel. It overlooks a postcard scene of rolling, tree-covered hills so, thankfully, they don't have a view of the parking lot and a gas station.

Tae's period started last night. So far, cramps haven't been too bad. Not as bad as sometimes. Should she tell Maggie about it? She's been getting periods for two years now; bad cramps or not, she always seems to need more sleep than usual. She rolls onto her stomach and closes her eyes. Not all the times she'd been touched by boys had been bad. Jalen was a sweet boy who moved away just two months after he'd moved into a house just down the street from her. He'd French-kissed her behind Rollfest Roller Rink, and it really wasn't bad at all. Had it not been for him, she might just be turned off to boys. And of course there was a kiss with LeAndra, but it had felt different than Jalen's. LeAndra and she had giggled during and afterward. They told each other that they were just practicing with each other to become good kissers for future boyfriends. But she was pretty sure that LeAndra had, or once had, a crush on her, and while she'd always liked LeAndra, she never pictured doing other things with her.

And what about the bath yesterday? Maggie had seemed worried about her; then she'd wanted to wash her back. But it was the voice she used that made her wonder. It was soft, as usual, but there was something different about it, too. A quaver…It made Tae feel not afraid exactly, but not safe either. One moment Maggie seemed motherly and the next—for want of a better word—strange—something she'd heard in LeAndra's voice a couple times, too. What if Maggie tried to kiss her on the lips? Maybe Maggie was gay, or bisexual. But that seemed impossible since she'd had all those boyfriends. If Maggie were ever to try to kiss her, it would be very weird. She loved Maggie, but not *that way*.

The good thing is that Maggie doesn't need to 'mother' her the same way that Quintana does. Maggie's not like that. Maggie shows her things and has so much to say, though at times she talks way too much, especially when she trying to read or daydreaming. And Maggie asks too many questions and seems to feel the need to tell Tae all about her life. Tae doesn't get that, particularly when it comes to the bad stuff which she'd rather forget or spin into a story. Lately, she's begun to wonder about Maggie's writing. She often talks about it, but rarely has Tae seen her actually put words on paper or on her laptop. Is Maggie as odd as Mrs. Tilders, just in a different way?

Since the drapes are pulled, Tae can't see the terrace, and except for a thin strip of light slipping through, it could be the middle of the night. Same way Mama always had her bedroom. Were it up to Quintana, the shades and drapes in the house would never be open. Quintana claimed to be a night owl, and said the sunlight gave her headaches. Tae and her three sisters had always refused to let her sleep around the clock. As the day would wear on, their knocks at the bedroom door grew ever louder. They'd worry that Mama would sleep her life away. Tae realizes that she's similarly predisposed. Maybe Quintana really is her mother, after all.

She drags herself into the bathroom to change her tampon, which she's certain needs to be changed. Good thing she got out of bed when she did, otherwise there would be a red smear on the white sheets. To think she's going to have to deal with this every month for the next several decades is too much for her to get her mind around. Maybe this is one reason women have children: for nine months when they're pregnant they don't have to deal with cramps, blood, and mood swings. But women who become mothers have issues, so many that Tae doesn't want to think about it. After washing up she studies her reflection in the full-length mirror in the dimly lit room. Still no Maggie…

Flinging her long, pink nightshirt onto the bed, she stares at her girl-woman's image in wonder. She cups her lemon-sized breasts, fuller if not larger than the last time she'd checked; her long, lean legs—some might call them skinny; a new indent at the waist, unnoticed till now because her hips are filling out; the nest of pubic hair, suddenly much more of it in the triangle above her legs. She stares long at this almost stranger. She veils the lower half of her face with several long braids. Her fingers flit and fumble as she gets acquainted with the toffee-colored skin of this new self. She's pleased but confused.

Any second Maggie will spring through the door bearing fruit and no doubt singing, "Rise and shine, Tae!" Maggie always seems way too cheerful, and Tae is beginning to dread her untimely good nature. Not that her mama didn't sometimes try to wake her in any one of many annoying ways, too… Maybe Tae should tell her that her period has started and how bad her cramps can be; not exactly a lie, just a slight stretching of the truth in order to keep Maggie off her back.

How she missed the lodge in Hocking Hills—not for its fanciness, but for its charm. She'd felt safe there, and she liked the routine they'd established; what a jolt when it came time to leave! Why hadn't they just taken a plane to Tyler's home? Why not just be done with this road trip? Because Maggie's got the purse strings, and Maggie claims that life on the road will help to make Tae a better writer.

And how she misses her own bedroom! It is hers and hers alone, despite the million intrusions on any given day. The only bedroom she's ever had, except when they lived with Granny in the country. No doubt one of her sisters has taken it over now… Mama is forever prophesizing how "the rug is about to be pulled out from under our feet," and any day they might have to move someplace cheaper, where she and her sisters will have to share a room. What she wants is a rug that's nailed to the floor—and so far there hasn't been one that could give her a sense of security or permanence. She misses her bed, her desk, her creaky, half-broken rocker, her tower of used paperbacks. These things give her a sense of who Taezha Riverton is, and all this traveling from motel to motel is no substitute for home.

She takes out the photo of Uncle Tyler and stares at his blurry but handsome face. Then she puts on a bead ring he once made for her and stares at her hand.

Why hasn't Quintana called more often? She's only heard from her only a couple of times, and she'd expected her to call daily, if not several times per day, not that she would always answer. But she feels hurt by the lack of attention. Maybe Quintana knows this. While Tae misses her—on an off—she doesn't miss her sisters, except Tamala, who has just passed ninth grade, even though she is sixteen. Tamala is the sweetest of her sisters, but she was sick much of the time, so she often missed school. Caring for both Tamala and for Quintana has fallen on Tae more than her other two sisters, and she sometimes missed school. When Aunt Serafina used to visit, she'd say, "Taezha, you don't have to mother your mama, you know? That's not how it's supposed to be." Many other things in the Riverton household weren't the way they were supposed to be, but anything else wouldn't be normal—at least not the normal to which she's become accustomed.

She gazes at some photos of her family—ones which she'd decided to take with her at the last minute before driving away with Maggie. Lingering over each, she promises herself to be careful to never lose them.

Two days later, Tae and Maggie are still at the same motel. Neither is happy about it, but as Maggie says, "It's a practical decision." A decision made because of Tae's cramps and Maggie's jangled nerves. Maggie thinks that Tae almost hurled because she'd eaten an entire pack of mini-donuts, followed by some sugary pop, and too many cherries. Tae isn't so sure. Yes, it was dumb to eat all that stuff, but she tells Maggie that it's because of her period, plus she's probably allergic to the motel.

"What's wrong with it?"

"Where to begin? "The air conditioning works okay, but it's loud and the hallways are long and dark. It smells like dirty feet, don't you think? Could that be mold?"

"Maybe it's from a dragon's under-wings." Oh, that clever Maggie…

"A fat spider just after it got squished on the bottom of your shoe!"

"Good, Tae, but spiders don't smell."

"Have you met them all? The big juicy ones are rank in that moment right after death. Perhaps that's their spirits as they fly off to the next world!" Tae comes to regret those comments because shortly afterward, she suffers several bouts of diarrhea. The image of the spider returns to bite her.

Maggie brings her ice water, and later Gatorade. Knowing she isn't up for conversation, Maggie reads and writes in her journal. Tae is pleased but doesn't think she should mention it. She pops one butterscotch Lifesaver after another, channel surfs with the volume low, recalling how Maggie once reminded her of a white Serafina (actually Caroline reminded her even more of her aunt). Truth is she no longer does. Not much, anyway. Serafina was glamorous, as well as mysterious; Maggie is a little mysterious, but more than that, she's confusing and unpredictable. Tae once thought her strong, but lately situations seem to make Maggie nervous. More than anything, Tae wants to understand her. Maggie may not be like Aunt Serafina, but she certainly is like an aunt—*her white auntie.*

Tae's been writing story starts directly onto her laptop for the last couple of days, but the problem is they all sound dumb, so she deletes them.

Maggie's a writer, too, so why isn't she writing more? She has often told Tae, that she is her muse, so why isn't the so-called muse-magic working? Why is Maggie so worried about this person—Sulie—following them? Why is Maggie so kind, so good to Tae? It's not like she owes her anything. Why has she lately been saying, "When we get to Uncle Tyler's, everything will be better"? Now that she thinks about it, Maggie has been mentioning Uncle Tyler a lot lately. Not that Tae minds it; not at all. While she's grateful for his letters and the little presents he has sent her (especially since Aunt Serafina died), she doesn't really know him well. How can you really know someone through letters? Questions multiply in her head as fast as rabbits breed.

———————

They are both relieved to leave Morgantown, despite the one hundred-degree temperature and not knowing precisely where they're going next. Generally southeast, yes... Maybe they will stop in Charlottesville or Richmond, or go further south to Norfolk.

Wouldn't Maggie feel more comfortable with a particular destination in mind? Tae knows better than to ask, but if Tae were a cat, she'd be switching her tail. She isn't sure if it's because she hasn't felt well for the last couple days, but Morgantown has so far been the low point of the journey. Maggie's behavior was skittish and inconsistent: in the motel room she had checked her cell phone incessantly, and she was continually peering out between the drapes at the parking lot.

"Why do you look out the window so much?"

No doubt Maggie was worried that Sulie was stalking them. She'd paced in circles while Tae felt imprisoned in the small motel room with a paranoid.

Lately, Maggie's left eye seems larger than usual. And the right eye appears to be a little droopy, like it wants to nap. So much for having fun on the road; the scenery will soon change, she hopes.

The next twenty-five miles feels longer than it should because Maggie is insisting on silence in order to listen to a strange intermittent noise coming from the engine. Tae can't hear it. Traffic is ridiculous. Maggie keeps looking out the rearview mirror, just as she did from the motel room window. Tae puts in her earbuds and turns up the volume. She is feeling that strange exhilaration that she always does before a storm; her skin isn't tingling yet, but she knows it will start any minute. She wants to tell Maggie how Quintana calls Tae her "little weather vane" because she can always predict a storm.

At last they pull up to a McDonald's. "How many Anywhere, USAs do you think there are, Maggie?"

"Not now, please. My head hurts, so do my knees." Maggie closes her eyes. Tae waits. Maggie appears older than usual. Maybe she hasn't been sleeping well.

"I drank too much wine last night. Then I had a strange dream. Something about my parents waiting for us at Tyler's..."

"Maybe it's because a storm is coming. A bad one! I've always been able to predict."

"I've been thinking...haven't decided...but maybe..."

"We shouldn't go on?" Tae finishes. "Don't you think we should just stick with the plan?"

"Just like you have a feeling about the rain coming, I have a feeling about—I don't know—things not going well for us. It's complicated. The world is not always as friendly as we might like it to be."

"Whoever said the world friendly? Remember who you're talking to, Maggie. I know all about disappointments, but I also know that it's what you make of your situation. Maybe you've got dark lenses over those blues eyes of yours."

"Let's have a bite to eat while we consider our situation." They both order a chocolate shake, and Tae also orders fries.

Three hours later, they are halfway to Richmond, Virginia. They listen to CDs together—everyone from Alicia Keys to Dave Brubeck—and it helps the time pass. The sky is still partly sunny. Tae points at the thickening clouds, but says nothing. Maggie has been in a calmer mood since she made the decision to continue the journey to Tyler's. Still, she's acting oddly. Could it be because of the bath? Sometimes she acts like her mother, or her best friend; other times, little more than a stranger. At last, Maggie confides her fear of Sulie.

"Why are you worried about her following us? We only saw her once."

"Actually, I didn't mention the other two occasions."

"Maybe you just thought it was her..."

"My fear is that she's singled me out. Who knows why? She could be a mental case."

"If she's following us, shouldn't we tell the police?"

"Do you really think the police would do anything? They'd probably think that I'm the crazy one!"

They drive for a while without speaking. The clouds race into each other. The air outside is thick as yogurt. When they get out of the car at a rest stop, Maggie suggests that maybe they'll end up being storm chasers, and Tae tells Maggie that becoming a storm chaser would be her second career choice. Maggie slaps her wrist, only half-kidding.

"How come you're always asking me about what I'm writing?" Tae wants to know. "And what about you, Maggie? When was the last time you wrote something?"

"I've been working on several poems that I haven't quite finished. Also, I have notes for a novel about an elderly couple who die engulfed by flames."

"Your parents…"

"Since my parents' deaths, I really haven't accomplished much, so maybe I am an imposter. Maybe I only wrote for their approval; but now that they're gone… Anyway, don't you know that I've got my little muse sitting right next to me?" Tae isn't sure she wants to be anybody's muse.

It must be horrible to lose parents the way Maggie lost hers. No wonder she hasn't written much since they died. But why would she want to write about a couple that not only died in each other's arms, but whose bodies went up in flames?

Tae feels sorry for herself for never having known her father. But she knows that he's out there somewhere. Maybe in North Carolina… As for her mother, who really isn't her mother, would her death really be so upsetting? Of course she would miss her, and she'd certainly feel bad, but maybe not as bad as when she lost Aunt Serafina. She could always connect with her aunt, feel an affinity with her aunt. All Tae really knows about her father is that he'd been on leave from the navy the night he spent with her mother. She imagines it was brief but sexy and romantic.

A lonely sailor and a pretty woman looking for love and getting just a taste of it… She and Aunt Serafina used to make up stories about him: where he'd come from (a small town in Oregon or Utah) and where he wound up (maybe in Chicago, still searching for Tae's mother, who was of course, not Quintana, but whom? Or maybe he had retired from the navy and was living in a fishing village in Italy). Their little game was so much fun. Of course, she hasn't played it much since losing Serafina.

So, who is this Uncle Tyler, anyway? Kinder than most white men, but definitely a man of mystery… She only has one small picture of him standing against a tree trunk and gazing off in the distance; arms folded, clad in blue jeans, a dark T-shirt, brown hair combed back. She notes how tan he is, almost movie-star handsome, and though slight, he's well-built with muscular arms. She must have taken out the photo hundreds of times from her wallet since receiving it a few months ago. Will the three of them get along? Will he be as nice in person as he's been in his letters? How long will she and Maggie stay with him? Does he have many friends? Does he lead an interesting life?

From Maggie's Journal

Detroit, 1972

Trying to stare down Jennavette in gym class counted among the most unpleasant moments in junior high. Our locker room was a large supply closet. Thirty girls at a time stripping off school clothes and donning ugly blue shorts and white T-shirts. Wouldn't have been so bad, but life had suddenly given me (as well as cookies and pop-tarts) a bulkier body, complete with pubic hair, breasts, and hips. The trick was to change as quickly as possible. After changing, we had to find our 'spot' on the gym floor and remain there until we were picked for a team. Since grade school, I had a history of not being picked for a team, not because I was too delicate a flower, but because I was too clumsy. In junior high it was made worse by added pounds, which made me self-conscious and overly talkative.

One particular day when I was feeling especially defiant, Jennavette told me to shut up. "White girl, what did I just say to you?"

"You're not my boss!" I said, before thinking.

One of her minions later handed me a note: "Meet me after school, or else!" Knees trembling, stomach in knots, I waited outside after everyone else had left for home. An hour went by and no Jennavette... She wasn't book-smart or pretty, but instead was street-smart and angry in a body that resembled an African fertility goddess (who on some level was to be respected). She must have thought I resembled a white fertility goddess, because the following day, she laughed when she heard that I'd waited for so long on the schoolyard. She never bothered me again.

Chapter 14

Sitting-still is making Tae crazy. Listening to music doesn't seem to help. How she loathes being a passenger. Is it because of the boredom of the road? Or is it the coming storm? Weather vane that she is, she's sure that her restlessness is due to the storm. Winds have picked up and Maggie is gripping the steering wheel with both hands.

Maggie almost collides with the car in front of her but at the last moment swerves and skids to a stop on the shoulder of the road. She refuses to look at Tae, who can tell that she's angry. "Please don't talk now. I need a minute," Maggie says without raising her voice. She speaks in such a low tone that it almost seems to Tae that she is growling. They remain on the side of a busy highway for several minutes. The darkening sky helps to relieve Tae's boredom. She can't bring herself to cast her eyes on Maggie, whom she sometimes loves and sometimes hates. Does Maggie have mixed feelings about her, too?

"I know I'm a goof-up, Maggie, but do you love me at least a little?"

She also wants to ask Maggie if she is having a problem with her race. *What if I were even darker than I am?* She bites her tongue but the question dangles loosely, ready to fall from her mouth.

"Sometimes I don't like what you do, but I love you as if you were my own!"

As if she were her own…what? Child? Kid sister? Friend-with-benefits? Tae knows better than to ask.

And then the storm hits. For the last half hour traffic has slowed to a crawl, with several cars pulling off the highway to wait out the downpour. Maggie decides to keep inching along. Time weighs heavy. Maggie mentions that she saw Sulie in her little yellow car on the shoulder of the road a few miles back.

Once they reach the motel parking lot, Maggie suggests that they leave their luggage in the car until the rain lets up. Even so, they are drenched by the time they reach the lobby. Maggie jokes about how they must look like drowned rats. She gets a ratty-look on her face by twitching her nose and rubbing it with a hand cupped into a paw. While it's far from Tae's favorite animal, Maggie's rat-attack strikes her as hilarious. They double over in laughter. Maggie has a hard time coming to her senses as she registers for a room.

"Will that be a King or a Double?" asks the pinched-faced little woman (not unlike a rodent herself) behind the counter. Maggie immediately sobers up. "A Double, naturally."

Even in the elevator they can hear the booming thunder. Their room is located on the fourth floor. Maggie suspects the elevator has only made it to the second floor when it stops and the overhead light goes out.

Maggie slides down the back wall and pulls her knees to her chest. She is trembling as Tae kneels and throws her arms around her. It is dark except for a dim red glow behind the alarm button. They soon find out that pressing the button does no good.

"The power outage is probably affecting the entire city. What if it takes days?" asks Maggie.

"You're always thinking the worst. Someone will rescue us."

"I hope you're right, It's only been five minutes and already it's terribly stuffy."

Lucky for them (and particularly for Maggie) the lights come on in the elevator. They begin to move upward after Tae presses the button for the fourth floor. There are mirrors on three walls, which neither had noticed before. Is it only Tae who sees an ageing, messy-haired woman, or does Maggie see that woman, too? Does Maggie see the vibrant young girl standing next to her, a young woman who is calm and caring and fully at ease with the situation?

Tae does what she always does when entering a motel room: she bounces on the bed she's claimed as hers. It's merely to test out the mattress (or that's what she tells Maggie). She can tell even without lying on it that this one will be hard. "How long will we be staying in Richmond?" Before getting an answer, the bedside phone rings. It is the woman at the front desk checking to see if they are okay and informing them—as if they don't already know—that power has been restored. Maggie's polite, but just barely. *Yes, yes… They're okay…A complimentary breakfast? Isn't breakfast included?* Maggie must have misread the brochure: she'd thought that it read 'complimentary' when it actually said 'continental.'

Maggie silently fumes as she paces their temporary quarters. She wonders aloud about asking for an upgrade to a deluxe suite—at no extra charge—but then decides against it, as they'll only be staying one night.

When Maggie goes downstairs to collect the luggage, Tae remains in the room. She channel-surfs, uses the bathroom. The fan is loud, but the sound of the toilet flushing is even louder. Loud footsteps are heard in the long hallway. She peers through the peephole at a woman leading a little boy who is having a temper tantrum. He's kicking the walls as she drags him along. Next, she checks the view, but it faces only a small rectangular pool with a fence around it. No one is in the water, of course. When they'd first arrived, her heart was set on swimming if the weather cleared, but she doesn't know what she wants to do now.

What's taking Maggie so long? Has Sulie kidnapped her? Has the woman at the desk called the police because she knows that Tae is a minor and that Maggie is clearly not her mother? Hadn't someone at the last hotel told them that Richmond's crime rate was high? Maybe Maggie is being robbed at this very moment—held at knifepoint—or worse: at gunpoint! Maybe she has been gagged and thrown into the backseat of a car. Maybe she is bleeding, or crying, or even wishing she were back inside the disabled elevator…

That's it! Tae lets the door slam behind her and isn't about to wait for the elevator. She takes the stairs to the lobby where there is now a small but growing crowd. The line at the Reservation desk is at least twenty deep.

Maggie is nowhere to be seen.

As Tae races to the parking lot, she takes her ringing phone from her jacket pocket. Maggie? The call from Quintana. Tae tells her she can't talk; she will call her back.

The red minivan is in the parking lot, but no sign of Maggie.

Again, she races, this time back into the hotel. "Excuse me," she says after elbowing her way to the front of the line.

"You'll have to wait your turn," snaps Lady Pinch Face.

"It's an emergency! Have you seen my auntie?"

"I saw her walk into the building about five minutes ago." Maybe the lady's face isn't as pinched as she'd thought.

"Thanks!" she shouts, darting toward the elevator. Somehow they must have just missed each other as she was heading 'down' and Maggie 'up.'

Maggie is in the room and acting like she's been there awhile. Clothes are strewn about the floor. "Tae, I strictly told you…"

"I was so worried. What took you so long?"

Maggie explains how one of the suitcases—her own—hadn't been improperly zipped. Clothes had spilled onto the wet parking lot, so she'd had to wring out several items before repacking. Now she'll have to find a laundromat… Oh, and then she was asked for directions by a woman with three young children in tow. It took forever for the woman to recall the name of a street, so Maggie could type it onto the GPS.

Tae sobs. Now it's Maggie's turn to do the hugging.

Chapter 15

Another dream about Heidi Atterwall. Maggie is questioning her, grilling her, in attempt to get Heidi to talk about her life. At last, she breaks the inmate down, and Heidi, faltering now and then, expresses how she was raped, not only by her father, but by an uncle, too, with her mother watching and smiling. Heidi is crying and Maggie is congratulating her on facing repressed memories, telling her: "Now you'll be able to express yourself creatively." Heidi continues to cry, telling Maggie that Maggie just doesn't understand. Now Heidi must relive it all over again. "My death is on you!" she screams at Maggie, who wakes up drenched in the acrid sweat of the guilty bystander. What she can't remember is whether all, or part, was a nightmare, or if it had actually happened. What actually happened, years ago, was that she had hung herself and Maggie was the one to find her body dangling in her prison cell. Maggie wakes to find her fingers scurrying across her chest. Where are her breasts?

Next morning, Maggie and Tae walk the streets of Richmond in search of a laundromat, but gone is the spring in their steps that they'd had in Morgantown, or the little town (she can't recall its name) outside Hocking Hills. Is it the steamy air or something else? For Tae's sake, Maggie tries to act as if she is looking forward to the day—to the road ahead.

This is only the second time they'd washed their clothes since beginning the journey, and no way is Maggie going to wear the same clothes another day. She's never been the sort to mind wrinkles, but the odor wafting from both their suitcases was off-putting. Tae says it reminds her of athletic socks after a five-mile run on a hot day; Maggie claims it is worse.

It's only 9:00 a.m., but it feels like mid-afternoon. There's a bench up ahead where they can rest. If Maggie doesn't sit down she might keel over. She should tell Tae, but she doesn't want to upset her. No choice but to 'soldier on' (who said that? It's not one of her usual terms), but she doesn't want to pass out either.

"I think I'll sit for a minute or two," says Maggie.

"The laundry should be in the next block. Can't you make it that far?"

Instead of answering, Maggie plunks down. Hundreds of tiny, sharp needles shoot from one tonsil to the other. She sips warm bottled water and manages to wash most of the needles down.

The air in Lola's Laundry is only slightly cooler than outside, but at either end of the large room are two enormous fans. Maggie stands in front of one and waits for it to teleport her somewhere else—anywhere else—and is disappointed five minutes later to be at the same spot. During her countless laundromat moments, she was usually alone, but now she is with a girl that she is mentoring, one she also hopes will become her muse. At times Tae is certainly that, but at other times… She's an interesting girl—complex with a colorful personality as diverse as the spectrum. Lately, Maggie sees the world through Tae's eyes, not her own.

Tae is sitting on a white plastic chair at the end of a row of several other white plastic chairs. Maggie is slouched on a chair, directly across from her. Tae is wearing the black derby, now a little travel worn, and is madly typing on her laptop. Her slender body, as sinuous and slinky as a cat's…she's oblivious to her whereabouts, and to the uncomfortable air. So unlike Maggie, who feels puffy, disturbed, and otherwise ill-at-ease with the world.

The rumble-whir of the giant fans lulls Maggie into a state between waking and sleeping, where thoughts and images come unbidden; she's powerless to dismiss Sulie who stares at her with this impossible-to-read expression, always one step ahead and knows something that Maggie doesn't know.

Images of Sulie morph into Quintana pacing barefoot upon her driveway on a hot summer evening, her chin cradling her phone, a can of beer in one hand and a cigarette in the other…Then last night, Quintana's voice loudly admonishing Tae, warning her, "I'm your mama, and I'm talking to you! Don't go visit Tyler. He isn't your real uncle. Hear what I'm saying, baby girl? You are still my baby, aren't you? You know what I'm talking about? You better…" Those words replaying now in Maggie's mind above the din of the fans.

Had her parents been alive, Maggie wouldn't have done this…

Then memories of the bridge and the ledge… Maybe there will be a pier on the ocean for her to plunge into. A large wave could simply carry her out. But no! This is a different time in her life. Obstacles certainly, but nothing she can't deal with. Some might say she's crossed a line that should not have been crossed. So what? What's wrong with mentoring a young person? Helping her become who she is destined to become?

Tae continues to type. Maggie is relieved by how oblivious Tae is to her mood, and her plight. At some point, she moves into Maggie's row of white plastic chairs, two seats down from Maggie. Just a few customers were here when they first arrived, but now there are several. A rotund woman in shorts and a sleeveless tube top with a baby under one arm and three more in tow. Two are toddlers with runny noses, chasing and pushing each other. There's also an older girl of maybe five or six, petite and prim, sitting by herself with a stack of books on her lap

Maggie smiles for the first time all day. She so wants to be this girl, off in her own little world. And if she can't be Taezha the Writer, she really doesn't envy her young friend because, after all, Tae is stuck with her—anxious Maggie who worries about everything, who has been drinking too much each night.

 When they get to Tyler's, the world will right itself. It must. She'll quicken the pace of this journey. Despite Quintana's warnings, Tyler is who she must see. He'd said they could stay as long as they liked… that it was an open invitation. It's the only one they have. If he would only answer his phone… Tae has been trying to call him for several days. Still, no answer, and he doesn't have an answering machine.

Chapter 16

Maggie scans the crowd at Virginia Beach. If only she harbored a few good beach memories, times in which she felt, if not pleased with her appearance in a bathing suit, then at least satisfied. Damn all those fashion magazines she'd read at Tae's age! And always the awareness of not being anywhere near as stunning as her sister… Yet the crashing surf of the vast blue ocean now washes out the self-conscious moment. Almost. At any rate, she isn't as perturbed about her body as she used to be, especially since she's now clad in a long purple caftan. A smaller beach and she'd stick out like a swollen thumb, but not on this expansive shoreline.

Tae is sprawled on a beach blanket and clad only in blue bikini. She knows Maggie well by now, and she instantly knows the source of Maggie's discomfort. In a sleepy voice, she tells her friend to chill out. It's unnerving. Maggie loathes the role of the twitchy, petulant child, but at first feels clueless about how to break free of it. After daubing sunscreen on her nose for the third time in a half hour, she tells the girl in her most maternal voice: "You've got to let me put some sunscreen on your shoulders, dear."

"But I don't burn!"

"Silly goose, you've never been to an ocean beach!" Tae ignores Maggie and runs down to the water. Maggie watches her through binoculars.

After Tae returns, dripping wet and lower legs and feet covered in sand, Maggie insists again that she protect her skin.

Maggie is aware of her fall from a once held position of high-esteem in the younger female's eyes. Her role as mentor, while not completely gone, is now greatly reduced from what it had once been. She reminds herself that all teens distrust authority figures. Why should Maggie be perceived differently? Maybe her whiteness is secretly abhorrent to Tae. Not that Maggie will ever be able to ask her. Why not? A road trip like this brings out all kinds of warts and wounds and ugly little imperfections that one can keep hidden within a more superficial relationship. It makes her almost resent Tae's presence; her perfect little self.

All the young guys watch Tae as she plays in the waves and walks along the wet sand. When Tae finally returns to her blanket on the hot sand, Maggie almost yanks Tae's braids and tosses them off her back, then forcefully slathers her shoulders and back with lotion. Doesn't she realize that the sand sticking to her shoulders is causing Tae's skin to sting? Doesn't she see her wince?

How lovely it is to be inside, away from the glare and the beach crowd. They shower the sand and stickiness off their skin, and then change into almost matching sundresses before going out to dinner. The Surfside Bar & Grill provides seclusion and shade, while still overlooking the sand and ocean. At first, both are too tired to talk. Maggie snaps several pictures of the door leading to the beach.

While they nibble on salad and bread, they don't mention their earlier moods, and conversation drifts to Tyler's place; their imaginations have already taken them to his small farm.

Before going out to the restaurant, Tae had at last reached him by phone from their hotel room. And now, waiting for seafood entrées (salmon for Maggie, and shrimp again for Tae), the two recall his friendliness. This time he hadn't been so guarded and quick to get off the phone. Again, he mentioned, half-jokingly though maybe he was serious, that he had set the table for dinner and was feeling kind of like he'd been 'stood up.' After admitting to Tae that he was only joshing, he switched topics, informing her that he had the following boarders: two horses, two pigs, two sheep, and would now have two human females to add to his collection. Tae had laughed, but now his comment bothers Maggie, as it strikes her as more than a little sexist, though she keeps this to herself, not wanting to bias Tae's viewpoint. But to be counted along with the livestock!

Tae assured him before ending the conversation that they'd be seeing him in only a few more days. "Can't pin you ladies down, can I?" He then added how he understood, as that was always the way he operated in life, and how he really didn't understand those who were too exact.

Dinner continues to go well. Service is prompt and the conversation turns lively. First they discuss the trip and some of the places they've been: Hocking Hills, Athens, Morgantown, and Richmond. Tae can't decide which place has been her favorite: the lodge at Hocking Hills or here at Virginia Beach… Then it's on to books and languages: Tae wants to learn Chinese, Russian, and maybe Ancient Greek; Maggie has studied French and Latin, and wishes she had studied both of those more intensively. "You still have time to learn at least one really well," Tae says. The conversation turns serious as they discuss mortality, and Tae confides that she worries about her sister, Tamala, and how her asthma seems to be growing worse every year.

It amazes Maggie that they still have so much to say to one another considering that they've been constant companions for more than a month. She can't help making a comparison with her boyfriends: after several days together, a breakdown in communication was inevitable, except for Vince the Fourth. Tae complains that her nose feels burned, but before Maggie can reprimand her, Tae begins to tell her about the dream she had the night before. They usually report dreams to each other at breakfast, but this past morning, both were too conscious of packing for the next leg of the journey. Aunt Serafina and Uncle Tyler had starring roles last night.

They were in the front seat of a car and Tae was in the back seat. Tae was much younger than now. Uncle Tyler said, "Your mother just asked you to buckle up back there." And she had answered, "Mom's not here." Aunt Serafina flashed her a wide grin. "What you talking about, girl? I'm right here!" Tae woke calling out to her over and over again.

As they finish dinner, an unexpected silence falls between them. Maggie wants to tell Tae the truth about Serafina being her mother, but she'd promised Quintana that she wouldn't. Is it possible that Tyler is Tae's father?

"Don't act so astonished, Maggie. I'm not...You've thought about that possibility, too, right? I mean, I wasn't born yesterday. Why else would *Uncle* Tyler pay me so much attention? Think about it: He started doing so right after *Aunt* Serafina's funeral. Did Auntie Quintana tell you this secret?"

"No, she didn't," Maggie lies. While Maggie knew about Quintana not being Tae's real mother—that her real mother was Serafina—she'd never seriously thought Tyler was her father. Although she had little regard for Quintana, she'd kept the secret. "But let's suppose Aunt Serafina was your biological mother. Since you've been raised by Quintana, she might as well be. But if Tyler really is your father...then what?"

"I'll let him have it! You just watch me pound him to the ground! But if it's true—and my dreams rarely lie—why hasn't he told me? My main reason for seeing him, Maggie, is to learn the truth about my parents. I've suspected it for a long time and my dream just confirms it. Still, I want him to tell me himself."

"Maybe he didn't feel like he could raise a child on his own? And now he's ready to accept you into his life."

This puts a different spin on things. If it's true that Tyler really is Tae's father, there's the chance (the hope?) that he'd want Tae to live with him, despite her age. Where will that leave Maggie? Three will definitely be a crowd. As she sees it, there are three options: 1) remain in Tyler's town, but relocate (this way she could become Aunt Maggie); 2) continue on the road trip further south and crash for a time at Jocelyn's condo in Florida; or, 3) she could return to Michigan and beg for her old job back. The last option is the worst one. Once they get to Tyler's she'll re-establish contact with Jocelyn, in hopes her old friend will take her in—if it comes to that. A person always needs options.

Maggie decides against dessert, though Tae orders strawberry shortcake. Envy doesn't even begin to explain how Maggie feels, considering the sweet tooth she's always had. Maggie has put on over five pounds since they began the journey. She knows it because her pants are too tight to button at the waist. In fact, several buttons have popped off in the last few days.

The dessert arrives. When Tae pushes the plate between them on the table, Maggie says, "Sure, Tae, maybe just a couple of strawberries. Thanks."

They stroll along the three-mile boardwalk. A warm gust of air grabs Maggie's floppy-brimmed hat and runs off with it. Tae chases after it, as does a gull. Girl wins; gull loses and flies away with a complaining squawk to join a dozens of others perched on a pier. Maggie thanks Tae and decides against putting it back on her head. Tomorrow, Maggie declares, she's going to jog the length of the boardwalk. "But Maggie, you don't jog!" says Tae, laughing so hard tears trickle down her cheeks. Maggie refuses to join in the laughter. She'll have to find a way to make Tae realize how her righteousness manifests into smugness. Tae apologizes, but Maggie raises her brow. Apologies are no longer accepted.

"By the way, I saw Sulie this afternoon," Maggie says to change the direction of conversation.

"Where? Did she see you?"

"We passed each other right here on the boardwalk. She was just a few feet from me, but I couldn't shove my way through the crowd without making a scene. I tried calling her name but she didn't turn around."

"Maybe just a Sulie understudy. Was she dressed as usual?

"The beret minus the trench coat…I know it was her, Tae."

"I want to believe you, but why would she be following us? It doesn't add up."

No doubt, Tae has a more logical assessment of the situation.

· ─────────

For the last hour a worldly looking man has been sitting alone at a table for two next to hers in a beachfront bar. Mostly he's been busy chatting on his phone. She doubts he's aware of her. It's been several years since she met a guy in a bar. Not one of her favorite venues for meeting someone, though back in her college days...

Despite the chatter and the Top 40 selections playing in the background, being outdoors and close to the beach on a sultry summer evening makes her feel vibrant and alive. She is dressed in a long, black skirt, sleeveless white blouse, and silver bangles on one arm. Her face has more color than usual. She's wearing her hair down instead of in the usual ponytail. For once her eyes appear approximately the same size—or so the bathroom mirror conveyed. She hasn't been bothered by hot flashes lately. Open on the table is a small notebook she's been using to make story notes about a suicidal elderly couple. Her new notes are scanty and vague. She's overly-conscious of the man next to her. She begins doodling as she slowly sips a vodka & tonic. He's speaking softly on his phone in German; a few minutes later in French. After his second call, he notices her discreetly noticing him and asks if she might like to join him. Not wanting to disturb him, she shakes her head. Is she an imbecile to pass up such an invitation?

"Then how about if I join you, unless, of course, I'd be disturbing you?"

"No, I mean, yes—by all means—join me!" Her enthusiastic tone is over-the-top and probably a turn-off. He will probably drink his glass of wine quickly and bid her adieu… Turns out that his name is Chad Trilling and he's been all over the world: Thailand, Mongolia, Peru—all work related trips, though he's always combined work with pleasure. Without stating the exact nature of his work, he bats his long black lashes, and she is taking the bait that actually hasn't been cast her way. He's tall with deep-set, brown eyes, balding on top, but with a single long dark braid down his back. Wearing khaki shorts, a black T-shirt, an open white short-sleeved shirt and sandals, he has fantastically tanned legs; muscular, yet lean.

She leans over the table; her breasts perched like doves waiting to be fed. Suddenly, conscious of their expectant pose, she sits back in her seat. His chin rests on one of his hands as his eyes stun her into submission. Next thing she knows, she's in his room.

The last time she'd had sex was five years ago, the night after the death of her parents. Andrew the Sixth had been a gentle lover, though she'd clawed, cried, and screamed her way to a frighteningly lonely orgasm that made her feel like she was falling down a bottomless well. It had been enough to satiate (as well as to half-scare her to death) until now. Yet until now, it hadn't been so much the sex she has missed, but the merging with another to dissolve falsely imagined contours. That's what she desires now and thinks she's going to get with Chad. Instead, it's pure fucking: urgent, needy fucking on her part, raw and all-consuming. He senses her animalistic frenzy and rubs his face between her parted legs, stroking with his tongue. This arouses her all the more. They come separately, in spastic jolts. He asks her if it's been a while. She admits that it has.

The first, in an even longer time, since she's longed for an after-sex cigarette... She lies back on the pillow, sublimates with a red plastic coffee stir. He lies next to her, vaguely amused by her pretend smoking. She thinks of her protagonist, Pauline, from her once nearly famous novel. Pauline thought sexual favors would buy her freedom, and sporadically Maggie described the various acts she performed on Ray and how they didn't get her anywhere. When Pauline realized there would be no release for good behavior, she no longer felt anything sexual toward her captor, and then in turn she no longer initiated or responded. Maggie considers telling Chad about this part of her published book, but decides against it.

It's as if Tae has been watching from the corner of the room, and Maggie feels ashamed. What is she doing here having sex with a man she doesn't even know? And what is Tae doing? Maggie had told her that she'd be gone only a couple of hours, but now it's been several. What if she returned to their room and Tae wasn't there? Not that she could blame the girl, who understandably felt like a prisoner by now...

They don't meet each other's eyes or say much until he tells her they know someone in common. She sits up with a start. Turns out he'd met Sulie on the boardwalk earlier in the day... Must have had her beret pinned to her head, otherwise it would have been snatched by the wind. He'd gathered, from Sulie's near perfect French, how there were two females—a woman and a girl—from her hometown who kept appearing wherever she went. "She's a strange little woman. Intriguing, in her way," he says.

How does he know that that is how she perceives Sulie?

"I have no idea why she's been following us. At first I thought it was just coincidence."

He looks at her dubiously. "Where else are you headed next?" he asks.

No way is she going to fall for it, revealing everything just because they've had sex.

"Listen, Tae will be wondering where I've been all this time. It's been…It's been …" She can't find the word, and thankfully, he has the decency to put his index finger gently across her lips. She licks it. She knows her one-night stand with Chad will never amount to more. Phone numbers are exchanged. He kisses her cheek and whispers that he'll call.

She will say nothing to Tae about Chad until they leave Virginia Beach, although moments after Maggie returns to the room she knows that Tae knows. It's been almost five hours since they have seen one another. Tae has been stuck in the room except when she went to the lobby to buy a drink from the vending machine. Then she finished one story and began another. Tae confides that she's begun a series of Sinbad & Sarie tales: all about a crime-fighting dog and his owner, Sarie, who happens to be a detective, just like Sulie. It's curious that she doesn't ask Maggie about her evening. Maybe she'll tell her that she ran into an old acquaintance and how they'd spent a long time catching up, but why mention anything if she doesn't ask? Maybe she should just tell her the truth. Part of her is eager to tell Tae more about her evening, but she can tell that Tae senses something is off-kilter, so Maggie isn't about to convey details.

Could she read Tae's story? "Maybe some other time," says Tae from her bed. Nonchalantly channel-surfing, she adds, "Guess it's getting late."

True, it's almost 1:00 a.m. Maggie takes a shower and wonders if she'll see Chad Trilling the next day, though she thinks it's unlikely. She replays the scene as she showers and then, in the dark motel room, facing away from Tae…

"Remember how we promised each other we'd get up to see the sunrise," Tae whispers in a tone of disbelief.

"I promise," Maggie says.

But Tae has grown skeptical of promises made by all the adults in her life.

Chapter 17

Tae watches the sun come up from the balcony of their hotel room. The eastern sky is painted with pink and lavender swirls, and then the sun-king rises in slow procession above the horizon. If only she could witness this miracle on the beach, she wouldn't feel so agitated—pacing the room and waiting for Maggie to wake. Also, she wouldn't be having so many bad thoughts about men… If only Maggie could be more like she'd been at the beginning of the trip—or better yet—like she'd been in the early summer before they left Flint. Maybe this *is* the real Maggie: a loser who makes promises she doesn't keep; another adult telling her what to do. A fake.

After Maggie returned last night, Tae smelled sex on her like she always did on Quintana. A sweet but rotten odor… And there was a look about her—messy and kind of school-girl silly. She knows that most people, even at Maggie's age, enjoy sex. So, maybe this means that Maggie isn't actually gay, or about to become gay, and Tae can breathe a little easier. But, if Maggie ever bats her eyes at her again…

She picks up a coffee stir from the floor next to Maggie's bed, twirls it, pretends it's a magic wand, and shakes it over Maggie's head. The wake-up spell doesn't work. As she takes a swig of warm, flat pop from a can on the bedside table, she wonders, as she has often wondered before, if she did something to make Maggie attracted to her (not that Maggie was always stirred up around her). Maybe Tae is, like Quintana sometimes called her, a vixen, or a "hot little number trying to work voodoo on folks." She feels guilty about being provocative.

Today, or maybe tomorrow, Maggie will tell her about what happened last night. Tae wants to know, but she doesn't. If Maggie gives her too much information, Tae will tell her: "Where I'm from, we have a saying: 'Not even a ho tells her business!'"

What cool places will they see before getting to Uncle Tyler's house? As much as she likes to travel, the long car rides and the many motels have now become boring. She'll tell Maggie as much, that is, whenever the snoring woman wakes up! Tae is getting hungry. She hates being stuck in the room. One more half hour then screw Maggie! She'll leave a note and go to the lobby restaurant to have breakfast on her own.

———————

Tae approaches Sulie in the lobby restaurant where she (Tae) happens to be waiting for Maggie. At first she wasn't so sure, but the little woman standing there with a toothpick between her lips, wearing a black beret and an unfashionable beige coat, had to be Sulie, the notorious Private Investigator. She walks right up to her and greets her with a "Hello, there." Tae's a little surprised at her own boldness but has a hard time believing this strange little person could possibly be dangerous. They speak for a couple of minutes.

Maggie joins Tae almost an hour later. She thanks her for being considerate enough to leave a note stating that she was at the restaurant, and lays on thick praise about how Tae is maturing right before her eyes. Tae wonders about a possibly deeper motive on Maggie's part, but decides to take the compliment at face value.

"Guess what?" she says to Maggie, "She didn't run away or say: '*Watch your backs,*' or '*I've got your backs,*' or anything like that. Mostly, all she said was, '*Funny how we keep winding up in the same places!*' And, oh yes, '*Give Maggie my best*'."

"And then what?"

"Then she told me to have a nice day."

"Maybe Quintana hired her to follow us," says Maggie.

"She doesn't have that kind of money," says Tae.

"Maybe her new boyfriend…"

Why does Maggie always think the worst of everyone? True, Tae doesn't think much of Jayvon, but why does Maggie always criticize, judge, or act paranoid? Maggie changes the topic and apologizes about missing the sunrise, adding how maybe tomorrow they'll see it together. This means they're going to stay at least one more night. Wonderful…*Not*!

After breakfast they hike along the boardwalk. Maggie admits to being on the look-out for Sulie, as well as a man she met last night. A nice man—tall, slender, with gorgeous eyes.

Oh, no! Here we go. Now she's going to tell Tae all about her experience last night. What is it with adults needing to tell all?

Another surprise: Maggie switches topics and informs her how they'll be staying just one more night and then take off for the Outer Banks. She whispers as if Sulie might overhear every word.

Tae dances on the boardwalks, spins and leaps. Her own spontaneity amazes her; they both laugh. Maggie reminds her, as she frequently does, "Let's remember to live each day, so why don't we go dancing and tear up the place tonight?"

Sometimes Maggie comes through for her. She really does. It makes Tae wonder why she sometimes gets so pissed off at her. Maybe it's not Maggie that sends her over the edge, but her own mood swings. She envies Maggie's more stable state of mind. Maybe that's one thing to look forward to about getting older.

And then there's Quintana…

From Maggie's Journal

When Caroline was a Teacher/Detroit, late 1960s

Before Caroline became an artist of some local repute, she was a teacher. I must have been about thirteen when she taught art at an elementary school near the Detroit Tigers' baseball stadium. Her students loved her and soon wanted to quit going to their other special classes (even gym), not only to make collages and drawings, but to hang out with her. She had her favorites, but never showed favoritism, or tried not to, since they were all her students. Most lived in ramshackle houses or thin-walled apartments and slept next to one, if not several, siblings. Few had regular meals, except for the free ones at school. Rarely did adult males live with them, and even more rarely did their biological fathers. The population included Appalachian whites, blacks, and Hispanics.

She went above and beyond for the few years she taught there, spending her December paychecks on Christmas boxes for the neediest in her classes. As her chosen assistant, I helped fill her shopping cart at K-Mart or drugstores (these were the pre-Walmart days). Even though I didn't go with her when she delivered the Christmas gifts to their homes, I loved picturing the delight on her students' faces. I thought my sister's many kindnesses (not merely the material ones) would single-handedly repair any strained race relations that existed in the city. Naturally, her compassion couldn't heal all the broken lives. That she couldn't, thoroughly frustrated her, and teacher burnout turned her to ash and cinder much sooner than other teachers. Many students never forgot her and would continue to look her up—even years later. Decades later, it was the impetus for me to apply for the school library job on Flint's north side.

———

After a family on our street sold their house to a black family, I was shocked at the vicious comments circulating through the neighborhood: "There goes the neighborhood!" or "Can you believe they sold out to a nigger family?" one neighbor would say with a shake of the head to another, who would then repeat it to another. What did they mean? Could it be that they were against integration in this Great Lakes industrial city? Maybe they were all for it, provided it didn't happen on their street? Little white sheep following each other into the safe suburbs… Thankfully, no one in my family thought that way. Incredibly, within the span of five years, my neighborhood on the northwest side became solidly black. My family was one of the last to move. A source of pride for me at the time, but years later I discovered the real reason we hadn't taken off with the rest in the great migration—the white flight: my father had too many debts which needed to be paid off before we could move. Hardly an ideological decision… Glad I was unaware of it at the time.

The Drugstore Holdup/Detroit, early 1970s

I've written two stories, four poems, and countless journal entries about the holdup. I did so in order to come to terms with it. It was a hot, late Saturday summer afternoon. This would turn out to be my first and only outing on what I thought would turn into another long, boring day. Caroline always took forever in the make-up aisle of Ashton's Drugstore and that Saturday had been no exception. No doubt, I'd been more than willing to accompany her there, as there weren't many places a thirteen-year-old, especially a thirteen-year-old girl, could go on her own. It was one of those summers when friends were always busy, and I considered my parents way too boring to hang out with.

In the back of the store at the pharmacy check-out, Caroline flirted in her charming, this-side-of-outrageous way (that both amazed and annoyed me) with the pharmacist, Lenny. How bumbling and oafish I must have appeared next to my pretty and sexy older sister! A study in contrasts… Little time to feel my usual self-consciousness, for standing next to me, rubbing against my shoulders, was a dark skinned man asking Lenny for little blue pills. When Lenny told him he'd have to have a prescription, the guy pulled out a gun, pointed it at Lenny, and demanded all the cash in the drawer. Everything happened too fast, but too slow: the thief told us quietly, in a low voice: "Don't move!" ('Us' consisted of Caroline, Lenny, and me.) I couldn't have moved if I'd wanted to. Caroline, always the defiant one, began to back away.

Next thing I knew, he had the bag of cash, was pointing the gun at Caroline and commanding her to follow him. She'd been taken hostage because she'd moved when he told her explicitly not to. Was it to be the last time I'd ever see my sister alive?

The teenage boy working at the front cash register raced past me to press the alarm button, which was located in the back by the pharmacy. Then Caroline reappeared. Turned out she had been used as a human shield so the robber could make a quick get-away.

After the hold-up, I never returned to that drugstore, nor did I take walks by myself through the neighborhood. Was this why fearful whites were fleeing to the suburbs? Caroline tried explaining the desperation of those unable to put food on their tables, and how some resorted to drugs. All part of the vicious cycle of poverty, she told me.

Chapter 18

Maggie doesn't blame Tae for hanging out with a group of kids her own age or slightly older. Is it obvious to them that she's watching them on the sunny beach? She hopes not. Her plan had been to begin re-reading *Anna Karenina*, but she hadn't realized how hard it would be to concentrate. Still, she continues to hold open the thick paperback, though not a page has been turned since she began the undertaking… At first, there are six of them—all girls, sitting in a circle. Even though it probably isn't true, they appear to be the best of friends…the atmosphere of intimacy makes Maggie envious. Every so often, one or two of them will get up to splash in the surf. After a while, a few of them drift away, leaving just two girls besides Tae. (Later, Tae will remark how they told her she had an exotic beauty and wished their tans could be as nice as hers.) A couple of surfers join them, and Maggie can hear the girls giggling.

Sitting on her beach chair, wearing a black cover-up that conceals only the tops of her pale legs, Maggie begins to mope. At first she eagerly awaits Chad's call, but as the morning wears on, she realizes she won't be hearing from him. Embarrassment gives way to disappointment, then relief—not that she wouldn't have met him for lunch, but there would have been an inevitable awkwardness that ridiculous striving men and women employ when they're not all that interested but feel like they must be at least polite. Tae, out of duty, stops by, and Maggie explains how she's glad Tae has met some friends. Before waiting for Tae's response, she tells her how once she's taken a walk, her plan is to head back to their room. She doesn't add that the beach is exhausting her, as is being hyper-conscious, not only of age differences, but from worrying whether the white kids are including Tae in their conversations. It makes her wonder if Tae had been darker skinned, whether she would have dared to take her on this road trip. Maybe not… This thought is reprehensible to her. Is it nascent racism on her part, or merely anxiety over society's judgment of her?

She tells Tae not to worry about having dinner together, and then gives her some money, as she knows Tae will probably want to have a bite to eat with her new friends. "They're not my friends," Tae responds, though she's secretly delighted at her newfound freedom, and at the sudden trust that Maggie is now displaying. "You know what I miss? You in a good mood like you are now!" says Maggie, cuffing the top of Tae's head. Big mistake, as Maggie immediately regrets her playful show of affection. Ordinarily, Tae doesn't mind Maggie doing this, but like any other teenager, she wants to appear as adult-like as possible. "Sorry," Maggie whispers, as Tae waves at the girls who are now watching with mild curiosity.

Maggie and Tae agree to meet at the dance at 7:00, though Tae claims she will be back to the room earlier to change and rest up. Maggie uses her hands as megaphones and exclaims as Tae's beginning to make her way back to the group: "I can't wait to check-out this outside, tropical dance!" And even more loudly: "Don't worry about having to sit next to me! Maybe we'll have to leave the dance a little early so we can catch the sunrise and also get an early start."

After making sure she'd given Tae the other room key, Maggie collects her beach bag and strolls along the boardwalk. She always feels older when she isn't around Tae, even though Tae can be—at times—a little hard to keep up with, and on occasion even exasperating.

She braces herself against a stiff, salty breeze, and then takes it on, licking the brine from her lips. Waves are high and the spindrift sprays across her face. Squinting in the bright sunlight, she searches for Chad—or Sulie—not that she thinks they would be together; there's no reason to think that would be the case, but she doesn't want to be caught off-guard—whether she comes across them together or alone. When she thinks about her wild time with Chad last night, she feels even more ridiculous, more isolated. Why does she not yet realize that these brief connections with strangers always make the next day's mood even lonelier? Of course she'd enjoyed the sex, made all the more intense by having 'no strings attached.' Still, she feels more fragile than ever. Had he secretly been repulsed by her less than perfect body? All those gross dimples on her uppers legs and upper arms? But the room had been dark…

How grateful she is to have Tae as a travel companion. She could not have made the trip alone. Had she taken it with someone her own age—male or female—she wouldn't be experiencing this fresh perspective. Still, she's known all along that a day might come when Tae will want to return home. How could Maggie blame her? If their trip had been a short one, it would be one thing. If Tae is, in fact, sick of traveling, then Maggie will know better than to take it as a personal rejection. If she were a teenage girl, how would she experience rambling around the country with an aging woman?

———

The glistening, black waters of the nighttime Atlantic lapping the shores of a coastal resort, plus the illumination from tiki-torches, creates an amorous atmosphere on the open-air dance floor. A live band would make it better yet, though the selected Top-20 hits being played by a DJ named Jimmy T sound sweeter here than on the radio while driving along the highway. Maggie is dumfounded that Tae isn't spending more time dancing with the young people she met on the beach, and she can't help but wonder why Tae is spending so much time sitting with her now. Is it because she's tired of them, or just feeling sorry for her?

"Can't I just sit with you because I want to?"

"I just don't want you to feel like you have to…"

"I missed you today, and I'm annoyed with a couple of them… Amber and Lisa… I told them about our situation. Maybe that was my mistake, but I'm not like these rich white girls. You wouldn't believe all the stories I've heard about European vacations, winter ski trips in Colorado, the homes complete with movie theaters and bowling allies... My life is so different than theirs. It was hard to know what to say to them. I felt as distant with them as I do with kids at school."

They observe the dancers on the crowded floor. Mostly teens and twenty-somethings, but a few older couples who are enjoying themselves, as well. Tae sips a Shirley Temple; Maggie, a vodka & tonic. When Maggie first arrived, Tae was out on the dance floor and it appeared that she was having a good time.

"Don't you want to join them? Isn't 'Someone Like You' one of our favorite Adele songs?"

"Maggie, why don't you come out on the floor with me? Remember that time at your apartment? I know you have some smooth moves."

It's been years since Maggie has danced. The last time must have been at a wedding reception for the daughter of one of her parents' friends. It doesn't take much more persuading on Tae's part. She won't bother telling Tae how badly her knees have been hurting the past couple of days. Tae would call her an old lady. Maggie hates that expression.

The two dance together. A couple of boys try to cut in, but Tae ignores them. Maggie and Tae laugh and twirl, and Maggie is able to forget about her bad knees. Before they know it, it is eleven o'clock, and then eleven-thirty. They slip away from the other dancers. Tae doesn't bother to say goodbye to her new acquaintances. That's just how it is with life on the road... Determined to see the morning sunrise, neither has to persuade the other to return to the hotel for some sleep. Maggie has never seen Tae this exhausted, and she is sure that the girl's thinking the same about her. Before drifting off, Maggie whispers, "We had a pretty good time, didn't we?" Sleepy Tae smiles and nods before drifting off. Both sleep so deeply that neither can remember their dreams the following morning.

Chapter 19

What did Tae expect? A romantic encounter simply because the place would have been perfect for one? Thankfully, she hadn't suffered what Maggie had endured—a one night stand. Don't women, like Maggie and Quintana, lose self-respect? And what if the white boy hadn't glanced her way at the dance? What a loser he turned out to be when he'd asked her if she was black. "What does it matter?" she'd shouted and flipped him off, something she usually did only to stupid adults when their backs were turned. Self-respect was her prize for the taking by not looking over her shoulder at him as she walked away. If only she hadn't found him so easy to talk to… If only she hadn't been attracted to the way his sandy brown hair fell over his eyes (she'd so wanted to run her fingers through it), and to his deep voice with that soft Southern accent.

It had all turned out for the best because Maggie and she wound up having a pretty good time. Not that Tae had faked it, but part of the reason she'd laughed so hard on the dance floor was because Maggie couldn't dance. Plus, too many drinks had made Maggie slur her words. For once, she had acted silly without trying.

Could it be that it's time to go home? Home to that noisy, smelly, grimy place where she could never hear herself think; where she spent most of the time being angry at her mom for being a drug user and a drunk; angry at her sisters because they were always screaming, singing, and hating each other and the world. But her bedroom was her sanctuary, the place where she'd written so many stories and poems.

And then there were the better times with Tamala. She loved that girl so much she could never do enough for her, especially when Tamala wasn't feeling well. Tamala was the only one who ever appreciated her stories. Tae now knows that she'd written them to entertain her; they always seemed to have helped her feel a little better. As much as Tae misses her, there's not much else there for her. So, no; she doesn't want to return yet...if ever.

———————

Neither is particularly sad to leave the crowds of Virginia Beach. Tae has not written much, and Maggie has not written at all... Now is probably not the best time to bring it up, so she doesn't. Instead, she tells Maggie about how she loves listening to the surf hitting the beach. She feels a sense of being home—not her home, but some greater home: comforted in a way nothing else in nature has ever comforted her. Maggie always feels this way when near the ocean. She tells Tae about her first visit to the seaside and about how travel must involve exploring places that have history...going to exotic countries with interesting terrain, shrines, museums, places with open-air markets where people speak in foreign languages. Seeing *The Seven Wonders*...

Maggie declares: "Before we get to Tyler's, I have someplace else in mind for a short stay—not saying where..." She turns the car around and heads inland. It is hard to determine if Tae has heard her or even taken notice of the fact that they're no longer headed toward the Outer Banks.

Even though Tae is sitting only a couple feet away, those damn earbuds of hers make it seem like she's in another world. To decrease the distance, Maggie decides to tell her about her night with Chad.

"It's been years since I did something like that—meeting a guy and just going off with him. I really don't recommend it. That he reminded me of Jason the Second probably had a lot to do with it."

"I remember you telling me about Jason. Why was he like Jason?"

"I guess because he knows several languages. In other ways, too...

His courtship was similar, too. One thing led to another, and then I found myself in his room."

"I hope you practiced safe sex, Maggie. That's all I can say. Even though you probably won't get pregnant at your age, you can still pick up an STD. Yes?"

"Right, but, oh, could he kiss… He knew exactly where and how to touch—"

"Enough! Puh-leeze! TMI! It's *me* you're talking to. Remember, I am only fifteen, and I really don't need the details."

Tae effectively shuts Maggie down. Maggie's cheeks burn with shame. What has possessed her to want to divulge the specifics of her sexual encounter? Once again she'd crossed a line…Why? To feel closer? It was one thing to tell Tae what had gone wrong in her past relationships with men. More than a few times she's come close to telling her everything; thinking the more Tae knew, the closer they would be. Still, she's aware that some of her secrets need to wait a few years until Tae is older. Maybe, too, she wants Tae to realize that she has no sexual interest in her. Maggie loves her like a friend or a daughter. She's attracted to her youth and her intelligence, and most of all her energy, but that's all! How many times has she told herself this? She would never do anything more than hug Tae. A few times she's had fleeting thoughts, though she's never allowed herself the luxury of lingering over visions. She knows herself well enough to know that she would never go further. Tae is not Maggie's Lolita! She can easily imagine Caroline accusing her of that. It wouldn't surprise Maggie in the slightest. So maybe that's the reason she'd brought up her one-night stand. In years to come, they will both be able to look back at this time and feel no embarrassment or shame.

Or so Maggie hopes.

Chapter 20

Tae realizes in a thunderbolt sort-of-way that she is sick and tired of this trip. Bored, too, with all the talk about writing and becoming a writer. All Maggie's questions about Tae's thoughts and feelings have finally driven Tae nuts. How can she be fifteen but feels like she is forty? Maybe even fifty. Maybe the real crazy lady isn't Sulie but Maggie... Maggie, who, a couple days ago, promised that today would be the day they'd be going to Uncle Tyler's and staying in a *real* house and eating *real* food. True, she doesn't want to return to Flint—at least not yet. Seeing Uncle Tyler has always been the primary reason for her agreeing to this ridiculous adventure. Seeing him and finding out the truth about Aunt Serafina being her mother and him being her father. Then yesterday Maggie told her that maybe they would stay a few nights more at the ocean, in an area called the Outer Banks. And then—just thirty minutes ago—the plan was changed again, because now they're headed someplace else.

Does this mean they'll get to Tyler's in a few days or a few weeks? Or maybe not at all? *Are we forgetting to enjoy each moment, Tae? To live each day is so important.* How many times has Maggie reminded her of this? She's used to stupid adults (ad-*dolts*!) putting whatever it was on 'hold.' They're all psycho and fake. Most of the time whatever *it* was would never happen. Why can't they just say what they mean? Doesn't Maggie think she can deal with the truth? Shouldn't Maggie have realized by now how truly tough she is? Except when she has to pee... Dang! Except when she has to be a passenger for too many miles....

Now they are an hour beyond the exit that they could have (*should have*) taken to reach Uncle Tyler's house near Monroe. Instead they are on their way west—or so says Maggie—to a destination somewhere near Asheville. It means another couple of hours in the car. *But Maggie, I really have to go! C'mon, find a place!* She had made her request ten miles east of their present location and still no buildings in sight. Maggie suggests a wooded area just up ahead. Good thing Maggie can't see the face she's making: a look of disgust and absolute loathing.

Finally, Maggie spots a roadside restaurant. She tells Tae that it is a good stopping point because there they will be able to discuss the plan over lunch, and Maggie thinks at least part of the plan, Tae will find acceptable. Yeah, right.

At a restaurant called The Diner, they both order chicken noodle soup and split an egg salad sandwich. The soup tastes like it's straight from a Campbell's can, and the egg salad has more mayonnaise than egg, but it doesn't matter since over the course of the past several weeks they'd eaten at some splendid restaurants.

And it isn't just Tae who has become tired of the road, restaurants, and motel rooms. Maggie is convinced that Sulie is a spy, no doubt hired by her sister or by Mr. Hardin. If not for Sulie's peek-a-boo presence, then Maggie wouldn't hesitate to drive directly to Tyler's, but now they will have to drive back in an easterly direction on some of the same highways. She explains this to Tae while simultaneously noting from the corner of her tired blue eyes that they are being watched by an elderly white couple in a booth across the room. Has Sulie hired others to help her? She immediately dismisses the idea. It's not like they are on the FBI's Most Wanted List. Tae notices Maggie noticing the couple. She smiles and gives them a wave.

"Maybe they think I'm related to President Obama…possibly a niece, if not a daughter. Yes?"

"Knock it off, you goose! You know we've got to get our plan worked out, though it's nice to see you're in a better mood than earlier."

"Who says I'm in a better mood? I'm really not. I know my skin's lighter, but do you think I look a little like Sasha or Malia? Remember that lady who came up to me in Virginia Beach and asked me if I was related to them? Maybe that was my fifteen minutes of fame. You think so, too?"

Maggie switches the topic and tells Tae how picturesque it will be in the mountains around Asheville. Maybe they will find a cabin near a spring or river, or better yet, a waterfall. They would be far enough out of town so as not to be tempted to drive in every day (such city girls they are at heart!). There they could write to their heart's content. If it works out, maybe they will stay for the entire month of August, and maybe even part of September. That should be time enough to make sure that Sulie is no longer in pursuit.

Maggie again changes the topic. How would Tae feel about being homeschooled at the cabin? And if not there, then it would surely be worth considering if they wind up staying any length of time with Tyler. Why not get a jump on things as soon as they get settled? Her goal is to teach Tae both the ninth and tenth grade curriculum in one year. That way she'll be able to graduate on time and start college at eighteen instead of nineteen. In Asheville, Maggie will try to obtain a list of the books that they use at the local high school, then simply purchase them online and have them sent to a P.O. Box. That is, of course, if they end up staying for a long time…

Tae makes a face at having to return to school (so to speak), but Maggie reminds her of the importance of getting her high school diploma and doing well so that she'll be able to get into a university. "I know, Maggie. You've only told me a gazillion times!"

The white-haired couple is still eyeing them with disapproval, maybe even disdain. In no way do they look at peace with the universe. Their single consciousness seems to be judgmental. Maggie will later realize how much they reminded her of her parents.

Chapter 21

Being in the mountains is completely different than Tae imagined. Maybe it's because she's been feeling dizzy. Not all the time, but mostly when she stands up too fast. Maggie hasn't complained about feeling odd, so no point saying anything to her. Not yet, anyway.

They've now been at the cabin near Asheville for three days. A real log cabin! The living room, the kitchen, and the dining area are all located in one large room. They each have their own bedroom, for which Tae is grateful, especially since she can lock the door with a latch. Maggie keeps calling it a perfect writers' retreat. Tae guesses that she's probably right but can't muster anywhere near the same enthusiasm. She wishes they were at Tyler's; they should have been there days ago.

The weird part is that while Maggie doesn't seem relaxed, she appears to have no problem writing. She begins early in the morning; stops at noon for a bite to eat with Tae; reads for a couple hours; returns to her writing, stopping only for dinner, followed by a walk and a shower. Then she once again takes pen in hand and works until midnight. Is this what she's going to do every day until they leave? Maybe Tae is Maggie's muse after all! There's no TV, just a radio (only one FM classical music station comes in clearly). Tae has her iPod, but she is tired of listening to the same old tunes. Since there is no Wi-Fi, she can't download anything new. It's so quiet that she begins to call her sisters more often—especially Tamala, whose asthma had worsened earlier in the summer and still isn't under control. Tae hasn't worried about her during the trip, but now there's time, too much time, not only to worry about Tamala, but about everything else.

When she'd told Quintana about their delay in getting to Tyler's, Quintana had sounded strangely relieved. Could it be because Tae will then learn the truth about the identity of her parents? Tae knows that Quintana has never been a big fan of Tyler, but wouldn't she want Tae to be living in an actual house, leading a normal life? (That is, if everything works out and Tyler wants them to stay...) Just once since Tae has been gone has Quintana asked her what she would be doing about school this fall. Maybe she simply takes it for granted that Tae will be back in Flint by then. Drinking and drugs have probably permanently screwed-up her thinking. Just today, Tae told her how tomorrow Maggie and she will be going to the school in the city to pick up the ordered textbooks (of course, she didn't let Quintana know which town), and how she'll have to hit the books early, since she'll be completing two years in one. Quintana didn't sound impressed or surprised. Strangely, she wanted to know more about the cabin. Maybe she knew not to ask about its location. Tae had wanted to tell her the real reason they were at the cabin, but she was under strict orders not to bring up Sulie. Why make everything sound complicated, right?

Tonight, after a small supper of beans and rice, Tae finds herself thinking about the God-question. Every time she seriously ponders God's existence, the following day signs seem to appear which help to strengthen her faith. She makes the mistake of telling Maggie.

"Do you really think that God causes an event to occur for your personal benefit? Oh, baby..."

"Listen, Maggie! Something's going to happen tomorrow. It always does after God comes to me."

Maggie's arms seem to be permanently crossed over her chest.

"Why are you looking at me *that way*?" Tae asks.

"What way" Maggie counters.

"It's kind of like you find me sexy or something." Tae gives her a sidelong glance.

"I find you charming...and funny. I enjoy your lively mind, and

your energy. You take away some of the dullness, some of the pain…
That's no small thing, believe me. You are attractive, but I'm *not*
attracted. Get it? Anyway, that's what you do for me. Tell me, what
do *I* do for *you*?"

"Besides taking me on this expense-free road trip? I guess you've
shown me the world… But sometimes you act strange—more gay than
I could ever be or want to be. Is this is how most white ladies act?"

"Well, Tae, I'm not 'most white ladies.' And I'm not gay. I've told
you my theory about how most people—most straight people—are
actually bisexual, right? Most never act on their impulses… Once I
kissed a woman, but it only happened once…okay, twice. But I have
never, and would never, contemplate having sex with a minor. You
do believe me, don't you?"

Tae nods. Several weeks ago she trusted Maggie more than anyone
she'd ever known, but now she doesn't always feel safe with her. It isn't
just the way that Maggie sometimes looks at her. What she'll never tell
Maggie is that she can clearly see how Maggie seems to really dislike
herself. Tae sees her as a lonely woman who doesn't know what to
do with the rest of her life. Whatever regrets that Tae may one day
have in her own life, she won't end up like Maggie or Quintana, and
hopefully not her own mother, who was almost certainly Serafina.

Chapter 22

For the first time in weeks, Maggie can think clearly. It must be the clean, cooler mountain air, as well as the solitude and the simple yet cozy, well-stocked cabin. She knows that she's done the right thing bringing Tae here. It helps, too, that she spoke with Tyler and went to town for the textbooks. The high school signed them out to her at no fee, provided she'd enroll Tae for the winter term. Nothing wrong with a little white lie, Maggie reasons.

During these moments of clarity, she realizes that her parents hadn't always been judgmental; both had inquisitive minds, and each could often be caring and compassionate. As a girl she'd enjoyed taking evening walks with her father. He would tell her about his trials, and she could tell, as he deliberated aloud, how he wrestled with his conscience. *(Should he have given a stiffer sentence than he had to the woman who'd bitten off her husband's ear? Should he have given hard time for the swindler—a regular guy who'd simply fallen upon hard times?)* Sometimes he left his work in his briefcase and asked if she thought her mother loved him. It was probably then that Maggie loved him most. She'd do her best to reassure him, adding that her mother just didn't know how to show it. Often he'd described his youth and how his uncle—a card shark—took him to the West Coast when he was fifteen. He never failed to add how Uncle Bob had showed him the time of his life—he'd left Michigan as a boy but returned a grown man … He hadn't been home much when Maggie was a girl, but when he was, he was devoted to family. Sometimes he went bicycling with her on Saturday mornings.

Her mother's face was always in a law book, but when she would glance up, she saw—really saw—both daughters. *How is my girl?* she'd ask when in a room alone with one of them. She had a way of making Maggie feel like there was no one in the world but her, though she now knew her mother had made Caroline and her father feel the same. Times with her were both intimate and intense, even if too brief. Consistently, a woman who rarely complained and never confided… Besides becoming an attorney, she was also a cool-headed manager who made sure the household ran as seamlessly as possible. Other positives: allowing Caroline and Maggie to sleep in on the weekends, and making sure that they weren't overly involved with friends or after school activities. And teaching them how to prioritize would later serve both well.

Tae is working on one of her stories at the large oak table. Maggie wishes that she, too, could write directly onto her laptop; she's tried on many occasions but never felt comfortable. Tae had decided, and Maggie had readily agreed, that mornings were the best time for schoolwork, but only after Tae had been out for a walk to one of the nearby streams or ponds. This left afternoons and evenings for Tae to write.

———————

How fast time races by! Not so in the car… They've just driven twenty miles to town. As they eat apple pie and sip tea at a cafe, they again discuss the possibility of Tyler being Tae's father. It is Tae who brings up the topic. His unfailing interest in her, especially since Serafina's death…the small, but many presents he has given her—it all begins to add up. She takes out the faded photo of him from her wallet. As they compare her similar high forehead with his, they overhear two waitresses discussing an accident that happened a few miles away.

A small, yellow VW Bug went over a cliff and then burst into flames. Rumor has it that the charred remains belonged to a short, middle-aged female. Not much else is known, or if it is, nothing further has yet been released to the public.

Maggie and Tae widen their eyes. Maggie gulps and Tae shifts uncomfortably. Yellow car… Short, pale, middle-aged woman…

"Are you thinking what I'm thinking?" Maggie whispers. She places an index finger to Tae's lips then glances around to see if anyone has overheard. As much as she'd like Sulie off their trail, she certainly doesn't wish for the woman's death.

"It's probably not her, right?" says Tae.

"Maybe I've grown accustomed to being followed… But if it was her car that went off the cliff, then I guess I'll miss her presence just behind us."

Why does Tae feel like Gretel lost in the woods and imprisoned in a witch's cottage? But she has no Hansel, and the walls of this dwelling aren't made of candy, and Maggie is not a witch fattening her up to taste. It's after 2:00 a.m., but she can't sleep. Except for the sound of Maggie snoring in the other bedroom, it's too quiet. Maybe she'll sit at her desk and work on a new story. She could write about Hansel and Gretel from a cannibal's point of view. Better yet, why not write about Rapunzel? Innocent black princess locked in a tower by a whacky old white witch. Maybe it's a slight exaggeration to think of herself as a prisoner over the past few days, but still…

Maggie's eyes have looked strange lately: her bigger eye, even bigger; and the lid over the smaller one, so puffy that the eye seems to have all but disappeared. It is now hard to believe that Tae ever thought her pretty. The only meal that tastes good is pickle sand-wiches: dill pickles on multi-grain bread (one of her old favorites). If they run out, maybe she'll go off food and drink only water for a couple of days. Surely, Maggie will get the message.

She pulls out half a sandwich from beneath the bed and removes it from plastic wrap. She'd forgotten a napkin or paper towel. Crap.

Had it been Sulie in the accident they'd surely be at Tyler's by now. Their bags had been packed and they'd been ready to drive there when

Maggie got the not-so-bright idea to check the local news. The victim's name was Erika something-or-other—neither she nor Maggie had heard the last name. A photo of her showed a woman of about Sulie's age with similar straight, thinning hair. Other than that, according to Maggie, they didn't look much alike. Tae couldn't tell since she hadn't seen her up close (except briefly in Virginia Beach). The victim had thin lips, beady eyes, and a strangely long nose. Maggie claimed that Sulie had better features. Not a beauty queen, but cute like a fairy. Maggie's reaction had been odd: she seemed relieved, almost happy to hear it hadn't been Sulie. Of course this meant that Sulie would show up again, even in a far-from-everywhere place like this?

"Exactly, my dear… That's why we must stay here a while longer."

"How long is 'longer'? You seem so happy about everything: Sulie being alive still, us having to stay here…not to mention you being more teacher than friend!"

"I'm just trying to enjoy each day, Tae. Nothing wrong with that… I guess I'm relieved that it wasn't Sulie who went over the cliff. And why can't I be your friend and, if not your teacher, then your tutor? I know you're upset about yesterday."

"Whatever!"

There's no understanding Maggie, so Tae might as well stop trying. But then yesterday, Maggie had thrown Tae's cell phone to the bottom of a nearby pond. Thinking about it makes Tae's blood boil, even now. According to Maggie, Tae had been spending too much time texting her sisters, and more recently, Tyler. His texts were always fun because he spelled out most of his words a little too carefully. It cracked her up. Having only Maggie to talk to made life boring; especially since they didn't have Internet here (they had to go to the town library to get online). They should have smartphones. Why didn't they? How could Maggie have been so nasty? Bad enough she'd taken the phone and wouldn't give it back, but then to have actually tossed it into the pond? The real kicker was that afterward, she'd said: "There's work to be done, Taezha." Lately, Maggie hardly ever called her Tae. They took trips to town a couple times a week, but usually only for *provisions* as Maggie called groceries and other necessities. "It's all about survival and hard work, Taezha."

What Maggie doesn't know is that earlier today, Tae decided to take a vow of silence. She'll show Maggie how serious she can be, all right, since there's no point in trying to change her mind. Tae will simply raise the stakes.

Now, back to her modern day version of *Hansel and Gretel* through the eyes of a hungry witch… Sitting at the small desk in her cramped cabin bedroom, wearing the black derby, Tae picks up her pen and furiously writes by dim lamplight.

The location of the cabin is almost idyllic: close enough to Asheville, yet far enough away from crowded public places to allow Maggie to experience Thoreau's back-to-nature solitude. Along with taking photos of the cabin's doors at various times of day, Maggie snaps pictures of the wildlife in the early evenings, including raccoons, foxes, pheasants and owls. Roosters crow from sunrise to sunset. She's lived in too many cities.

She hasn't liked what she's been writing. Could it be that she just needs time to adjust to the new routine? No, there's something more going on. She notices how certain thoughts loop. And sleep, as usual, has been a fickle friend. It's almost as if her mind is turning against her. How ironic this bucolic setting…

This morning she again finds herself riddled with self-doubt. If her parents had been alive, would she have embarked on this adventure? Had it been wrong to uproot Taezha? Her intent was to give the girl a chance at a better life, but was her plan not ill-conceived as well as poorly executed? She'd manipulated both the girl and her mother, and never having been a parent, and now to play the part of one, what gives her the right?

Then a worry of a different sort: when they finally descend from the mountains she might lose Taezha altogether, either to Tyler, or to Quintana, or possibly to new friends. She had taken the girl on this trip to broaden her horizons and give her opportunities, but can

Maggie deny that at times she views Taezha as her possession? How sickening! A new self-loathing envelopes her as she realizes that what she's done is wrong. Reluctantly understanding what it could come to—a kidnapping charge which Taezha, or perhaps Quintana, might one day bring against her—causes her throat to constrict.

But in the end, her judge and jury will correctly see that she has a heart. Right?

Next time they drive to Asheville, she will buy Taezha another phone—a Smartphone! After all, cell phones have become lifelines. Yet Maggie seldom receives calls or messages. Maybe no one cares if she lives or dies. At least out here in the woods there's solitude, if not concomitant loneliness. Oh, Maggie, you fool!

Chapter 23

Tyler wasn't sure that he was ready for their visit, but now he wonders if they'll ever get here. Maggie keeps postponing their arrival. "Typical female," his friend Alex warned. "I take it back. It's hardly typical for a woman to roam around the country with a girl she isn't even related to!" Alex the cynic. He can't get his mind around the fact that Tyler is allowing a woman into his home for God-knows-how-long; someone that Tyler has never even met. Assurances from a fifteen-year-old shouldn't be taken as gospel. "She's not just any fifteen year-old, but the daughter of a woman that I was once wild about," Tyler has told his long-time friend more than once. He's also tempted to tell Alex how his big-hearted welcome is partly because he gets damn lonely at times. The other part, he'd never admit to a soul, is how his grandmother Nana has been downright excited about the company—especially about Taezha. Nana had been gone for years now, but not really…

———————

Over two weeks have passed since they arrived at the cabin—two very long weeks! At least Tae no longer has the dizzy spells she had when they first arrived. Not every moment has been terrible, but she's had about enough of Maggie the Task Master; Maggie the Strict Schoolmarm; Maggie the Bitch; Madame Maggie who keeps thinking of herself as Tae's mentor, but is she really? Almost every day is identical to the last. Little wonder that Tae's poetry hasn't been any good lately; in fact, most of her drafts have been worthless.

Any day now she might just hit Maggie up for a plane ticket back to Flint. (Before the trip, Maggie had said that Tae could return anytime she chose.) Tae didn't see how much longer she could put up with this writers' boot camp. Doesn't Maggie see that she's taken all the fun out of writing? Also, she's beginning to doubt they'll ever get to Tyler's. It'll make Maggie crazy-sad when Tae tells her she's had enough, maybe even psycho; but it's Tae's life, after all, and she's tired of being Maggie's little puppet. She flips Maggie the bird behind her back.

Maggie dives into the wastebasket and retrieves one of Tae's poems. She tries to revive it on the table with her surgical tool (a blue pen) by circling a line that she says is worth using in a future poem: "Muscular nude mountain girls throw rocks at the sky." It sounds kind of dumb to Tae (both her line and Maggie's idea), but whatever... She hasn't yet told Maggie that she's not so sure she even wants to become a writer, an *author*. There are plenty of them; why must she be one, too? What Maggie views as opportunity, Tae sees more as a rigid routine sucking the life from her with Maggie as a vampire, feeding off her life-juices, sucking away her vitality.

Tae's diary reveals this to be true: *M. woke me up at 7. Ate breakfast then got dressed. From 7:30-9:30 worked on poems, drank coffee with lots of milk and sugar. From 9:30-10:00 went for walk...10-12:00 worked on school work...12-12:30 lunch...12:30-3:00 more school stuff...3-3:30 another nature walk...3:30-5:00 writing discussions with Maggie...Get this: FREE reading time from 5-6:00...Dinner at 6...6:30-7:00 DOWN TIME—I'm allowed to text and check voice mail, make calls...7-9:00 writing time...9 – 10:00 shower and FREE reading time. Lights out at 10. Goodnight, Cruel World!!! (Daily Breakfast: small bowl of cereal...Daily Lunch: cheese and an apple... Daily dinner: pickle sandwiches)*

Maggie's routine is similar, except she eats a more varied diet and doesn't have school work. (She keeps going on about how she needs to lose weight—Tae can't tell if she's gained. Who cares anyway?)

While Tae's doing school work, Maggie revises, reads, or naps. On weekends, they clean the cabin. Their 'fun' days are Sundays and Wednesdays, when they go to town to shop or have a bite to eat. Tae varies her usual diet in restaurants. There's little to say, except to discuss what they're writing or reading.

Finally, she has a phone again (sadly no bells and whistles, but she's not complaining) and can text her family, LeAndra, or Tyler. She writes him the question that's been burning in her mind for so long: *R U my dad?* but deletes it. No, this is a question she'll have to ask in person because she wants to see the expression on his face. Same with her question about Aunt Serafina. Lately, she longs to be around pretty much anyone besides Maggie. Sometimes they argue. Their latest disagreement went like this:

"Your poem's okay, Taezha, but something's lacking. It seems a little flat. Don't throw it away; maybe one day you'll be able to return to it and turn it into a wonderful piece…"

"What do you expect? Life is a little flat lately. Wouldn't you agree?" Tae begins to pace.

"Life can't be a constant party. Is that what you think?"

"No, but I hope I'll never be ready for a life as boring as yours. *No can do!*"

Tae stops pacing long enough to spit at her with her eyes. Maggie averts her gaze before the venom reaches her.

If Tae had known that the trip would turn out this way, she *never* would have left home. What was so bad about her *real* life, anyway? She always did well in school and every year received awards. Besides Maggie, other adults had helped her to survive the ugliness, the violence, but no one could take away the painful knowledge of her mom being a failure, or the hunger on the days when there wasn't enough to eat. The hands and lips of her mother's male *friends*, not only all over her mother, but on her sisters and her, too (it hadn't happened all the time, but a few too many—especially to her older sisters). All the shouting matches, then the tearful making up… The whole ordeal starting over again… Quintana getting high because there was too much of one thing and too little of another… Life constantly out of balance, toppling her over in craziness and chaos… Tae's fear of being a complete loser… Still, it hadn't always been so bad, especially when Aunt Serafina was alive.

She tells Maggie about how she once lived with Mrs. Tilders, and about how she had while suffered in her care. And just when she is about to tell her how trapped she felt, she bites her tongue, though she manages to say how much she misses Quintana and her sisters. She now wonders how she ever could have seen Maggie as her 'white' auntie. If only she could tell her how Mrs. Tilders had made her clean cat poop; scrub herself in the bathtub until it hurt; plus, all the times she'd been made to sit in the corner for no reason. Living with Maggie is nowhere near as bad, but just like her time with Mrs. Tilders, she cries herself to sleep at night. The difference now is that she is careful to weep silently so that Maggie won't hear her. Her tears are tears of longing, tears of absence, tears of missed connections and unanswered questions… Every photo she had of Quintana and her sisters was submerged with her phone.

Maybe Tyler can help her to reconnect.

Chapter 24

Maggie tosses and turns for several nights, worrying about Taezha's eating habits: she's been consuming the same food for almost the entire time they've been there and has lost weight. Worrisome, as she's all elbows and knees. Then Maggie has the recurring nightmare about her parents. She stands before them in their black robes. They sit next to each other, facing the court and judging her, criticizing not only her life, but the lies she's been telling herself about being a writer. The images are grainy, black and white like an old film, except for small blue carnations pinned to their robes. The scene shifts: they are now inside the cabin, watching Maggie and Taezha. Maggie tries to blink them away, but they refuse to go. "Oh, Maggie, what have you done now?" they demand. When she doesn't answer, they confer. So typical... Scene shift: Taezha busily stacks up a Leaning Pisa of books. When they collapse, Taezha claps and the tower rebuilds itself. Maggie watches as she waits for their verdict, though she is certain that she has been found guilty. Truly, she has made such a mess of everything.

She wakes with a start, covered in sweat. Her tinnitus is driving her crazy. Enormous pangs of guilt, accompanied by a fresh layer of self-loathing. There were earlier variations of this nightmare, though none ever quite this bad. She's always been a screw-up—she knows that—certainly more so than Caroline—but her family still loved her, right? She falls asleep again and dreams of Heidi Atterwall in her prison cell writing poetry. Maggie can almost read the words. This time it's Taezha's face. Again she wakes gasping. How does Taezha see her? What kind of monster has she become?

She makes an effort to become as quiet as possible—whispering whenever she speaks to Taezha, sitting still for hours at a time. Writing, thinking, reading…hot flashes are bad again—sometimes one an hour… She adjusts the lighting, never content with the way she's adjusted it. She darkens the room. Without lights, the rooms are full of shadows, even at noon. These are old habits; ones she thought she was free of once on the road. She thinks about the ending of *Pauline's Revenge.* (After knocking him out with chloroform, Pauline had put Ray's body in the trunk of her car, and then, in the middle of the night, had driven the car into a lake. Despite Pauline's newfound freedom, she'd always be imprisoned by guilt. It's an ending with which Maggie has never been completely satisfied.)

For a couple days she even worries that she's pregnant, as she hadn't used protection in Virginia Beach. No reason to get anxious about not having a period at her age; rarely does it mean pregnancy. She'd only had a small one a few months ago. Still, she purchases a pregnancy kit from the town drugstore. When she finds out she isn't pregnant, she feels relieved, but also a strange wistfulness, too, in knowing this will probably be the last time she'll ever have to contend with the issue.

If she could time travel, she'd go back in time and set fire to her parents' cabin after their funeral. Setting it ablaze would have helped to bring closure. Why didn't they light a fire after taking their pills and die engulfed in flames? That way, she and Caroline wouldn't have known it was a double suicide. Tragic deaths, but at least accidental ones, and the loss would have been easier to deal with. To think they hadn't wanted to remain here with their daughters—it was more than a rebuke—it was, and still is horrifying. Caroline disagrees, and though she was certainly upset by their untimely deaths, she also believes that the elderly have the right to end their lives however they choose. Maggie agrees, but not when it comes to her parents.

The fire fantasy is what led to her note-taking about an old couple who lights their own funeral pyre.

She refuses to re-read what she's written after writing it; that is, she won't read it for months, or even a year. When she can't write and is sitting still, Maggie thinks about how she twice cheated death: her leap from the bridge, and the time when she came close to jumping off a ledge. Then her thoughts drift to her two miscarriages, and to her abortion. At least she no longer jots down names for her forever unborn.

One morning upon waking she notes how her nightgown is twisted above her waist and is soaking wet. She's certain her breasts are gone: she feels for them, cups them with her hands to make sure they haven't disappeared during the night. They're still there. More than one reason she's glad for Taezha's presence: it keeps her from doing stupid things, like stealing from stores—usually drugstores. Never much—only small, inexpensive items: a pack of gum or socks. During her dark times, it was one of the few things that eased the. Luckily, her kleptomania has been in check since *stealing* Taezha.

The worst part about living in this cabin is that there is no music, though both have been singing in the shower with greater frequency. (Taezha's iPod battery has expired. Nothing can be done about it until the next time they go to town.) The kitchen radio works, but stations come in scratchy and fuzzy, if not completely garbled. It's only in the car that they can listen to CDs.

Maggie hasn't worn a bra since they arrived at the cabin. She asks Taezha if she finds this offensive and Taezha giggles and says she hasn't even noticed. Maggie doesn't believe her. Well, she hasn't completely let herself go. Every morning, she puts on make-up and removes it before bed. She wants to appear pleasant to look at. Is she?

It's now been three weeks since they arrived at the cabin. Maggie knows that she's been too strict with Taezha. Who is she to demand that she develop good study habits? This morning she concluded that there is absolutely no way that the girl can lead an ordinary life here, and if she truly wants to write, then she will, not matter where she resides. Still, Taezha needs to feel settled. They both do. Maybe they will at Tyler's, and if not there, then somewhere else. Right now the ordinary sounds extraordinary. If it weren't for the fear that Sulie is out there lurking, waiting, then they would have already packed their suitcases and been on the road to Tyler's house. Does Taezha think it was Sulie that they saw in town yesterday? One thing she'll do before they leave is call Caroline and have it out with her. That is long overdue.

Chapter 25

Now that Maggie knows the truth, her fears seem ludicrous. They could have gone to Tyler's sooner had she not allowed Caroline to wield so much power over her. They have been hiding out from Sulie, whom Caroline has practically admitted to hiring, and to what end? Does she really think that Sulie will kidnap them and return them to Michigan? Caroline probably hired her just to keep an eye on them.

Over the years, Caroline has made it a point to know Maggie's whereabouts. It began when Maggie would run away from home as a girl. She knew all Maggie's routes. She also knew exactly how to lure her home: *We can go to the store together and I'll buy you some gum.* How quickly Maggie would climb into the passenger's seat! Once again outwitted by her big sister, and upset with herself for losing her steely resolve.

When Maggie was in her twenties and thirties, Caroline more or less left her alone, which was necessary since Maggie moved from state to state. Then in her forties, and now in her fifties, Caroline began, once again, to see it as her duty to keep tabs on her sister. After their parents' deaths, Caroline had become especially ardent in her mission. Why hadn't Maggie realized sooner that Sulie was Caroline's hired-hand?

Earlier today, when Caroline answered Maggie's call, she feigned surprise until Maggie called her on it. "Yes, I suppose I knew you were in the mountains of North Carolina, but not exactly where. Let me guess: you're now headed to Tyler's, right?"

"Soon…if it's any of your business!"

"It's not your first mistake since you left town, but it could be your biggest one."

"What makes you say that?" Maggie begins to pace.

"There might be things you don't know, but now probably isn't the time to reveal them. You do realize that what you're doing is wrong?"

"You've been talking to Quintana, haven't you? At first I thought it was she who hired Sulie, but she couldn't afford that."

"I don't know what you're talking about."

"You don't? How transparent you are! You really think I'm that slow on the uptake?"

"Not at all… You just have a skewed view of reality. It's nothing new."

"So, you're admitting that Sulie is *your* watch dog?"

"I'm admitting nothing. This conversation is pointless. But heed my words: it's time to come home!"

Maggie doesn't recall who hung up first. It doesn't matter. What matters: Sulie is a paper tiger, and so is Caroline. Now is the right time for them to pack their bags and drive to Tyler's. She hopes they'll still be welcome. Before informing Tae, her phone chirps again. Since it's probably Caroline, she doesn't bother checking caller I.D. "Yes, now what is it?" she snaps. "Hello, to you, too!" responds Andrew the Sixth. In a more appealing way, he, too, implores her to return to Flint, and tells her how much he misses her. She would have felt more flattered had his call not come so soon after Caroline's. Cutting him off, she only agrees to think about it. "There's never going to be anyone but you, Maggie. Just remember that." Except your wife, she almost adds, but doesn't feel like expending the emotional energy to do so.

After she informs Taezha that tomorrow will be their last day at the cabin, the girl flashes a grin at her that Maggie hasn't seen in weeks. Maggie can't stop grinning too, that is, until she realizes the reason for Taezha's elation has more to do with getting away from Maggie than leaving the cabin. Everything's going to be better once they get to Tyler's, Maggie promises. Maybe they'll be able to find—at least for a time—some semblance of a normal life; that is, provided Tyler will continue to accept their presence. Even if it's asking too much of him, it could prove worth the effort. It appears to be the only remaining option. Maybe living there will dispel the nightmares about her parents. She just hopes she doesn't start having new ones involving Caroline. She really does love her sister; she's always been the constant in her life.

Driving through hilly country in the red minivan on the way to Uncle Tyler's, the cabin fever of the past few weeks seems to have broken and Tae wonders about the road ahead and what life will be like during their stay with him. Each hill they drive up and fly down feels like an adventure. The early September sky is brilliant blue, and though it's late summer, the trees are still deep emerald green. It's like she's suddenly noticing the physical world again.

Maggie won't admit to feeling anything close to excitement, saying instead that the time at the cabin had been good for them both, and how *all* writers must, now and then, experience a "dark night of the soul." Tae isn't exactly sure what Maggie means and suggests the What If game rather than spend more time belaboring dark states of mind.

Tae says: "What if we are exactly who Tyler's been searching for? He's been lonely and we soon become a family."

Maggie says: "What if I finally find a husband and stay married for the rest of my life?"

Tae: "It'll be a great place to write! What if he wants us to read aloud everything we write?"

"He'll understand our commitment to writing. He'll be our muse. I don't mind sharing him that way. Do you?"

"Not at all! What if I make new friends and finish school there?"

"What if he's a storyteller and gives us lots of ideas? Not that we need them."

"I think he has a porch swing on a big, old fashioned porch."

Maggie asks, "How do you know?"

"He either told me about it or I dreamed it. Does it matter? Anyway, what if you two fall in love? He could be your lucky number seven!"

"Oh, we're probably getting ahead of ourselves. Wouldn't you agree?"

"That's the whole point of this game. Yes? Didn't you just say he's to be your husband?"

"What if Sulie is with him on the porch when we arrive? What if they escort us to the airport?"

"Now, you're reaching… He wants us to stay. Remember? He told us so."

"You're right, of course," Maggie says. "According to the sign we just passed, it's just a little over one hundred and fifty miles away."

From Maggie's Journal

Detroit, 1960s and early 1970s

After I'd gotten to know some of the students who were bussed to my elementary school in the 1960s, I became more aware of race. Why weren't many Negroes on TV? Why did my father wonder aloud if Negroes got married in churches like whites? How could he not know that they did? Long after the word 'Negro' fell out of public discourse and had been replaced with 'African-American' or 'black,' my grandfather was still calling them 'Coloreds.' After I ate lunch with a couple of black girls, why did several white girls refuse to have anything to do with me? And this was in 1980 in a high school on the fringe of city and suburbs!

When Caroline was in college she had a couple of black boyfriends; one was a teacher, and another an attorney. Mom was fine with it, but not Dad. While he had nothing against them—no doubt they were well-educated, fine, upstanding young men—he didn't think it right that they ever be more than friends. (He never mentioned this to her.)

"Dad, I didn't think you were prejudiced!"

"Mag, I'm not, but I wouldn't want my future grandchildren to suffer. Think about it: the whites wouldn't view them as white, and the blacks wouldn't view them as black. The poor mulatto children would be trapped between two worlds and accepted by neither."

I'd seen several biracial students in junior high. They seemed just like other kids; I didn't see why it was such a big deal. What kids mostly seemed to notice was whether or not you were from a good family. Those who had parents who worked and did okay, unlike those whose parents didn't work, or were from single-parent homes seemed to suffer. I wanted to tell him this, but knew it was pointless. Caroline must have known too, as neither of those boyfriends ever came for dinner.

Moody Dog Blues

I got them moody dog blues
Looks like they're here to stay…
That sucker-punched feeling –
Never goes away…

So won't you sit be me, Honey?
Won't you sit by me, Gal?
I know you know about me
(You should by now…)

Let me rag on you, Sugar,
for just a little while
about them moody dog blues
Looks like they're here to stay…

—*Tyler*

Chapter 26

Tomorrow everything will change, and maybe that's for the better. Tyler is aware that he is a little too settled in his ways for a man in his early forties. For almost a week now, he hasn't been able to eat his normal three-square meals per day. Doesn't help that Kip, going on eleven, has been acting strange and not eating much… When the day comes that old Kip won't live to see the next sunrise, at least Tyler won't be alone in the house, though he's never really been alone in the house. As usual, he takes his morning coffee into his grand-mother's bedroom on the second floor (his room is on the first floor). The floor boards of the old farmhouse creak as he makes his way to the window where he opens the shades halfway, and noting—as he always does—how one can only see a portion of the green yard and even less of the faded red barn. He sits on the bedside, fingering the faded blue satin comforter.

Nana, I think you're really going to like Taezha. She's as smart as a whip, but also sweet and caring—you know? More than a little, she's like Adele. I've spoken some to Maggie, and she sounds nice too, though I don't yet know much about her. Enjoyed her book and can't help but wonder if she's a little like her character, Pauline, but maybe not since Pauline was a victim-type. No author photo on the back. Taezha tried sending me a photo of Maggie from her phone but it didn't come through. All that high-fallutin', hi-tech crap…but shoot, my phone's simple, like me. Nothing wrong with that, right? Taezha and I have been playing a game. I'll ask: 'Is Maggie's hair brown?' 'Maybe,' she says. 'Is she a looker?'

'Maybe…' she says, just to keep me guessing. She must be a good-hearted gal to bring Taezha all the way down here from Michigan. Shows she must think highly of Taezha, too. Granted, it's a little strange the way the two of them have been traveling around together.

He can't think of what else to add in his update, then gazes down at his large, rough hands, browned by the sun, and is overcome by a tremendous peace that he always feels when inside his grandmother's room. So clearly can he still conjure up what it felt like to be a little boy on her lap… All her wonderful hugs… He visited her daily when she fell ill. No place on earth as sacred as this room. On his way out, he's always careful to shut the door halfway, just as she liked it. Every evening he returns to pull down the window shades, but never lingers, as he does in the mornings. Sometimes he'll pick up her brush on top of the clothes bureau and study the fine white hairs entwined in the bristles. Not today, as there is too much to do before his guests arrive.

Next, he surveys the two other bedrooms on the second floor that he has made ready for his guests. He's as nervous as a new innkeeper. What if the sheets are too musty? What if the flowers he put in vases on the bureau make them sneeze? Don't go there. Don't over-think it. Stand tall and be a good host. No one's perfect. They'll like you for yourself because you're okay. "You're more than okay, Tyler—you're a prince!" Nana used to say, though he never let it go to his head.

He surveys Taezha's room from the doorway. Simple but inviting: a twin bed, a rocker, a bookshelf with several old, dusty *Hardy Boys* books that his dad had read as a boy. Also, a *Norton Anthology of American Poetry* given to him by Nana. He likes poetry, even reads it aloud. Always a slow reader, but he refuses to let that excuse him for not reading more. There are a couple of dolls on top of the bookcase. One is made of porcelain and is in mint condition; a gift given to Nana when she was a girl. The other is a baby doll that once belonged to his mother. Big tufts of hair had either fallen out or been yanked out making her seem as if she'd been dragged around more than a few times. Maybe Taezha won't like white-skinned dolls (not that dolls have skin). Pictures of Taezha make her skin look more toffee-hued than brown. Maybe just a shade lighter than her mother. He'll tell her to put them on the closet shelf if she doesn't care for them. (Somewhere in the attic there are others, but something about dolls has always frightened him.)

The quilt on the bed was made by Nana: blue and yellow patchwork. Since there isn't much on the wallpaper of faded roses, save for a small mirror and a painting of fruit in a cheap – looking frame, he hopes the quilt will make the room cozy. Will she notice how the wallpaper is peeling in places? He gazes at the desk under the window. A writing desk he'd recently made for Taezha. Inside the single drawer he'd placed a recently purchased pen and notebook.

He lingers a little less in the doorway of Maggie's room. It's much like Taezha's room, except that the quilt (also one of Nana's) was made with darker colors: autumn red and gold. There is a small mirror, identical to the one on the wall in Taezha's room, but in place of the painting on the adjacent wall is a simple wooden crucifix. It's been there as he can remember. He'd always known this room as Grandfather's room because Nana made Grandfather sleep here after she'd discovered he was sleeping with a stripper from town. Tyler had never met him. This room has a writing table, too, which once belonged to his grandfather, James O'Rourke. It was where he'd written many of his plays (locally famous). Nana hadn't told Tyler much about him beyond basic facts. He'd only stayed in this bedroom a year before she threw him out entirely; got rid of him by pointing Grandpa's own Smith & Wesson at him. "Goodbye to bad rubbish!" she'd proclaimed. Tyler could tell that behind her anger, she continued to love him, for she'd quickly defend him if anyone else dared put him down, saying, "All of his tomfoolery notwithstanding, he had a fine mind." Bound copies of five of his plays lean against a King James Bible.

The window in this room doesn't allow as much light as in Taezha's room (he hopes it will suit Maggie). Maybe she won't see how badly the walls are paint-chipped, how worn the furnishings. At least not right away.

He returns downstairs because Miss Sophie is at the door. Miss Sophie, his cat, has been with him for five years longer than his dog, Kip. She's fifteen going on sixteen, and Kip is now eleven. He's always been grateful for his bond with him since Miss Sophie is just too damn independent to belong to anyone. Strange cat, though. She'd be gone for days, only to return and follow him everywhere in need of constant attention. Her homecoming is always one of celebration, but after a few hours of being talked-to and petted, she inevitably turns into a pest. Maybe once Taezha and Maggie arrive, Miss Sophie will change her ways. She talks too much for a cat; then again, maybe she isn't a cat, but the reincarnation of his mother, Adele. His relationship with Miss Sophie is ambivalent, just like his relationship with Adele.

Miss Sophie persistently meows at the kitchen door until he lets her inside. When he opens the screen door, she gazes at him as if to say, "What took you so long, Buddy-boy?" He doesn't know how he knows, but he's pretty certain Miss Sophie thinks of him as Buddy-boy and even this irks him (Adele had often called him Buddy). Nana knew Miss Sophie, too; in fact, it was Nana who named her. The black and white, long-haired cat still sleeps on Nana's bed, whereas, Kip, a Border collie, won't go near the room and sometimes whimpers outside Nana's bedroom door. At times, Kip reminds him of his grandfather. Kip had never gone anywhere near Nana, always acting terribly guilty.

There's a riff he plays on his harmonica: "Moody Dog Blues." *"I got them moody dog blues/Looks like they're here to stay…"* One of several tunes he's come up with over the years. Kip enjoys sitting next to him on the porch as the sun sets, listening and thumping his tail in a slow wag of appreciation as Tyler plays. Will Tyler explain the true identities of his animal companions to Taezha and Maggie? Will either of them understand? Or, will they see him more like a plain and simple country gent…

His parents were exact opposites. It's a wonder they ever hooked up in the first place. He'd known his father better, though he died suddenly of a heart attack when Tyler was twelve; and only ten when his mother slipped away from an overdose. More of his time had been spent with Neil, who was more a father than Adele had ever been a mother; still, it is she who Tyler recalls more clearly. A hippie chick who laughed often and loudly… Sometimes right in the middle of screaming at him or someone else in the house, she'd burst out laughing. Not in this house, but the abandoned mansion near Asheville. Because there'd been so many people living there when he visited as a boy, it never seemed large. (The opposite of how places usually seem smaller when we're older.)

The day she left his dad, she'd thrown clothes into a garbage bag, donned an enormous floppy hat, and with too hard a grip had grabbed his wrist. "Mama, you're hurting me!" he'd cried, but she hadn't heard him because she was too busy yelling at his dad. She took him to live with her at a commune, but he was often left alone. When Adele died of a heroin overdose he didn't cry. His dad showed up the following day and told him to pack his things. The memory still plays out when he can't sleep.

His cell phone rings, loudly playing the ring tone of an old dial up. He'd left it somewhere—maybe in the kitchen—but just now he can't get up from the rocker in the living room, because Miss Sophie is curled up on his lap. He knows that if he doesn't oblige her, there will be hell to pay. Her eyes sizzle. The phone stops ringing.

In a corner of the pole barn he throws old blankets over his birdman statues. When was it that he began carving them? Years ago, maybe after he'd come home from the Navy… He won't keep them hidden from Maggie and Taezha forever—maybe he'll show them his collection of miniatures first.

His phone rings…again. Maybe it's Taezha. Maybe she will tell him that Maggie is holding her hostage for another couple of days. He's beginning to have doubts about Maggie. Doesn't she realize the importance of this visit? In all fairness, she thinks he's Taezha's uncle, after all. Unless Quintana had let it slip. Overall, he doesn't trust Quintana, though he's inclined to trust her on this issue. He finds his phone on the kitchen counter, but again he's missed the call. The call hadn't come from Taezha after all, but from Alex, his friend and card buddy, who also happened to be assistant manager of the local hardware store where Tyler had worked until recently. Two weeks ago Alex had let him go. Not that he was fired; it was more a case of being let go because they were downsizing, like so many places. He replays Alex's voice message twice: "So, we're meeting at my place this Friday. You in, Tyler? Let me know."

He grunts at the phone. He knows Alex kept him on as long as possible. The little he'd made barely paid the bills anyway. Repairing furniture helps, but now he doesn't exactly know how he'll make ends meet. His birdman statues hadn't sold at the area art shows.

Calling Alex back, he explains about his soon-to-arrive house guests. "I'll let you know mid-week if they're still here...or if they plan to stay until Friday, or beyond. I think that they probably will... How about if I have my people call your people?" Tyler laughs nervously and begins to pace like he usually does when he's talking on the phone.

"You already got yourself in too deep. If they're going to be long-term, why not swing by for some cards?" Before ending the call, Alex tells Tyler that he senses a mystery. "You holding out on me, Tyler?"

Miss Sophie peers at him accusingly from the kitchen doorway before scampering upstairs to Nana's room, where she'll surely spend the afternoon. If it weren't for the need to maintain communication with Taezha, he wouldn't mind misplacing his phone forever. He's especially bothered by a comment that Alex made about women ruling men and running their lives. Alex knows little about the situation—and it's going to stay that way!

Chapter 27

He leans back into his high-backed cane rocker across from Maggie, who is swaying slowly on the porch swing. The early evening air is still; once in a while a scent of sassafras rides up to their noses on a cooler waft of air. When he brings out Nana's secret lemonade (a little gin mixed into it), he thinks about sitting next to her, then decides she might consider it a little too forward. He notices that the two sides of her face are disturbingly mismatched. On the left side, her eye is larger, the brow more arched, the lips fuller and the cheek paler. Her right eye isn't only smaller, but has dark circles and lines suggesting a sort of world-weariness. Kind of like the way she described Pauline in her novel; still, Maggie doesn't strike him as a victim. He can't help but notice how fond she seems to be of Tae. This must bother Quintana no end.

He takes a swig of his hard lemonade. Which is the real Maggie? It's not just her face, but her voice, too. Sometimes it's loud and her words collide and crash in mid-air; other times a soft lilt, a strumming murmur. She seems to linger over her syllables in an appealing, almost Southern way. Which voice will come from her next? He can't help but wonder if she has split personality disorder. Most of what she says seems to make sense, though at times she sounds very old school, especially when talking about books and authors. Even though Taezha likes to talk about books, she doesn't come across quite as bookish. He feels easier around the girl…his daughter. She's enjoyable, delightful even. Today is their third day here, and already he's begun calling her Tae.

"Tell me, Maggie, does Tae know the truth about her real parents?" He leans closer; their knees almost touch.

"You mean about Quintana not being her mother? I think she has guessed it, though she doesn't know for sure." She stops the swing from swaying and crosses one leg over the other.

"So you know the truth…that her mother was Serafina?" He can tell by watching her expression that this comes as good news—though not really news—just confirmation.

"I think Tae will be pleased. She always talks about her. Now she'll…"

"And I'm her father…" Maybe he should not have told her this so soon. Maybe he should have given her a chance to get to know him first. "I thought I'd wait to telling her…"

"Yes, you'll want to wait for the right moment, but I doubt she'll be shocked." She begins to rock the swing, its creak mingling with the crickets in the yard.

Though he had not intended to reveal more about his past with Serafina, he can't seem to stop his tongue. Maggie just sits there with her somewhat attractive but unusual face as it all comes pouring out of him.

It had been the most incredible weekend of his life. He was twenty-two, on leave on from Basic Training. They met in a small blues bar in Chicago where she had a singing gig, which happened to be her first. He wasn't her first, but he didn't know that then. They connected as soon as their eyes met. He was one of five or six people; most of the Chicago crowd wasn't there yet. After listening for a couple minutes he was transported to someplace lovely yet sad. Suddenly, he believed in the possibility of love. They'd held hands as they strolled down the Chicago sidewalks on a sticky summer night. They kissed, talked, and played in a fountain. Gazing at Lake Michigan, she told him how she was from the state directly across the lake. "Isn't it amazing," she'd asked him, "how you can't see the other side and it isn't even an ocean?" Her plan was to move from Michigan to New York. To hit the big time! (During that weekend she'd repeated that phrase many times.) She liked Chicago, but there was something about New

York that absolutely fascinated her, that called to her. "That's where Billie is from. You do know who Billie is, right?" Billie Holiday may have been her idol, but already she had her own style. Her voice, her talk, her walk—all worked together to put him under some kind of magical spell, one that would affect him for a very long time.

He doesn't tell Maggie all the details, though he does mention how Serafina's love spell changed him: he'd felt clever, energetic, like he knew more than he actually knew. It was the reason that he'd been brave enough—after her set was over—to ask if he could buy her a drink. She accepted. They did the town together, and after he went back to his base, and she to her home in Michigan, she wrote that she was pregnant, but wasn't going to keep the baby, wasn't ready to raise a child. Rather, she was going to follow her dream and move to New York City, to become not just a singer, but a famous one. He kept sending her letters. What he didn't know at the time was that after the first few, she never received them; instead, they were intercepted and rubber-banded by Quintana, who concealed them high on a closet shelf in the bedroom where she slept with Serafina's baby (who she'd agreed to raise, so long as Serafina helped with rent).

Serafina didn't return home for five years. She cried when she saw the gorgeous little girl—her little girl—not only because it reminded her of the weekend together with Tyler, but because Taezha could never know her as *Mama* (or that it had been she who'd named her and not Quintana). She cried when she came across the stack of Tyler's letters, of which there were sixty—one each month for five consecutive years. After reading them all, she wrote back to inform him that her career had taken off, plus there was now a good man in her life. She let him know that while she thought of him fondly, no longer would she open his letters, though he could write to Taezha only if he referred to himself as her uncle. At first, Quintana didn't think this a good idea, but finally agreed to give the girl mail from Uncle Tyler. She'd been six when Quintana read her the first letter. It was after the second or third letter that she wrote to him and continued to do so for the next nine years.

"What does she know about your relationship with Serafina?"

Maggie asked, as they strolled around his property.

"Only that we were good friends, and that we met in Chicago."

Kip follows them down to the brook. Maggie marvels at a giant pine—the tallest tree around. Is she this easy to impress, or has he simply been taking nature for granted? Everything on his many acres is like an old companion: from the trees to the pole barn. And his most faithful companion today has a limp which wasn't there yesterday. Poor old Kip… He tells her that he knows that Tae is disappointed that his animals are gone; maybe one day he'll acquire others. She assures him that Tae is like a new person these days, that she has never seen her like this: so impressed by him, and enchanted by the area, at home in her room, as well as captivated by Alex's son, Nick. "I'm sure she thinks she's died and gone to heaven!" Tyler laughs but can't help feeling deeply pleased.

Chapter 28

Tae can't get over how much she resembles Tyler; the same long legs, tall forehead, the shape of their eyes—despite their different skin tones. Twice she's been ready to ask, but chickened out. If he really were her father, why hadn't he told her before now? If not in a letter, then in person… Maybe the reason she can't ask is because if he denied it, then her heart would break. For so long she's carried the hope.

She takes over the porch swing in early evening. Maggie and Tyler are out for a walk with Kip. Pen in hand, she opens her notebook, studies it. Minutes go by, a half hour. The page remains blank. Nothing worse than a blank page… Maybe she should write straight to her laptop—the words always seemed to flow over the keys. She'd rather think about dark-haired Nick and how lucky she was to have meet him. The way he looks at her with those piercing blue eyes. He's cool (and hot!), yet also warm and friendly…and classy—so unlike the white boys she'd known at her old school. And like her, he's a loner. Another similarity: he asks questions. Unlike Flint, her life here is sweet. Lately, she feels a lightness and wishes she could write about it, but first she needs to really think about how it all happened. Reliving once more those first memories as if they were butterscotch Lifesavers, rolling them over on her tongue and trying to recapture the heavenly taste of them. Maybe he'll become her muse and she will write the best love poem ever written! She knows she has it in her.

No words are written, but a small heart is drawn on the page, then two hearts side by side. One is upside down. Never has she met anyone quite like him. She's been attracted to lots of boys before, but never has she fallen so quickly. Blue eyes and curly dark hair; pale skin. Tyler had said something about Nick's grandfather having been born in Greece. How exotic! Within minutes of meeting the tall, handsome boy, she felt like she was hurtling from a cliff. Is her attraction obvious? If so, she might die of embarrassment. Does he feel this way about her? He must, for just two days after they'd met, he began stopping by Tyler's house on his way home from school, and then again in the early evening. They don't sit together, but prefer strolling back and forth between their houses. Lots of time for talking, as the houses are about a half-mile apart. She can tell him everything—and almost has—because she's certain he can see right to her soul. He has a way of nodding his head, of listening intently. He is the protective type, she suspects. He's told her about how his mom left and how devastating it was. She'd left only a goodbye note on the kitchen table—that was it! The note said that she'd met someone else and wished good luck to both his dad and to him; and how at some time in the future she would contact Nick. Both he and his father had waited for her to return. Nick still dreams about her.

He'd switched topics to the car he's been fixing up that would someday be his, but then stopped right in the middle of telling her about it, and kissed her as they were sitting against the trunk of an oak tree. The earth moved. She's sure of it. It stole her breath and made her knees tremble.

If only she could tell Maggie, but she can't. Not yet, anyway. Little does Maggie know, but she'd again come through for Tae—again saved her from misery. When will he kiss her again? What if he doesn't? Maybe she'll be the one to make the next move… Okay, back to that poem she's been planning to write… Something about the dream she'd had the night before. In it she and Nick were on a boat, diving off it into warm blue water.

The page remains blank. Try again. Tomorrow.

Chapter 29

As much as Tyler wishes he could spend more time with Tae, it's been amazing getting to know Maggie. He can't believe how much he's confided in her and wonders if it would be wise to tell her about his brief but passionate affair with Serafina. As they walk, he asks about her novel, *Pauline's Revenge*, and how it felt to have written an almost-bestseller. He admits to not being much of a reader, but he'd read her book recently and liked it. Pauline sure got her revenge, didn't she? Then he makes a comment about how complex and mis-understood Pauline was: strip away the layers and she was likeable, even light-hearted. She had hope, even if it was a dark sort of hope; and that's what makes the book appealing, at least in his humble opinion. (Now that he thinks about it, there were definite likenesses between Pauline and Maggie.) Has she written other novels? If not, she should, and he'd be sure to read her next one, too. While he doesn't much understand writers, he can't help but think his house would be a dandy place to work. She agrees.

The neurons are firing now, old boy… Since she has no plans as to where she and Tae will venture next, maybe she—they—could stay indefinitely, and Tae could attend the local high school. This, he'll wait to propose after she knows he's her father. Quintana will certainly have a problem with it, but screw her, anyway. She's his daughter, anyway. And it doesn't sound like she's been a particularly good mama for Tae. And if Maggie could pay a little rent, it would free up some of his money issues. He'll wait a week or so before making the suggestion, drop a few hints to plant the seed. Since being let go from the hardware store, he really hasn't been sure how to make ends meet. More than once he's thought about putting the place up for sale, much as he hated to even think of it. Maybe a full house was just the hand he needed.

He's telling her about the hardware store, the reason he was let go, and how his side business of furniture repair has slowed to a crawl, when Tae and Nick appear out of nowhere. They laugh like they've known each other a long time. Tyler doesn't recall ever hearing Nick laugh before. Such a nice kid, too… Tae seems to have an easier time directing her gaze at Maggie rather than at him or Nick. It makes him wonder if eye-contact is difficult for her. She must have a shy side he hasn't known about until now. Definitely his daughter…

Nick begins to explain how he'd introduced Tae to his dad and showed her the race car he's been repairing, but Tyler is still ruminating about how to ask Maggie for rent. Nick turns away and gives Tae a little push on the shoulder. She gives him an ever harder one back. Seeing them together—pale skin contrasted with darker skin… so much like his own had been next to Serafina's that it makes him wince. If he recalls correctly, Tae's mother was darker than Tae. Races mix more these days than they did fifteen years ago. About time, too… Not that everyone would agree.

The horseplay going on between Nick and Tae brings him back to the present. They begin chasing each other through the long-shadowed yard. Kip, forgetting his limp, bounds after them. Tyler sees the concern in Maggie's face. He can tell that she isn't sure about Nick. Probably has something to do with the fact that Nick is eighteen—three years older than Tae. Soon, just not now, he'll do his best to reassure her that Alex and his son Nick are decent people. Nick helps out at the hardware store and has proven to be reliable. He's also book-smart. Maggie should like that.

His gaze turns toward Tae. She's laughing and whirling in the late summer twilight. Like Serafina, she's definitely not the sort to just sit around. Similarities between them are striking; not only in their physical appearance, but something deeper—a certain light from the eyes—the melodious quality of their laughter. One difference is that Tae is less sultry. For a moment he feels jealous of the boy receiving her attention. He's never felt this way, not that he can recall anyway. Is this what it's like to be a father?

He feels Maggie's eyes watching him watch Tae.

He crouches to pet Kip.

"You have everything here, don't you?" says Maggie, gesturing from the two barns to the blueberry patch, the Christmas pine area with the thick woods beyond. "Even a gazebo… Lucky you!" She sighs as she watches Tae and Nick. He does look more than a little like a young Greek god… Certainly, Maggie can see why Tae finds him handsome.

"I should probably tear down that old barn."

"All it needs is a few nails pounded down here and there. Maybe a fresh coat of paint…" She then announces that if she and Tae decide to stay much longer, she'll be happy to pay their way.

"I'm just a poor old bachelor. I can't offer you much, but please feel free to stay as long as you'd like." He wanted to add how he hoped that Tae would decide to attend school here, but knows that it's too soon for such a serious discussion. He doesn't know if he'll be able to make that kind of commitment, not to mention that it might make Maggie feel like she had to skedaddle, and the poor woman only just got here.

Why did Maggie choose Tae to be her travel companion? It's obvious that she sees herself as Tae's aunt. But no denying it's a different sort of arrangement. Doesn't Maggie have friends her own age? Men must find her good-looking enough to want to curl up with her at night. Maybe she's sick of relationships. Still, he's picking up a vibe that she's interested in him. There's a heat coming from. If it weren't for his fear of Quintana pulling the plug on everything, he might be experiencing a kind of hope he hasn't known in years. Quintana… Damn her! He's almost certain that she'll end up meddling in his life. Like she always has… There must be something he can do about it.

Chapter 30

Maggie rises briefly to stretch from her morning post: a stool behind a covered fruit stand. The air is stifling, especially for so late in the season, though she's never been in North Carolina in September before. Maybe it's typical for it to be hot. Funny, the places she's found herself. Places she never could have imagined, like Tyler's small farm in North Carolina. Tyler himself had been only a name when she and Tae were back in Michigan, and now she can't get him off her mind. If only he'd come down to the stand with a thermos of coffee for her, like he has on several mornings. Kip is getting worse and hasn't eaten in two days. That's got to be the reason.

Tae's absence has had an enervating effect on her, too. Lately, she has been seeing a lot of Nick—too much, in Maggie's estimation. He seems like a nice boy, but too old for Tae; in the end, he'll break her heart, or she will shatter his. The three year age difference matters: she's simply too young for him, though she is probably more emotionally mature. He's obsessed with NASCAR, and until now Tae could have cared less about cars. Plus, he is a peacock. The writing is on the wall. Why doesn't Tae see that?

Not only does she miss Tae, but even the smallest whiff of patchouli fools her into thinking that she's still in the house when Tae has actually been gone for hours. What Tae doesn't know about herself is that she's the sort who creates enormous voids in peoples' lives when she isn't around even though she is only fifteen.

Maggie is certain that her own wake in the lake—behind her

boat-of-self—is puny in comparison; she leaves the waters mostly undisturbed. No one has ever truly missed her, nor will they. This truth doesn't matter, though at one time it would have. Since she has left so many men over the years, it now makes her feel somehow less culpable. Another fact: while she's been in love several times, no one has ever really been in love with her. Not in all her fifty-two years. Sure, a few have declared they were, and many had liked her well-enough, yet she is certain that she just doesn't evoke the intensity of feeling that someone like Tae does. Nick is clearly a victim of her influence. But, ultimately, Tae will grow bored and need to move on. Someday Maggie will speak to the survivors, if there are any.

After Kip gets better, if he does, Maggie will ask Tyler about his feelings for Tae. Unlike other men, he seems connected with his emotions; hence, more capable of articulating them. One thing is clear: he's fallen to Tae's charms, just as she has.

Gazing down the long dusty road, she sees a blue dot. More than likely a car… No reason to stand on the roadside waiting for the object to manifest itself. Also, she doesn't want to seem desperate for customers, though she's as bored and lonely as she'd once been as a girl selling lemonade. Has Tyler ever considered selling his statues at the stand?

Almost every evening he plays his harmonica on the porch, either before or after whittling one of his bird-men. All have wings, but some are two-headed with four arms; a few have one eye, and others, several. They could well be visitors from another world. The ones which look more like humans have obvious roles; among this group are bakers, farmers, and musicians (to name but a few). There is a china cabinet full of smaller ones in the formal dining room, and larger ones are grouped in a corner of the pole barn. (He hasn't, of course, mentioned the latter, but she came across them and couldn't help but peak under the canvas covering.) With ritualistic formality, he'd unlocked the cabinet door when he first showed them to Maggie and Tae. After taking them out with great care, he'd set them one at a time on the dining room table. Tenderly, whispering each one's name, as if afraid if he spoke too loudly, or handled them too roughly, that they might awaken. He, too, had seemed otherworldly at the time.

Why hasn't he shown (or even mentioned) the larger ones in the pole barn?

A woman behind the wheel of a small blue Mazda has been parked in the driveway for several minutes. At first she thought that it might be Sulie in a different car, but then Maggie realized it was Helen, a busybody neighbor who lived less than a mile away. According to Tyler, before Maggie and Tae had moved in, she used to check on Tyler about once a month. Since their arrival, Helen evidently hasn't felt quite as comfortable doing so; her last visit had been over two weeks ago. After having noticed Tae on the couch reading, she'd pursed her lips and curtly told Tyler to have a nice day, adding that her only reason for stopping by was because folks in town wondered how he was doing. Translation: *Helen* had been wondering.

It takes her forever to emerge from the driver's seat. Instead of venturing over to see Maggie behind the stand, she retrieves a large cardboard box from the trunk. Her short silver hair glistens like shiny metal. Despite her tanned and slender legs, isn't she a little too old to wear such a short white denim skirt? Her legs are surprisingly taut and smooth, with no signs of spider veins, though she must be a good ten years older than Maggie. Her leathery tan, expressionless forehead (no doubt, compliments of Botox) and dark eyeliner make her appear more suitable for a minor role as an ageing warrior woman pretending to be a kindly neighbor in some bad sci-fi film. At least this she-devil has brought honey for them to sell; Tyler's down to his last few jars.

"You're still here, I see," says Helen, after setting the box on the stand.

"Would you like to speak to Tyler? I think he's out back," Maggie says, pointing to the larger of the two barns.

"Actually, I'm glad just to see you. The gals in town, and I, would like to get to know you better. Why don't you join us at church or at one of our music nights in the town park? We don't bite. I promise. Just one word of caution: having 'live-in help' really isn't politically correct these days." She appeared pleased with herself for giving Maggie such important information.

Live-in help? Could she be referring to Tae? Does this idiot think Tae is 'help' because her skin is slightly darker than her own? What gall!

"Where's Tyler's old dog? Is it Tippy?" Helen asks, flitting to another topic.

"No, it's Kip. He's in the pole barn, not doing so well. He hasn't eaten in a few days… Tyler's pretty upset." Why has Maggie even bothered to give her so much information? How much more is this nosy neighbor going to pry from her? Maggie locates a folder she always carried out to the stand. In it an envelope with Helen's name on it—payment for the last case of honey that Tyler sold. Usually, whenever a car pulls up, Tyler and Kip are the first to greet the visitors—not that there are many. Kip must be worse today.

Maggie agrees to stop by the park at some unnamed date, just so Helen will take the hint and leave. Sensitive socialite that she is, Helen sniffs her little upturned nose in response and manages a forced and phony smile, before getting back into her car and mumbling something else that Maggie doesn't clearly hear, something Helen wanted her to pass along to Tyler. Maggie nods without asking her to repeat what she said. No way is she going to further delay leave-taking of this busy-body.

She finds Tyler crouched over the large black-furred body of his trusted companion. He's sobbing and doesn't turn in her direction, but mumbles, "Kip's gone." She immediately enfolds Tyler in her arms. No point in telling him about Helen stopping by; not now anyway. What can she do for him? There must be something. Almost an hour later, they go inside. She makes him a peanut butter sandwich and pours him a large glass of lemonade. He smiles wanly through his tears. The heat of the day makes it difficult to breathe.

After a solitary walk the following evening, Maggie sits on the porch swing attempting to read. Is it her ears ringing or is it a swarm of insects chirping or rubbing their legs together out in the grass? Lately, the nights have been cooler, and at last she's able to don her faded blue cardigan. Even so, she can't seem to get warm. Kip's death makes the brightest of house lights seem dim. Large moths dance tirelessly around the porch light. Her energy is low, even though she's been writing more lately; maybe she simply needs more exercise to take off those extra pounds she had gained while on the road.

She takes out a letter from an envelope. It's from Sulie:

Dear Maggie,

We really should've spoken when we were in Virginia Beach. I'm sure, by then, you realized that seeing each other here-and-there along the road was not happenstance. I'm also sure that, by now, you know I meant no harm to either you or Taezha. My hope is that soon we'll be able to talk in person.

Sulie

All very curious… She doesn't notice Tyler sitting with head-in-hands on the broken porch step. He doesn't turn her way; she can tell by the way he hunches his shoulders and then doesn't relax them, that he's aware of her presence. Should she say something? Probably not… Gradually, his shoulder muscles relax—maybe because she hasn't interrupted his thoughts. Always a man of few words, his dog's death has given him reason to communicate only in the most minimal way: a grunt, a nod, a sigh—no questions or statements longer than a few words.

She longs to tell him how worried she is about Tae spending so much time with Nick…and hardly any on her school work, or her writing. But it's not like they're her parents and can order her back. Sure, they could call Protective Services—for all the good it would do. Despite not talking about it, she knows he's aware of how much she misses her younger friend. He misses her, too. Does he realize, though, how Maggie saw it as her own fault when, earlier today, Tae had stormed out after throwing an almost full glass of iced tea at her? He'd watched as Maggie mopped the kitchen floor. He'd seen her tears.

But he doesn't know the complexity of the story, so how can he possibly put the pieces together, especially since there are so many missing ones?

———————

Maggie and Tae haven't talked since the day some weeks ago that Maggie had scolded her for not spending enough time on school work or writing. A few weeks from now, they are supposed to attend the story award ceremony for young authors in Washington, D.C. Maggie is not sure how they will get there since her car's been acting up. Tyler doesn't think anything is seriously wrong with it, but even so, he's been meaning to look it over. There's no reason, he said, that the red minivan won't be road-worthy by then, but Maggie has been having serious doubts about the trip...for other reasons, too. A shame, since for so long she's been thinking about how this would be Tae's formal debut as an author.

Maggie had not had a similar opportunity when she'd first begun writing. She only hopes that Tae won't squander this chance to launch her career. Is it possible that Maggie has been too much the stage mother? Is it possible that Maggie's true gift isn't as a writer herself, but in developing the talent of creative and hyper-sensitive young writers? How much she's wanted to show Tae how to always see with fresh, clear eyes. She will certainly keep the name, Taezha Riverton, in mind and search for her work online and on bookstore shelves in coming years. So, what should Maggie do when the time comes for her to move on? Where to go from here?

She could stay with her sister, though anything beyond a week would be intolerable for either of them. The only other person that Maggie can think of crashing with is Jocelyn, who had predicted that one day, when Maggie was middle-aged, she'd do something whacky; something of such magnitude that it would prove to be life-changing. It looks like Jocelyn was right, and now Maggie can only imagine the smug look of satisfaction on her old friend's face. It's been decades since they last saw each other. First, maybe she'll shoot her an e-mail and see if she responds. Jocelyn could help her become better at meditating, at learning the healing power of herbs. Perhaps Maggie could read her friend some poetry, and maybe inspire Jocelyn to write once again. People don't outgrow the need for 'best' friends, do they? But then Jocelyn's husband, Josh, probably wouldn't want Maggie around, and she'd wind up feeling like she was in the way.

Two other options…First one: she could return to Flint. Not all bridges have been burned. Not that she has many social contacts there, but it's someplace familiar. Second one: she could continue life-on-the-road by driving around the country and moving on whenever she gets bored. For now, why not stay here with Tyler? Paying him monthly rent will help him stay afloat, so, it's a win-win. Even though their rapport is a little strained without Tae around, they are oddly compatible. Tyler tries his best to understand her. He is not one to ask many questions, yet he is a good listener, and there is something in the way that he cocks his head and folds his large hands upon his lap when she's speaking that attracts her to him. He seems interested in her, too, though she doubts that he could ever feel the same for her as he once did for Serafina. Also, Maggie is attracted to his simple faith.

"There is more to existence than what we see and know. That's it in a nutshell," he'd told her. He reminded her of Levin in *Anna Karenina*. For Tyler, faith is simple; for her, so difficult. Maybe she can learn by observing him.

The next night at dinner she tells him about Sulie. She describes her as a strange little gum-chewing woman she met at a bar in Flint. Not only about her trench coat, toothpick between her lips, beret, and strong opinions, but how she and Tae have seen her on-and-off during the trip. She'd like to hear his opinion of her, but he just gazes at her blankly. Her cheeks burn. Not to be derailed from the topic, Maggie tells him how she called a guy she knew in Flint, a cop who'd agreed to run a background check, but he came up with nothing. Sulie's name was probably an alias. With luck, she's harmless. She can tell by the way he rubs his chin that he finds the revelation a curious one. Maybe he'll mull it over and offer his opinion tomorrow. Maybe now he needs to be left alone with his grief for Kip.

From Maggie's Journal

Detroit, 1980s

Wayne State University: It took me nearly a decade to receive a four-year degree. From my first day, I noticed how integrated the campus was compared to my high school. In classrooms and area restaurants there was a wonderful mixing of everybody; though in most places on campus there were far fewer blacks than whites. I soon discovered that few females—white or black—felt safe walking alone at night. Then a friend was mugged, and another was raped.

My father asked me the racial identities of the mugger and the rapist. I refused to answer. Both my parents implored me to move back home. Instead, I moved in with Caroline, though I stayed with her only a few months. I hadn't been there long before her house was broken into. It happened twice. The first time, our family (minus our father) was eating in the dining room. A guy wearing a ski mask and carrying a sawed-off shot gun seemed to materialize out of nowhere. Caroline rattled dishes and everyone took it as a cue to take off. We scattered, confusing the thief so much he left by the back door, taking nothing. Later that night, when my father wanted to know what he looked like (meaning the color of his skin) I replied that no one could tell because he was wearing a mask. He then asked if the man had been wearing gloves. I couldn't recall, but if I had I wouldn't have told him.

And then a couple weeks later…Someone was on the back stoop, jiggling the knob of the kitchen door. This time Jocelyn and I were about to enter the kitchen when Caroline whisper-warned: "He's back!" Jocelyn and I fled upstairs. She followed me into a bedroom closet, and my sister disappeared into a bathroom with a good lock. My brother-in-law alone remained downstairs with, we assumed, the burglar. Jocelyn was wearing several silver bangles on one arm; her trembling created a kind of other-worldly music. I thought for sure we'd be heard if the guy made it as far as the second floor. I tried to steady her musical arm, but my hands shook. Finally, we heard loud male voices coming from downstairs. I could taste vomit in my throat. Much later (was it minutes or hours?) we discovered that the voices belonged to cops. My brother-in-law had called for them. If it had been the same thug, he must have seen my brother-in-law and fled. Cops said this B&E artist had broken into twenty homes in the area in just one week.

How long would the crime wave continue? Would there be no end to the violence? I couldn't drive certain freeways because I worried about my car breaking down. Soon, I gave up driving city freeways altogether, as well as walking down certain streets, regardless of the time of day. Constant reports of drive-by shootings, murders… It began to feel like a war zone. I was dug in and watching from the trenches. From news reports it sounded like the crimes were mostly being committed by black men. This made sense, not only because of high unemployment rates among blacks, but because whites were moving out of the city in droves. Most, my sister told me, didn't have the same advantages that we did while growing up. Often, they were from broken homes, and too often fell between the cracks. Desperation drove them to it. I tried to understand, the way she did, but I became afraid of any black male, teenage or older, that I passed on the streets. "Hey, sexy lady!" they'd often catcall after me. I knew it wasn't me that they found attractive, it was code for, "Hey, white bitch!" I never responded.

Once There Was a Poet

He visited me in my office at the university
This brilliant, prize-winning, words-man
In the late afternoons he'd sit in a chair opposite my desk and stare at me
He was darker than
I was pale
I was flattered, but shy
We never knew what to say to each other
Once we agreed to meet for coffee, but we
never did…

—Maggie Barnett

Chapter 31

As her obsession with Tae's absence grows, Maggie pays increasingly less attention to her own appearance—especially her fingernails. Plus, she's gained ten pounds in the past few months due to midnight snacking when she can't sleep; not only are her clothes fitting snuggly, but her jeans have broken zippers. She shakes out her long, silvery-blond mane from a ponytail and examines her face in the bathroom mirror. "Not getting any younger, my pretty!" she tells herself, and then cackles.

There's nowhere quite like this wraparound verandah, and nothing quite as calming as swaying on the porch swing. The constant creak soothes her, lulls her into memories and fantasies. She sips the last of a second cup of coffee from the blue mug with a chipped handle, pulls a purple paisley shawl tightly about her. First time she's shivered in the morning.

She should be writing. Guilt washes over her and scrubs her inside and out. Guilt rides the wave of a hot flash. Despite the cooler weather, hot flashes have been occurring more often lately. She never sleeps longer than a couple of hours at a time and finds herself unable to relax, even with Tyler, who is one of the gentlest souls she's ever known.

This morning Tae finished her home-school work in less than an hour. Maggie is sure that it should take three or four. When she insisted on checking it, Tae had refused and stomped off, mumbling something about her plans with Nick for the day.

How vastly different are these days from those on the road. Their quasi-attempt at family life is difficult, but it does have rewarding moments—especially during evenings, when she and Tae sit together on the porch and listen to Tyler play his harmonica.

Those times remind her of when she was a girl at the cabin. There she saw more of her parents than she ever did at home. She especially enjoyed being there with them when Caroline was away at college. Too often in Maggie's life, Caroline had stolen their attention, just as Nick or Tyler now steal Tae's attention. Old patterns haunt her. She knows she must bite her tongue or Tae will reject her.

Miss Sophie jumps onto her lap and looks her right in the eye. Does the cat sense her fever? Is she a fellow sufferer? Tyler's remoteness over the last few days has made a moody cat become even moodier. Since Kip died, Tyler's been in such a fog of grief that he hasn't been able to find his way to the others, including Miss Sophie. Hopefully, he'll soon snap out of it.

Maggie finally stirs and gently sets Miss Sophie on the padded seat of the porch swing. For what it's worth, the rooms look better than before—less dusty. And the curtains that she bought in town make the bedrooms appear less plain. She still needs to find some for the downstairs windows.

During the past several days it has become clear that he's interested in a committed relationship. How could she help but feel flattered? Not only is he gentle, but kind and intuitive. Yet at the age of forty-two he seems to have no interest in ever moving from his land, and that makes him, in her view, provincial. How could a relationship with such a man last?

Besides, if Tyler knew more about her, he probably wouldn't be as interested in her. He would understandably be aghast not only by the number of men she'd lived with, but by the way she'd left them (usually without even leaving a goodbye note). And by the time she'd leaped from Detroit's Ambassador Bridge, two years after her parents' deaths. Not to mention the time on the ledge... If he knew that she'd had an abortion, and miscarriages, and then there is her history of kleptomania (only small things—no big-sticker items), and last but not least, the depth of her feelings for Tae. If asked, she'd be tongue-tied due to the complexity… Little doubt he'd not only ask her to leave, but insist that she did. Maybe soon she'll let him in on a couple of her secrets, just to see his reaction. Certainly not all of them… Has she even recounted all of them?

Not that Tyler doesn't have a past… Maggie knows about his experimentation with drugs after the navy; his short but intense passion for Serafina; his guilt about Tae. Then there were the years of blind dates with pretty women. One-night stands and brief relationships…

Tonight the sky is overcast and Tyler claims that they're in for quite a storm. "Around here, late summer storms are always the worst," he tells her. They hold hands as they sit together at the fruit stand. Right now, there is only honey and the last of the blueberries for sale. He thanks her for taking over for him. Life is certainly slower in the South. She tells him how she had intended on writing today but had frittered away the entire morning. "Maybe I won't ever write again," she tells him.

"You will, I know it. Just like I know when a storm is coming," he says.

She is less skeptical of an impending storm than she is about putting words on paper. And also, less nervous…

Tae arrives home in the late afternoon, hollers a 'Hello' at Maggie, and immediately disappears into her bedroom and shuts the door. Tyler, who hadn't slept for the first couple of days after Kip's death, can now be heard snoring throughout the house, especially downstairs. How can he sleep before a storm?

Maggie feels hyper-conscious and has a hard time sitting still; it's like the electricity in the atmosphere is animating her entire being. She forces herself to sit, then bolts upright again, paces… She doesn't know what to do with her worse-than-usual restlessness. She gets a strong whiff of perfume in the upstairs hall, a floral scent. A mission has presented itself. She follows the aroma up the creaky stairs and into his grandmother's room.

The door is half open, as usual. Perching on the edge of the bed, she watches a shadow grow on the wall and can't figure out what's creating it. A small framed photo on the dresser falls over—not to the floor, but face down. She picks it up, expecting to see a picture of Tyler, but it's clearly an old photo of a relative. Is it his grandfather?

Later, Tyler explains that it is, in fact, his grandfather. The picture frame has always been fragile. Once Nana put the photo away for an entire year, but then brought it out again, though she'd usually kept it face down on the dresser. As for the perfume: yes, he sprays it now and then to keep her memory present but hasn't done so since Maggie and Tae arrived.

Chapter 32

Since Tae had spent the entire day with Nick watching old Marlon Brando movies, she isn't upset about not being able to return to his house after dinner. Although Maggie claims otherwise, Tae can tell that she really doesn't like him. Why can't Maggie see that she is ready for a boyfriend? Why can't Maggie see in him what Tae sees? Maggie is usually fair-minded. Her reaction to Nick seems ridiculous.

She slams the bedroom door, a little louder than intended, and flops onto the bed. Although she doesn't spend much time in the room, whenever she's does, she enjoys it. It's much nicer than her bedroom in Flint, though she hasn't yet re-built the book towers. She loves the rocker, the patchwork quilt, and the view of the tree-filled yard from her window. Her only issue with the room was the two dolls; the first couple of nights here, she could have sworn they were watching her, staring at her. They reminded her of the way Maggie's eyes sometimes followed her. Tae's remedy had been to hide the dolls on a closet shelf.

Just now she feels awake, almost too awake—as if she could run a twenty-mile race. Actually, it's the way she always feels just before a storm. Strange, as the sky doesn't look threatening…

Tyler is in the kitchen washing the dinner dishes. (He had made spaghetti with meat sauce and Tae, who'd recently recommitted to being a vegetarian, had eaten only salad.)

She follows on Maggie's heels out to the wrap-around porch. There are various chairs and rockers on the porch, including the swing. All are wicker, ancient, and falling apart. Creaky old bones and probably as brittle… She tests a rocker, then the chair next to it. Worried that the chair might break, she moves down the line to a sturdier looking rocker. Maggie hogs the swing.

Dark clouds gather, making it appear later than it is. She wanders to the side yard, then over to the gazebo. It's a romantic-looking place with ivy enclosing two of the sides and a white glider in the center. Why haven't Nick and she sat here yet? Maybe she'll suggest it to him the next time he visits. Tonight won't be the best night for it anyway, as it's beginning to sprinkle. Must be all that electricity somehow making her blood move more quickly through her veins…

She finally wears Maggie down and Nick is welcome to visit. Problem is that his phone goes immediately to voicemail, but doesn't allow her to leave a message. She answers the first of two voice mails on her phone—both from Quintana. The same message both times: *Baby girl, call me! Something I've got to tell you.* Tae is passively curious, but doesn't feel like calling her back for two reasons: 1) She prefers texting Nick, and 2) She's still pissed at Quintana for never having told her that Serafina was her mother.

So many occasions when Quintana could have come clean, particularly after eighth grade graduation. Tae knows it would have been harder to grasp if she'd been told as a little girl, but why has Quintana kept it secret through her teen years? Truth is, Tae is pleased to now know for sure. Although Quintana will always be her mom, it's cool (in a way), or as some of her friends would say, it's "so *glam*!" that the talented and lovely Serafina was her birth mother. Still, Tae hadn't known her as a mother, but as an auntie. Why hadn't Serafina told her the truth when she'd stayed with her in New York? From what Tae knew about her life, it hadn't been an easy one. Maybe she'd had a drug problem like Billie Holiday.

Tyler told her that Serafina had always loved her, though from a distance, and had never— not for one minute—forgotten about her. How does he know this? They must have been pretty close friends (way more, if it's true that he's actually her father). Also, it now makes sense that her sisters, who are actually her cousins, are closer to Quintana than she is. No wonder Tae always loved the Cinderella story so much as a child. Maybe the next story she writes will be a remaking of the tale. (But wait!—that's been done before.) On some level, she's probably known all along that they weren't her *real* sisters. It wasn't only because she didn't resemble them—it went deeper than that. Weird, since Quintana and Serafina did look alike—especially their eyes which were large and sleepy. Serafina had been the bomb-shell beauty, while Quintana, even on her best days, could only be called cute or stylish; that is, if she wore the right outfit. What they'd really shared was a kindred spirit, though life had burned each of their candle flames to the quick, albeit in different ways.

She opens a new pack of Butterscotch Lifesavers and calls Quintana.

Main reason for not wanting to talk to her is due to Quintana always talking so nasty about Maggie and Tyler, though mostly she's nasty to Tae. This time, however, Quintana's tone is mild, even calm, as she tells Tae that she (Quintana) and her sisters feel like Tae's turned her back on them. Tae responds that it isn't true, since she'll be coming back for visits, especially around the holidays.

"That is, if your white-sugar mama will let you! And when was it that this trip turned into a permanent vacation?"

Tae lets the silence dangle on an invisible high wire between them. Then Quintana tells her something Tae doesn't have time to process. Their conversation ends abruptly without Tae being able to respond because everything—at least on Tae's end—happens at once: tornado sirens blare and Tyler is in the background yelling that she and Maggie take cover in the tornado shelter. Tae hurriedly tells Quintana that she's got to go and hangs up on her.

Maggie shouts: "Why not the basement?" He doesn't answer, as he's busy trying to locate Miss Sophie, as well as a flashlight. The sky is green and there is not a single breath or slightest sigh of air. He must be nervous. Tae realizes how she's never seen him like this; if she just hadn't heard what she did at the end of her talk with Quintana, she'd be thinking better thoughts about him... Miss Sophie is nowhere to be found. Wind from every direction whips through the trees and the sky is now an even darker green. One of the wicker chairs flips over just as they reach the door of the shelter. There is a strange smell in the air, almost like something's burning. Is this how electricity smells? A hard rain begins to fall. It takes Tyler forever to get the door open.

Steps lead into darkness. A switch is flipped.

The lighting is dim, flickering, yet bright enough to make out a plain, though not-unpleasant, little room containing a table, two chairs at the table and two cots. There's even a short stack of magazines in a box.

At first, all three sit as still as possible, trying to listen for sounds made by the wind. No easy task, especially for Tae. Their clothing is damp and the air down here is cool and musty. Tyler mumbles something about Miss Sophie. Funny, a man like him would even care about a cat. Maybe he's the sort who cares more for animals than people. It hits her that she really hasn't spent much time with him since she and Maggie had arrived. She's been meaning to, but it's not like Tyler is the kind of man to just sit around. If only Nick were here, she'd be able to ignore the adults and snuggle up to him and pretend to be a little more frightened than she really feels.

Maggie is quieter than usual. Her face as pale as chalk: Tae can see this despite the dim lighting. That's right, Maggie doesn't like rainstorms; it makes sense that she'd be nervous now.

"Weren't you once out in a boat with your dad and your dog when lightning hit the water?" Tae asks, saying it really for his benefit. Maggie nods and he takes her hand. They're sitting next to each other on one of the cots. Tae sits on the other.

It must be scary to be on a boat in a storm...

Tyler winces at the mention of a dog. Should Tae tell him about her invisible pal, Sinbad, and how she makes up stories about him when she can't sleep? Maybe not... Why did she bring this up knowing Tyler's probably thinking about Kip? Since he'd been a close friend of Serafina's (and maybe more), she'd felt an almost immediate bond with him, way back when they were just pen pals. Discovering the truth about Serafina being her mother, she now feels even closer to him. He's got a sensitive nature—artistic really—even though he doesn't much care about the written word. A way of seeing the world and showing it to her without even trying, yet there's a carefulness to the way he does things (unlike Maggie who plows through the days with almost brute force). And yet, if what Quintana had told her is true, do his good qualities really matter?

"How long do you think we'll be stuck down here?" Tae asks, knowing that the storm is not his doing, but still…

"Never can tell. The all-clear siren might go off within minutes, or it could take hours."

"Did anyone bring food?" She glances from Maggie to Tyler, then back at Maggie. Maggie shakes her head. Tae appears so panicked that he laughs and opens a cupboard revealing a box of crackers, cookies, tins of tuna, dried fruit.

"Nothing funny in fearing there won't be food, but maybe you wouldn't know what that's like," says Tae.

"Believe me, I've known plenty of lean times," he says, crossing his arms over his chest.

"Is that what led you to do what you did? Why you went to jail? I'd sooner starve!" Tae blurts out.

He stares at his hands. Maggie is confused. It's obvious that she doesn't know this little secret; Quintana must never have mentioned it to her.

"What does she mean *what you did*?" Maggie asks.

He says nothing at first. Tae and Maggie both stare at him.

"Did Quintana tell you? Or was it Nick?"

"Quintana… Nick's never said anything about it."

He cracks his knuckles. Tae notices how hairy they are. As if aware of her judgment, he drops his hands.

"Okay, here's what happened…" He then explains how it was shortly after his grandmother and Serafina died (both deaths occurred four years ago and within a few months of each other). He'd been depressed and unable to find a job. The small inheritance from his grandmother had been bound up in the county's slow-moving legal system. Money he'd borrowed from friends had kept him afloat for a time, but it wasn't long before it ran out; he wasn't the sort to keep asking for handouts. Times got so bad he'd resorted to eating dog food along with Kip. It often made him ill. One night when he could take it no more, he attempted to rob a convenience store in a nearby town. The police showed up just as he was crossing the parking lot with the twenty dollar bill (all that he'd gotten from the cash register) still in his hand.

He never fired the gun: the safety was on for crying out loud! Still, he got locked up for a year. Some good things about it: he got three squares, plus he came to terms with things… Alex had cared for Miss Sophie and Kip; he'd also kept watch on the house.

"Are you sorry for your crime?" Tae asks. He takes his time answering.

"Honey, I'm sorry that life was so grim that I became a thief. I would have felt much worse had I hurt someone or taken someone's life. Yes, I'm sorry I became so desperate, but I'd probably do it again if I ever fell on such hard times. I'm even sorrier you had to find out the way you did. If you had to hear it at all, you should have heard it from me."

The three lapse into silence. Maggie and Tae watch as Tyler whittles a piece of wood into one of his bird-men, a small one with the sad face of someone who'd been through hard times.

The wind tries its best to break into the shelter, but thankfully the heavy door keeps the storm at bay. An hour has passed since they had climbed into the shelter.

A curious look passes between Maggie and Tyler. They seem to be sitting closer than before. Despite his crime not having been as bad as Tae feared, it was still a crime. He had a gun, and he'd threatened someone. It was not any different than what the street thugs did back home… Yet she knows he's not a thug, knows he's a kind man. Who knows how she'd react if life ever got that tough? He's a far cry better than Quintana's boyfriend. She knows she can trust Tyler. Does Maggie think any less of him now?

He asks them to hold hands and pray for the storm to be over. Tae takes one of his hands, but Maggie declines. "You're kidding, right?" she asks, with an eyebrow raised.

"We don't know how bad it is out there. I know you're not exactly religious, but you're not opposed to the mysterious workings of the universe, are you? Many folks swear to the power of prayer," he informs Maggie.

"If shit's going to happen, it's going to happen. Sorry, but I don't credit it to fate or God. You two go ahead. I promise to mute my cynicism and be quiet while you bow your heads."

Tyler and Tae hold each other's hands and close their eyes. They close them out of piety, but partly because they don't want to see the smirk on Maggie's face.

"Please, oh Lord, deliver us safely from this storm. Not only us, but all those who are affected." Tae opens one eye and sees Maggie thoughtfully examining her own hands. Is she looking for cuticles or contemplating the possibility of an all-seeing God. Tae hopes it's the latter. Tyler keeps his eyes shut, as if trying to transport himself elsewhere; for the moment he seems unaware of either of them, as well as his surroundings. If only Maggie hadn't taken down the crucifix in the living room, and the one in the guestroom where she's sleeping. At least she hadn't taken down the one in his grandmother's room. Maybe Tae could hang the one from Maggie's room on her wall. It can't hurt, can it? The strange part is that he hadn't seemed to mind that Maggie had taken them down. The winds die down within minutes of Tyler opening his eyes. Tae wants to say something about it but can see for both their sakes that maybe it's best to switch the subject.

"Guess who's living in town?"

They both look at her blankly.

"Maggie, do I really need to tell you?"

Maggie covers her face with her hands and then peers through spread fingers at the girl. "Not Sulie?"

"None other. She's selling tickets at the theater. When Nick and I went to a matinee the other day, there she was! She was even wearing her black beret, but not the trench coat. She acted like she didn't know me."

"Did you ever think that maybe Quintana hired her just to keep any eye on you, since she doesn't exactly trust you, Maggie?" Tyler asks, jumping between the two.

"She doesn't have the money to buy me a pair of shoes, so why would—how would she be able to—hire someone to spy on Maggie and me?"

"Tae's right," confirms Maggie, who is clearly impressed by Tae's practical insight.

This leads to a short conversation about why Maggie hadn't worked a little harder at getting Quintana's full consent *before* the trip. Maggie explains how Quintana seemed to enjoy pulling their strings, saying yes one moment and no the next. Maggie had grown tired of the game, knowing that ultimately Quintana would give in.

"It's not like I haven't included her concerning the bigger decisions, such as home-schooling. Together we weighed the pros and cons," Maggie says defensively, then continues, "If there's anyone to be distrusted, it's Quintana. I'm sorry, Tae, I know you love her. She'll always be your mom, but there are other issues—things I can't tell you about now, but will someday."

The siren blasts the all-clear. Tyler lifts the latch and pushes open the door to survey the damage. Their heads pop up from underground like gophers.

Tae still can't reach Nick. He doesn't answer her calls or texts. "What if something has happened to him?" she asks Maggie. Tyler tries calling Nick's dad from his phone, and at last he receives a message: *No service available in this area.* Maggie tells Tae that everything will be okay. How does Maggie know? Is she psychic? Tae is nervous as a cat. Finally, Maggie gives up trying to reassure her and goes to bed. So does Tyler. Tae paces the floor until she finally gives in to exhaustion at 2:00 a.m.

Before falling asleep, all they know for sure is that the house and the two barns are still standing. No windows had been broken and from what they can tell, only chairs and potted flowers on the verandah have been knocked over. Still, it's hard to know how much has been damaged. They'd had no luck in their search for Miss Sophie.

Tyler thought maybe she was in the larger barn during the storm. Tae had wanted to take the flashlight to the barn, but Tyler said something about fractured tree branches that might fall. "Let's wait till morning," he suggested.

She wakes late in the morning to a call from Nick. It had driven him nearly crazy not being able to get in touch with her. His house hadn't sustained much damage either. Tears of relief run down her cheeks. They make plans to get together later in the day.

Downstairs, Maggie informs her that Tyler's gazebo received the worst of the storm, as it was severed into two halves by a tree limb that was hit by lightning. But now the sun is out, and it's already in the nineties and humid even though it's still before noon. Tae dresses in a hurry and tells Maggie that her homework can wait until tomorrow. She and Nick are going to meet halfway between the two houses. Life is once again exciting and wonderful; yet she is afraid, afraid that it could all be taken away so quickly: by a furious storm, for example, or waking up back in Flint.

Chapter 33

Maggie is dismayed that Tae left for Nick's without first helping her search for Miss Sophie. She'd spritzed herself a little too liberally with the patchouli then vanished. Maybe Tae doesn't care for the big-eyed cat? Most likely, it's that Nick comes first these days. Maggie won't be able to right the fallen porch chairs until she searches for the mouser who puts her so in mind of Lucy Lucinda (who she'd left in Flint with her young friend, Toby). She won't bother asking Tyler to assist her, as he's busy removing the larger branches littering the lawn and driveway.

After having little luck searching under beds and other crawl spaces in the house, she systematically checks for loose floorboards in the pole barn. Except for an area where Tyler repairs furniture, the pole barn is the least cluttered area. She throws back a dirty blanket in a corner and there are the birdmen that Tyler mentioned last night. Some farmers, a few artists, one or two businessmen, and a chef… All with wings which are either outstretched as if preparing for flight, or folded in a grudging acceptance of their earthly lives. She admires his talent but finds it curious that he doesn't sculpt anything besides birdmen.

How can it be possible that she finds herself physically aroused as she recalls the story he told in the tornado shelter about his time in prison? At her age! That familiar dampness in her panties causes her to first laugh, then hiccup. Familiar, yet so long since… Maybe she'll be able to get beyond her physical needs once she and Tyler begin sleeping together. It's worked in the past, so maybe it will again.

Here, kitty, kitty! Careful, Maggie, old girl: it's a slippery slope you're beginning to slide down once again. How can she even be thinking of Tyler with poor old Miss Sophie lost from the storm? At last, she comes across the safe but worried-looking cat staring up at her from a missing board. She appears perfectly capable of the short hop to ground level, but it's as if she's just been waiting for human rescue.

A grateful Tyler appears just as she's cradling Miss Sophie. Sweating profusely from gathering large branches, he expresses relief and gratitude by giving Maggie a lingering kiss. The cat leaps down (as if on cue), allowing him to take Maggie in her arms and spin her about. Next, he takes her face in his rather large dirty hands. "I Think I'm falling for you, Maggie Barnett," he tells her before kissing her again, this time more deeply, and for so long that the barn shadows have shifted by the time they come up for air. They make their way to the gazebo which the storm had torn as if it had been made of paper. She expresses her dismay. "No problem," he says, shrugging. "I can build another."

For several weeks, Maggie, Tyler, and Tae begin to feel like a happy family. Almost. Maggie plays the sometimes loving mother, but mostly the bad cop parent. She can tell that Tae secretly enjoys having limits, though she argues (just a little) and stomps her feet at a new curfew, as well as having to buckle down with schoolwork. "Tae, find your Spanish vocab and I'll quiz you. Remember, you have to take the test today. That was our deal." Tyler plays the quiet, but ever watchful, father. He seems to enjoy his role. Tae continues seeing Nick, but mostly on weekends. They eat dinner together; afterward they sit on the verandah in the evenings, occasionally with coffee and a dessert that Maggie has made. She enjoys doing something useful in the afternoons; it saves her from boredom, plus Tyler and Tae are always delighted with her pies, tortes, or tarts. Since their jeans are all getting snug at the waistband, they agree that maybe once a week is often enough for her rich and tasty desserts.

Maggie and Tyler begin spending nights together in his queen-sized four poster bed. She doesn't have to request removal of the crucifix, but by the second night, it's off the wall. While she's putting on a rarely worn, long silk nightgown, he lights several votive candles on the top of his dresser. Her libido's somewhat stronger than his, but she rarely fails to get him in the mood. He acts surprised by all the 'positions' she knows, and seems more than happy to have her show him. At least, he pretends *not* to know. She soon realizes he's more experienced at sex than his 'aw shucks' manner reveals. They both love snuggling afterward, and speaking in drowsy voices until they fall asleep. Often she wakes to find one of his hands on her breast. She doesn't detach his large but gentle fingers.

Then comes a night when Tae returns early from Nick's. Tyler is at Alex's house playing cards, leaving Maggie and Tae alone in the house. After telling Maggie that Alex plans to major in engineering in college, she confides that she's in love with him and has been thinking about having sex.

"You're too young!" Maggie shouts at her. "Maybe we should return to Michigan. After all you've seen with your mom, I thought you were smarter than that!"

Tae lowers her head, rolls her eyes, and looks anywhere but at Maggie.

"Well, I was honest and told you, but now I don't know why I bothered. I never would have said a word about it to my mom. We'll use condoms, of course, so spare me the lecture, and no, I'm not dumb. I'm way more mature than you think. I'm ready for this!" At last, Tae meets her eyes.

"You think you are… Most teens do. I know you're a mature and sophisticated fifteen, but you're still just fifteen! I guess I should thank you for your honesty. How do you know you love him?" Maggie purses her lips and shakes her unkempt, quickly-graying hair.

"I know what I know. And I know that I don't need any more of your questions."

Tae exits the living room, flipping Maggie off before she pounds up the stairs to her room. Maggie follows. At the top of the staircase, Tae swivels her head to face her formidable opponent. Maggie is only one step below her. In Tae's eyes, the cold gleam of someone with a plan. She slaps Maggie's face. If Maggie hadn't caught her balance by grabbing the railing, she might have fallen down the stairs.

Two hearts beat wildly.

"Do you realize what you…what just almost happened?" asks Maggie, still short of breath.

Tae races to her room and slams the door. Maggie bursts in to see Tae lying on the bed, popping those damn Butterscotch Lifesavers. Maggie waits in the hallway, then slams the door shut, opens it all the way, and slams it again. Tae is sobbing now, lying on the bed, face down. "How do you like it? It doesn't feel so nice when someone slams the door on you, does it?" Maggie hisses. She remains awkwardly in the doorway for a few minutes as Tae continues to sob. Why wasn't she better prepared for this sort of confrontation?

Maggie closes the door again—quietly this time and confines herself to her own room. She sits on the bedside and doesn't know what to do with herself. One hand trembles as it tries to still the other. She hates them—so pale and veiny. Her nails are chipped; some even show dirt under the jagged tips. The same body which felt sexy with Tyler now feels older, heavier. Tinnitus is worse than ever. Eyeing her sagging breasts in the mirror above the dresser, she turns away quickly, and again feels a surge of anger over Tae and Nick. How has it come to this? Does it bother her more because of her own feelings for Tae? Does this make her love for the girl perverted and wrong? Is she some kind of social deviant? At least Tyler wasn't there during their fight, or whatever the hell it was. The question now: What to do? Maybe it's time to return to Michigan, or venture somewhere else. Somewhere further than North Carolina; someplace where no one can find her.

All seems hopeless, dark…more dismal than her most depressed nights inside her Flint apartment. It was worse now, as she had come so close to having a better life here. But it's a life she now understands she probably can't have. She must let it go. Images of the bridge and the ledge return.

She drifts into the bathroom. Opens the medicine cabinet and stares at the bottle of sleeping pills. Why not? What's left? More disappointment, more loss…

Tae knocks at Maggie's door about an hour before Tyler returns, well before midnight. The two hug and immediately Maggie's dark mood lifts, at least a little. She boils water in the tea kettle and makes them both chamomile tea. They sit at the table in the kitchen nook and talk quietly, as if something is asleep within the house that neither wishes to ever awaken again. Maggie's the first to apologize. She hadn't meant to over-react. Tae emphasizes how she and Nick haven't actually had sex yet. Maggie exudes a loud sniff, sighs deeply, and her eyes dart nervously about.

"No harm thinking about it. I mean, of course you would. It's good you to want to talk with each other about sex, though it doesn't mean you're emotionally ready for it, right?" Tae nods, and this time knows better than to contradict her. As they're finishing their tea in silence, both hear a creak on the stairs leading to the second floor.

They listen and wait.

After a few minutes pass and they hear nothing more, they speak in whispered tones about the house ghost and of Nana's perfume and her invincible, invisible, watchful eyes.

The next morning, following a leisurely breakfast of scrambled eggs, fresh fruit, and freshly baked, extra-large blueberry muffins, Tyler departs to help his neighbors who are still clearing rubble from the storm. Maggie pours a second cup of coffee and tours the rooms, noting how the sunlight pours through the windows. It pleases her that Tae is upstairs sleeping. There had been no reason to tell Tyler about what had transpired the night before. She hasn't felt this at-home in a long time, despite the storm, and the blow-up with Tae. Considering how at-home she feels now, it mystifies her to think that she had given any serious thought about returning to Michigan. Definitely a different mood than the night before… Feeling like she's part of a family gives her a sense of belonging that she hasn't felt since she was a girl. It makes her almost giddy.

She tiptoes upstairs and peaks inside Tae's room. The door creaks as Maggie opens it, but thankfully, it doesn't wake the girl. An atmosphere envelops her that's almost as wondrous as being in love. Wondrous: that's not a word she often uses… Maybe she *is* in love. If so, it crept up slowly. Does Tyler feel the same? They both must be in love, given the way he kisses her so deeply, and the way she so lingeringly kissed him back…the way he tickled her as the two of them worked alongside each other at the kitchen counter shortly after telling him she was going to replace the downstairs shades with curtains…the way she'd giggled like a schoolgirl! Lately, she's caught him staring at her with a new intensity. It hadn't occurred to her at the time, but it must be because he's in love with her, too. Maybe at last she'll be able to write a love poem. Why not make the attempt before she begins excavating the strong, yet painful, memories from childhood and jotting more notes about her parents' lives? For the first time in a long time, all seems right with the world.

No Sulie sightings of late. Maggie's been eyeing the passersby whenever she goes to town, and always checks to see if Sulie is selling tickets at the theater box office. Next time, why not simply ask the manager if Sulie works there? Maybe Tae was mistaken. She finds herself waiting for another letter in the mail. The two short letters indicated that Sulie wanted to stay in touch, so why hasn't she? Strange little person… Will she forever lurk as a shadow-person in the back of Maggie's mind? If Maggie knows anything about anything, it's that she hasn't yet seen the last of Sulie.

———————

When Sulie has dreamed repeating dreams in the past, she's known enough to heed them, to follow the directions given to her. Yes, she's gone on more than a few wild goose chases, and maybe this stake-out will turn out to be yet another, but in her dreams lately, Maggie is working alongside her in the book museum. But what makes her think that Maggie would work at her (fantasy) museum? Especially, if she snatches the girl and sends her home… It's a sad day when you realize that you're dumber than you think you are despite psychic abilities.

From Maggie's Journal

Detroit Riots, 1967

Some of the looting was only a mile away, but it was a long mile. No one seemed particularly worried about it ever reaching our street. My parents refused to talk about what was going on in front of me, so I depended on Caroline for information. In the heart of the city, poor Negroes were rising up, she told me; they were angry and many of them had taken to the streets. I remember thinking often about that. It was a time of confusion and frustration for everyone. Lots of kids—all of them white—lived on my street. We were upset about a curfew that lasted for several days. To have to be inside your house on a summer evening was just this side of being in prison. During the daytime, we got together and listened to the rioting on walkie-talkies. The signal was never the greatest, but we listened with rapt attention to sirens (both in the background and on the walkie-talkies) and what we thought for sure was gunfire. Even after the curfew was lifted, we continued to hear sirens in the distance; they became commonplace. Thankfully, the riots did not. While the rioting never reached my street, it was a hot, tense, and strange summer. Nothing would ever be the same again.

Our favorite outdoor game in those days was Red Rover. Kids would divide into two groups facing each other on opposite sides of the street. You had to hold hands with whomever was on either side of you (unless you were on one end). When your name was called, you had to run full-force into the chain-link of arms on the other side and try to break through. If successful, you could choose the hostage of your choice as booty, and return with him to your side of the street. But if you couldn't break a link, you had to remain in the enemy camp, even though odds were that they didn't want you. I was always a weak link since I wasn't popular and had the brute force of a wet noodle. One particular hot summer night (this must have been after the riots), a particularly smart-assed kid, Tony, made my group yell: "Red Rover, Red Rover, let the Coloreds come over!"

Tony then yelled back at us: "Hell, no!" There were no actual black kids playing the game, as none lived in the neighborhood. It was only this that made me feel slightly less embarrassed.

Chapter 34

The entire month of October is as idyllic as domestic life could ever hope to be. No word from Quintana lately—maybe she has finally accepted the situation. Everything hums along. Maggie's hot flashes have been infrequent since arriving at Tyler's. She purchases curtains, which are perfect for the downstairs windows: off-white, tied backs with a slight flowing ruffle running down the edges. They remind her of ones her grandmother had once made. The effect is to reduce the austerity, not only of the old farmhouse, but the creased forehead of the bachelor who has lived there for so long. She continues to bake scrumptious pies and crème brulee.

Now she can relax and worry a little less about Tae changing her mind and requesting a plane ticket back to Flint. She's almost certain the girl feels the same as she feels: home at last!

Maggie no longer works at the fruit stand in the mornings, but at her desk. As always, she can't stay seated for long. Frequently, she'll go out to the verandah and begin to pace, resting only for a few minutes, before she's pacing once again. New writing rituals begin to develop: she hums and always has a glass of lime water on her desk, which she rarely finishes. Notes about her parents' lives accumulate: what it was like to live in a world of legal discussions; the difficulties they'd had raising two girls while both were attending law school; the especially trying times of her mother practicing law at a time when few women did. Maggie still hasn't written the penultimate love poem, which she knows is in her—somewhere—but promises herself that someday soon, she will.

Love is finally declared. She tells Tyler first. He's more passive, gentler than other men she has known intimately, so it's no surprise. What both amazes and pleases her is the way he is in bed: a wild man with a slow touch. True, he's the aggressor: it's as if he knows precisely what she wants done to her by his tongue, lips, fingers, and cock; all body parts in concert performing minor miracles with her body, inside her body. She's equally astonished and pleased by the way her body responds—not much differently than when she was younger. No doubt she'll never rival Serafina, but hopefully, what they have between them now has its own intensity, its own magic. They mostly make love at night when Tae is off somewhere with Nick, but also in the mornings, when the sun is just finding its way through the curtains. Lately, she's been feeling ten years younger. A marvel...

Tae unexpectedly begins to hang out with her more. They sip tea together in the afternoons, go for walks, and have lunch in town once a week at the town diner. Maggie always has tuna on rye, whereas Tae mostly orders grilled cheese with a dill pickle on the side. Diet cokes are gulped down by both (sometimes Tae orders a second). Their lunches remind them of being on the road. They recall their time in Hocking Hills; the flat tire incident; Morgantown; Virginia Beach. They also discuss their upcoming trip to Washington, D.C. where Tae will be presented with the award for her short story. Tae is worried that she'll be too nervous and will "pass right out." Maggie does her best to reassure her that she won't.

She is both relieved and pleased that Tae has been more focused on her studies, and that she is also finding time for writing and reading. Yesterday, she told Maggie that she's working on a new story about the ghost of Nina, an elderly woman. Nina haunts her family by tickling their feet when they're sleeping and scaring their cats. Sometimes they hear her giggling... She doesn't have a title for it yet. Maggie wants to know when she'll be able to read it and is assured that maybe within the next few days. Such a relief not to have to nag! Her mother used to nag Caroline when she was Tae's age by droning on and on, asking Caroline if she'd completed her work. When Caroline refused to answer, she'd refuse to allow her to watch TV or talk on the phone to her friends. If their mom was especially upset ('on the rag' as the girls used to call it), privileges were denied to Maggie, as well. And for no reason whatsoever! She never had to nag Maggie, not even once. Little was worse than hearing that nasal, whiny tone in her mother's badgering voice—that is, until she heard it escape her own throat, as she has on occasion—but not lately— when playing drill sergeant with Tae. What would Tyler think if he heard her getting on Tae's case the way she had, that is, until recently?

Miss Sophie frequents Nana's room less often these days, as do the three humans living in the house. Maggie wanders in and out, but rarely lingers.

The only real problem is that she still can't write the love poem that must be locked deep inside her psyche. She adds visualization exercises to her other pre-writing rituals, but to no avail. After staring at her ten-inch birdman statue (Tyler had given her the one he'd whittled during the storm), she pitches wadded-up drafts into the wastebasket across from her desk in the upstairs bedroom. Language flat and too many near clichés... The wooden face, so like Tyler's, seems to scoff at her. Not her room, but a borrowed one, and a life borrowed from some idea of what she thinks a contented middle-aged woman's life should be. She's ignoring her outlaw self, her true self, the less than socially acceptable self which she'd been cultivating pretty much her entire adult life.

But she isn't the only one playing pretend. She sees Tyler in the moments between moments; and in them, he seems sadder than anyone she's ever known. No one can ever replace Serafina, and Maggie begins to feel jealous of a dead woman—Tae's *real* mother. And both Maggie and Tyler know that Tae's ability to play the role of the sweet and dutiful daughter has even a more definite shelf-life than theirs. How careful they are with each other. Too careful. Their once idyllic family life is over.

It smolders for a few days before it completely extinguishes on the day that Caroline shows up with Lucy Lucinda.

––––––––––

It's a late Sunday morning when the two arrive. Dressed, but braless, Maggie's been having a fairly good writing session at the kitchen table—so lost in her work she's unconscious of time. During a break she savors her second cup of coffee and watches a green hummingbird flutter just outside the kitchen window. Before her, scattered on the table, are all the photos of doors from their days on the road. She'd had them printed at a drugstore in town the previous day. There are several dozen—more than she thought she'd taken. Those that she recalls open for her and allow her return passage.

Tae lounges on the sofa, reading Collins's *Catching Fire* (which, she claims, is even better than the first in the trilogy). Tyler is still asleep.

Even the lighting changes when Caroline walks in. "Are you just going to leave me standing here?" she asks, with cat carrier in hand, and a medium-sized suitcase on the floor next to her. Maggie notes that it's probably within limits of carry-on size.

"Sorry! You said you were coming, but you hadn't said when," says Maggie, bolting up so fast from the table that she knocks several of the door photos onto the floor. Why is Caroline standing there with a cat? Could it be none other than Lucy Lucinda? Maggie hasn't realized until just now how much she's missed her. (Her cat, of course, not her sister.)

"Anyway, my surprises, unlike those of some, are never outside the realm of possibility." Already that familiar accusatory tone… Maggie could stand her ground and simply not open the door—insist that Caroline turn around and get back inside the silver rental car in the driveway—but knows, as she walks toward the door, that she won't, and almost immediately, she falls into the role of little sister.

"As you may have suspected, I didn't just come here to bring you your cat, Mag." How embarrassing to hear her sister's old nickname for her in front of Tae. Then why was she here? Maggie intentionally waits for her to tell her the real reason for the visit, though Maggie is hardly eager to hear it. Caroline could have simply shipped Lucy Lucinda to her.

"Do you know how many cats this woman has left behind when she decides it's time to move on? This side of countless—that's how many!" Caroline says in lieu of greeting Tae.

"That's not true, Tae. Don't listen to her. Well, maybe there have been a few..." What's this intruder doing here? (Her sister, of course, not the cat.)

Caroline sits on the edge of the couch in her black and white checked pencil skirt—knee length, slit in the back. It's the sort that Maggie never could wear and look good in—even as a young woman. She keeps brushing invisible dust from her skirt with a look of disdain as she surveys the living room and adjacent dining room. It's obvious that she finds the place shabby.

Maggie and Tae glance at each other. Both notice how Lucy Lucinda and Caroline have brought with them the same critical, smug attitude: *We don't want to be here, but it's the right thing to do.* Lucy's dressed in her well-groomed short black and white fur. The two could almost be twins. The glints in Lucy's dagger eyes have already made the long-haired, black and white Miss Sophie turn tail and hide.

Once again, Maggie will be undermined by her big sister. She knows that Tae was impressed with her when they visited her in Detroit, but the way Tae now sidles over to Maggie on the couch tells Maggie all she needs to know.

Caroline continues to brush off more invisible dust from her skirt—as well as very real cat fur. Sitting a little taller in the straight-backed chair, she ignores the sound of the two cats hissing at each other from another room. Her eyes bore into Maggie's eyes.

Tae jumps up to referee the cats.

"I'm here, Maggie, to bring you and Taezha back to Michigan. Also, I brought along Lucy Lucinda because it turns out your old buddy, Toby, is allergic to cats. Got a call from his mom. Looks like he's going to have to exchange you two for Lucy... That is unless, of course, you'd like to take her back. I suppose, Lucy and you could stay with me until you're back on your feet."

At hearing what sounded like an edict, Tae rushes back to her former place on the couch. Why is Caroline so against them being here? This time she puts an arm around Maggie's shoulder. The two wait, both feeling like guilty criminals waiting for the judge to read the verdict.

"You took a minor from her home against her mother's will. Do you have any idea of the legal shit storm you're facing if Quintana decides to press charges?"

"It's not likely she will," Maggie tells Tae, then in as cool a tone as she can muster, addresses her sister: "Look, it's not like I kidnapped Tae. She wanted to go on the trip, and she especially wanted to come here. Plus, Quintana was just jerking my chain with all her equivocating. I did her a favor, at least financially, and she knows it."

"It's true!" Tae loudly pipes in. "Who sent you here? My mom, as you probably know, is *not* my real mom."

"But she is your legal guardian. The one who raised you… Anyway, Mag, the initial trip was one thing, though a bit foolhardy. But to decide to live in North Carolina with an almost complete stranger… someone who has a criminal record…"

"Tyler's no criminal! He's a good man and Tae—Taezha—will attest to the fact that he's been wonderful to both of us. In fact, he's upstairs sleeping, so ladies, let's please keep our voices down." Then it hits Maggie: her sister flew down here because she's jealous. Caroline, despite her wealth, lives a staid existence. Over-protected by her husband of a thousand years; kids grown and gone; art gallery shuttered; plus, she's hemmed in by her snowbird lifestyle (winters in Florida and summers in northern Michigan), there clearly isn't enough to occupy her mind. Her art isn't enough. When she discovered that Maggie was caring for Tae, as well as being involved in a new relationship, no doubt it was too much for the poor woman, and she's been beside herself with envy. She has swooped down on Maggie and plans to wreck everything.

"I'm on to you, Caroline," says Maggie with raised brow.

"How's that?" says Caroline, somewhat taken off-guard.

"The green-eyed monster's getting to you. Am I right? Admit it!"

"I don't know what you're talking about, Mag," says Caroline, yawning, "but I do know this is the last time I'm going to try to bail you out of what appears to possibly be the biggest mess of your life. If what you're doing here mainly has to do with your own writing, as I suspect, then come stay with us on Black Lake. You could stay there in the winters and have the place to yourself." Maggie doubts her sister's sincerity, but maybe she's saying this from a place of compassion rather than sheer nastiness.

"Thanks for the offer, Caroline. I'm sure you mean well, but I've got my own path to follow. I know it doesn't make sense to you, but not only is Tae playing a major role in my life's journey, I am in hers, as well. I wouldn't be here if not for her. Who knows what will happen once she's in college? Can I maybe take a rain check till then?"

"Hey, I'm doing you a favor and you're acting like you're doing me one. How do you always manage to twist what I say?" asks Caroline, voice raised in a whiney, tinny manner, so reminiscent of their mother's (at least on those rare occasions when their mother raised hers).

Surely, Caroline recalls the three times Maggie's lived with her before? She should realize why baby sister is less than interested in jumping at the offer—even if Tae or Tyler weren't in her life. First time Maggie had stayed with her was in her late twenties when things went sour with Jason the Second. She'd had an abortion which neither Caroline, nor their parents, ever knew about. Then, a year later, Maggie had returned to Michigan after going into labor in her seventh month, and given birth to a stillborn daughter. She can't recall why she hadn't stayed with her parents—probably Caroline had more loudly insisted that Maggie stay with her. One month after the sisters had again been living together, Caroline put Maggie in charge while she worked at the art gallery. For a time, Maggie felt like Caroline's year-old daughter was hers; that is, until Caroline set her straight. It was when she was living at Caroline's that she began to work on her first novel. Caroline had told her that the book was probably just a baby substitute. She can just imagine Caroline saying the same thing now.

Next, there was the untimely death of Maggie's old flame, a

stuntman, Eric the Fifth. A few days before his accident, her agent had unsuccessfully tried to sell her book rights to Hollywood. After his death, she found herself, at forty, broke from spending royalty money a little too freely in L.A., so she moved back to Michigan, once again with her sister. Caroline's kids were in college, which meant the bedroom she'd had years ago was again hers. That time, Maggie wasn't working on another book. Her clerical skills were rusty, and it took months before she landed a job. On one occasion, they'd been having a sisterly heart-to-heart talk in which Caroline wondered whether or not Eric would have been drinking alone so much (he had a massive hangover on the day of the crash) had Maggie not been so busy, so driven, trying to promote her book.

There had been other times, too, when it was clear that Caroline felt entitled to pronounce judgment upon her younger sister. And when she did, she always found Maggie guilty, though Caroline herself was accountable—or so it seemed—to no one but herself. And now, at almost fifty-three, Maggie knows what her 'dear' sister is capable of, and refuses to experience the guilt Caroline perversely seems to enjoy, seeing her sister, not only covered in, but buried under. A shrink once called it 'displaced resentment' over Maggie's birth—her very coming into existence.

"What's all the commotion down here?" asks Tyler, who almost falls over when he sees the well-dressed woman in the living room. Truth be told, it was actually the aroma of the bacon Maggie had made earlier, which brought him to consciousness, not their voices. After introductions are made, Tyler slicks back his slightly greasy, thinning brown hair and excuses himself to the kitchen for coffee, saying that he'll be right back.

"Maggie offered you a cup, right?" Caroline nods, then again wipes at the invisible dust on her skirt; Maggie knows it's his presence of which she's really trying to rid herself. Caroline and Tyler have never met, *though Caroline had been acquainted with Serafina*. According to Caroline, they originally met at an after-glow party for one of the gallery artists. Serafina had been high. It was early in her career when she was feeling the frivolity, but not yet the pain of fame. Caroline, prone to exaggeration, claimed Serafina actually got up on a table and danced in a risqué fashion. When Caroline heard about Maggie's relationship with Tae, she associated Tyler with Serafina's wild crowd of musicians and artists. After Tyler rejoins them, and Lucy Lucinda jumps onto his lap, Maggie notes a look of loathing on her sister's face.

What the hell is wrong with her?

Chapter 35

Never has Tyler realized how much he enjoyed making noise in his own home until after Maggie and Tae arrived. Gentleman that he's always hoped to be, he's as quiet as possible when they're sleeping. Yet this is the first night that Maggie has slept since Tae has gone to stay at Nick's. He trips over one of Maggie's books on the floor next to the bed. Now she'll wake up... Or maybe not... For once she seems to be lost to a deep sleep.

Tae has been at Nick's for the last couple of nights. Maggie had kept a vigil on both nights, hoping she'd return. Not tonight. His turn now...It's going on 2:00 a.m. and his daughter is still not home. Her first night away was the day that Caroline left. Maggie has spoken to her twice on the phone, but each time only for a few minutes. He knows better than to try to reason with that girl by phone. Never much of a phone person in the first place... Angry, not so much with Tae's actions, as seeing the effect it's having on Maggie. Never has he seen a woman so worried.

Pacing through the three large rooms of the downstairs, he worries that the creaky floorboards will disturb her sleep. He walks on tiptoe but then abandons carefulness. Maggie is not going to wake up, and even if she does, so what? Come to think of it, lately he's been tiptoeing about as he passes through *his own* rooms—going to great lengths to be quiet because they are writing. Not that either has ever said anything, but a couple of times Maggie furrowed her brow when he walked past the dining room (which has somehow been turned into her office). Tae usually writes in her room with the door shut; but sometimes she leaves it open. More than once, however, when he'd walked past, she quickly got up to shut it. A few times she'd even slammed it. He's tired of this nonsense.

He shuffles his large bare feet the way he always has, and picks up an orange gourd that Maggie had arranged with a few others between two teal-colored candles in brass holders on the dining room table. Staring at it with a murderous gleam in his eyes, he grins fiendishly at the thought of ruining her Martha Stewart centerpiece, and then takes care placing it back on the table. Gazing about at her womanly touches: curtains that add a feminine appeal to the rooms, candles carefully positioned on end tables, art prints on the wall. A new print that she has put up just this week: women in long dresses sipping tea in a garden. Nothing against Impressionism, but he has always preferred seascapes or landscapes. Maybe he should say something. He really should let her know but doesn't know how to tell her.

Then he reaches for a bottle of Jack Daniels that he keeps in the cupboard beneath the kitchen sink. This is the first time he's touched the stuff since his guests arrived, but this seems like the right occasion; in fact, there couldn't be a dandier time to down a couple of stiff shots. There's half a bottle left. He won't have more than three. If he were to drink more, he knows he'd kill the bottle. That's not his aim. Maybe he's fucked-up in other areas lately, but it's not like he's drinking like he did before he went to jail. Afterward, he'd vowed never to get crazy drunk again, and he hasn't.

He gulps down the first shot. Tilting his head back, he bares his teeth and enjoys the burning in his throat. What has he gotten himself into? And why did he tell Tae—especially the way he did—that he was her father? But if he hadn't said something, then maybe Caroline would have overstayed her welcome, and thankfully, that nagging bitch was gone! He celebrates her absence by downing another shot, and then toys with an old black derby that Tae had purposely left on the table. It was his from years ago. The last time he'd seen it was when he wore it that weekend in Chicago with Serafina. And come to think of it, Tae wore it when she was writing, but he hadn't recognized it until now. He begins to take shots from a shot glass. That way he can keep track of how much he's drinking. He doesn't want to wake Maggie and make a scene. Modus operandi is to unwind from all the tension of late.

Maggie…

What to do about Maggie? Until recently he thought—hoped—that they might have a future together. She is kind, smart, and attractive to boot! He enjoys all the cuddling, though she doesn't arouse him like Serafina did, or even a few of his other one-night stand ladies. One of her eyes is larger than the other, which bothered him at first. But he rarely notices it anymore. Still, she doesn't exactly turn him on, though holding each other feels good—somehow right—and it's fun to whisper together in the dark.

It's clear that she still enjoys sex despite her age. But the past couple of times he's had a hard time getting it up, and only thinking about Serafina finally got him in the mood. He'd never admit that the reason he likes the room dark is so he can better picture Serafina. It's not that he doesn't want to see Maggie's body, but maybe it would help if she'd stop taking his face in her hands—it makes him feel like a kid. Then there are those sounds she makes when he sucks her breasts: a cooing. Why can't he tell her what bugs him?

He toasts her with his third and final—yes, final—shot. She really has sweetened his life, but it may turn out that the effects of the sweetening will ultimately crush his spirit. Will he have to tell her that he isn't in love with her, or has she already realized it? He hopes she has; it would certainly make things easier. But he does want her to continue to live here—he'll have to be clear about that point.

Next, he picks up the gourd from the table, walks outside into the moonlight and smashes it on the driveway. Not as messy as a larger one, or a pumpkin. A niggling voice inside him tells him to sweep up. *Hell no, I won't!* Maybe just one more quick swig of the Jack and he'll be able to get some shut-eye and get rid of his own yowl-yak. He hopes Tae will return home soon. He dons the derby, then waits on the porch, and plays *Moody Dog Blues* on his harmonica.

He so wants to right things with his daughter. Not only is he proud to be her father but he loves her. He's understood this ever since he began writing her when she was little. He needs to tell her his feelings; soon can't be *soon* enough. If only she will forgive him for all the years he wasn't there. And it doesn't matter if her feelings for him aren't the same...he knows that it will take time for her own feelings to grow. Perhaps she'll never care for him in the same way he cares for her. How could she?

And he's troubled by complex women like Maggie who claim they don't believe in love, and that people just have feelings of varying degrees: first hot, then cooler; at first giving, and then needy. His belief in love has never wavered. Tomorrow he'll begin working on his new furniture project: making writing desks. There should be a market for them.

Chapter 36

Tae hopes that Nick will see the note she left him on the kitchen table. Mostly, she explained how she's still his girlfriend, but she'd added that she wants to slow down. What she really meant was that she'd like to just be friends right now, and then, at some time in the future, pick up where they left off, though even then it wouldn't necessarily mean she'd be ready to have sex. (She hadn't known how to explain this without hurting his feelings or sounding like she was contradicting herself, so she'd left that part out). Then she'd added something about how she had to get things ready for Maggie's birthday party tomorrow, which was partly true. Why couldn't she have been more direct? He's smart enough to read between the lines and will wonder if she's dumping him. She isn't, is she? Maybe she should just explain everything by phone? She could simply call him after he returns from school tomorrow. Maybe they could still kiss, but go no further. Lately she's begun to wish she were still in school. It might make sense to enroll at the high school next fall. He'll be a senior and she wouldn't be surprised if he no longer gives her a second look. Big man on campus and all...He'd be upset if he knew she was having thoughts like this. Maybe there'll be a class they could take together, a non-required one. Who knows if she'll have earned two years of credits by then (making her a junior), since make-up work keeps piling up. And if Maggie's still going to take her to Washington next week, she'll really have to hit the books.

The back of her left sandal is digging into her heel. She stops to loosen the strap. The walk feels longer than usual.

Who cares about stupid, old Washington, D.C.? Besides, since she hasn't been writing, she feels like an imposter. She hasn't been reading much either. When she told Nick about how she's been missing doing both, he looked at her like he didn't know what planet she'd come from. Nick's enormous Bud Light T-shirt, which she has on over her pale yellow one, doesn't provide much warmth—just like the shallow light from the sun now mostly hidden by a blanket of fog. How different from the blistering heat during summer!

What if Tyler—rather, her father—is sitting at the kitchen table drinking coffee like he sometimes does at this time? She doesn't feel like talking about *the issue,* but knows she can't keep avoiding it. Her left eye begins to twitch. She's thought of little else these past few days. The fact that he's her actual biological father still seems incredible. Since her first day here, she'd noticed how much her ears resemble his (small and elfin), as did the shape of her long legs and broad shoulders. Even their lopsided grins are similar, and also their lips—both full on the bottom and thinner on top. Only differences are the colors of their skin and hair. Has he yet realized that the black derby is his? The worst part of it is that she finds him attractive, even sexy for an older man, but of course she'll never say so.

Her thoughts make her queasy and her eye is twitching like crazy now. Maybe she should encourage Maggie to marry him. She wouldn't really mind Maggie as her step-mother, but that might be weird, too. Then with Nick bugging her about sex, and not knowing whether she should end the relationship...

Maybe if she does have sex with him she'll really like it, and she'll finally be able to answer questions about her own sexuality. She'll be able to forget the kiss she shared with LeAndra, or when Maggie washed her back, or gave her one of those looks that were beyond friendly or motherly. Thankfully, Maggie hasn't gazed at her like that in a while. Fine by her, but is it because Maggie has fallen in love with Tyler? Yet, there are times when she'll catch Maggie watching her.

Then there was the call from Quintana last night. Big mistake not only answering her phone (she thought it was Maggie), but also a major goof-up in telling Quintana that she knew Tyler was her father. Quintana had wanted her to put Maggie on the phone. "It wasn't Maggie who told me," she explained. "It was Tyler." Finally, Quintana spoke: "You haven't heard the whole story. I'm coming down there."

From Maggie's Journal

Flint, 2008

Despite being financially secure following my parents' deaths, I could no longer stand my own company—way too much solitude for my liking; all the deaths, including deaths of relationships, stalked me, and put a pall over the brightest days. Lots of time for writing, but I only scribbled in my journal… That's why I took the job as a media specialist at Jefferson Middle & High School. At first I wasn't surprised that most of the staff was white, though most of the students were black. It didn't take long before I didn't notice color at all, yet how could I help but see some of the students shying away from me because of my skin color? Some—thankfully, not all—had a hard time connecting with me because I was a middle-aged white woman. The only real problem during my early days there was when I served on a committee with intervention specialists—all black women. The school wanted us to come up with a plan for improving grades and test scores across the curriculum (the principal's idea for fending off blame from himself and his teachers). A couple of the intervention specialists didn't like me from the beginning. They spoke rapidly in hushed tones, and used terms they knew I wouldn't understand. Clearly, I was unwelcome, yet there was nothing they could do to get rid of me except shun me in the hope that I'd quit. But I stayed and tried too hard to make friends with them and for far too long. I experienced what I'm sure people of color have experienced time and time again in this country. While I haven't been able to exactly walk in their shoes, I tried them on and felt the pinching. So I, too, have known something of racism and have discovered what a hell on earth it truly is!

Then I found Tae.

Chapter 37

Maggie waits for Sulie to join her at The Down Under, a small bar just outside of town. At first she takes a seat at a table, but within minutes she sits on a stool at the bar. She's never been good at waiting. Uncomfortable on the bar stool, she returns to a table—a different one than the first. The bartender, an older guy, scowls at everyone, but especially at her. What's it matter if she plays musical chairs since the place is mostly empty?

Tonight Sulie is supposed to tell her the reason for having followed her across several states, as well as why she's now residing here in Monroe. Just yesterday Maggie received a letter stating how Sulie has wanted to get together with her before this, but was waylaid due to business out of town. Something tells her that there is nothing to fear from this strange little person. Even though Sulie is only twenty minutes late, it seems longer.

Maggie stares at her hands and sees dirt beneath a few of her nails, then balls her fingers up self-consciously. It's a good idea to keep them out of sight when Sulie arrives. After unfurling both fists, she stretches out her arms and notes the many rough edges from nail-biting (an old habit that she's recently resumed). She then inspects the back of her hands, her fingers. Even in this dim light, she can see that they are beginning to look old—deeply wrinkled around the knuckles. If only she could disown them...

Maybe Sulie won't show up. She's now a half hour late.

It won't be the first time that Maggie has been stood up. Back when she lived in New York City there was that evening she waited for close to forever in a Chinese restaurant. After having waited over an hour, she finally left. She'd been waiting for Todd the Third, who was always jealous about how much time she spent writing. Little wonder things quickly went south with him. Another time, back in Detroit, she'd had plans to meet a former professor at a coffee shop. She was going to read some of Maggie's poems. The professor was a well-known poet on campus.

The party last night had been for her fifty-third birthday. Not the best or the worst of birthday celebrations. The good news is that Tae is now back at Tyler's—for now, anyway. Though she's been acting strange lately, more secretive than before. The cake she made for Maggie turned out as lopsided as Tae's and Tyler's smiles. It was a rich and decadent dark chocolate cake. They gave her presents: notebooks, pens, and a coffee mug with a small bag of ground coffee. All hints for Maggie to buckle down with her writing. What Tae didn't realize is that Maggie has become more disciplined lately and has been writing every night for the past few weeks (except when Caroline was in town). Tyler had prepared an early Thanksgiving-style dinner for her birthday dinner, since she and Tae would be in Washington on the actual holiday. The turkey turned out dry, but the meal had been a valiant effort on his part. Alex and Nick had arrived late, but their presence added to the festivities (as well as creating fewer leftovers). Never before had she realized how much father and son resembled each other—both with curly dark hair, deep blue eyes. Similar dimpled and slightly crooked smiles. Maggie was surprised that Alex had shown up, given the not-exactly friendly vibes he'd been giving off, but maybe she was just paranoid. Turned out he even smiled at her a few times and was almost talkative, in a joke-telling sort of way. A toast was made to father and daughter. Alex had guessed about it more than a couple of years ago (though he'd never directly asked Tyler), but Nick was completely surprised. She was this side of amazed that Tae hadn't told him, as Maggie thought she told him everything.

Forty minutes have now passed. What's keeping her? She can't still be working. Why had she taken a job at the town theater anyway? If she had Maggie's number, she probably would have called, so Maggie might as well give her another five minutes before heading back to Tyler's house.

The only disappointment at the party had been Tyler's present to her. She thought for sure it would be a negligee. It's been years since she's had a sexy one. Before lifting the lid of a perfect and prettily wrapped box, she imagined the nightgown would be lavender and made of satin or silk. When she instead pulled out a gray wool shawl, she could barely conceal her disappointment. She saw that Tyler had picked up on it.

"It will keep you from getting a chill when she was writing. The upstairs rooms are drafty in winter."

She noticed a price tag he'd neglected to tear off, so it obviously hadn't once belonged to Nana. Then he let out a nervous giggle which sounded unlike him. Girlish even...

Tae helped him out by telling Maggie that she and Tyler had spoken beforehand and decided to have a theme for the gifts: they should all have something to do with writing. He'd also given her an expensive pen. Later, she found out that he'd given the same kind of pen to Tae. But, all in all, it was certainly better than the lonely birthdays of her recent past... She hadn't gotten much sleep that night, after realizing that her romance, the dizzying and delightful part, was over. Kaput... Maybe that birthday party will prove to be the last time she'll ever feel a sense of family with Tyler and Tae. For now, anyway, she'll continue to play her role as surrogate mom and surrogate wife. Even if she hadn't been part of Tae's life when she was little, Maggie is here now, and she certainly loves her like a daughter...and a friend.

Where in the world is Sulie? Yes, it's Sulie she's waiting for. She could be anywhere.

Or nowhere at all...

Finally, in walks Sulie, sans trench coat, but clad in her usual jeans and black T-shirt with long, thin hair pulled back into a messy ponytail. Toothpick between her lips... She apologizes for being late. "Sorry, Maggie... I got the job of sweeping up all the goddam popcorn kernels!" Maggie doesn't know which is stronger: the relief of not being stood up or her curiosity about this woman who's been on the periphery of her life for so long.

Sulie begins to tell her how much she's enjoying the area and continues to explain that the reason she's taken a job at a movie theater is two-fold: 1) she likes movies, and 2) she adores popcorn. Here, she can watch all the films she wants and chow on all the popcorn she wants for free! Is she imagining it, or is Sulie wearing patchouli? Sulie's aroma isn't quite as strong as Tae's. Mixed with the scent of popcorn, no doubt.

"Everyone's been so friendly and laid-back. This almost feels like home—not saying the ultra-conservative views of the locals haven't been driving me crazy…"

Maggie finally has to interrupt: "We can go no further until you help me understand how it is we both happen to be sitting here together. Out with it, Sulie!"

Sulie sits back in her chair and stares a little too deeply into Maggie's eyes. "Remember when you saw me in that gift store in Hocking Hills? Well, you were right to think I'd followed you from Flint. I did, but the only reason I continued to dog you two was because you'd dropped your handwritten travel plans on the floor in your hurry to escape me. So, yeah, that was me in Richmond and Morgantown, too…Reasons I've shadowed you are twofold, maybe three. First, while it's nice that you see yourself as Tae's aunt, can't you see that this sort of intensive mentoring of Taezha is wrong? Wrong as desert rain… Second: you living with Tyler is wrong, too, but for other reasons… You know that I'm obsessed with you, Maggie? Mostly because I know so much about you—including your future—without even knowing you… Like my ESP is in overdrive. My psychic abilities are usually sharp, but they're super-strong regarding you. Not only can I read your thoughts, but I know your fate. Right now, you're thinking I'm gay and have a crush on you, right?"

Maggie nods.

"Years ago, I was in love with a man. He and I were soulmates. Always hated that term until I found out there's more than a little truth to it. The sex was fantastic, as was everything else. He died in a plane crash a couple of years after we met. I know you were living with someone who died tragically, too. Am I right?"

"Yes."

"Unlike you, there has been no one for me since," claims Sulie, who continues, "but I'm okay with that. You see, I'm not straight or bi or gay, I'm asexual. Anyhow, now I am and have been for several years. There are more of us in the world than anyone cares to admit, but that's a whole other conversation. Am I open to change? Sure, if change is possible, but I have my doubts. My main goal is to live near you. One day, I know, you'll be ready to shake off this place. And, ta-dah: there I'll be, waiting to escort you to the next phase of your journey."

"What do you mean, 'next phase'? I'm perfectly content. Why does there have to be a *next* phase? Tae's so much better off here. Plus, I'm in love with Tyler," says Maggie, squirming in her seat.

"You sure about that? Can you really see yourself remaining with him indefinitely? How about married? Then there's Taezha. No doubt she's better off now, in some regards, but isn't she practically living with her boyfriend? I sense some inner turmoil going on with her." Sulie's small hands are folded together on the tabletop and she's leaning forward as if she's brokering a deal.

"How do you know if she's even got a boyfriend? That's weird."

"Certain things I just know…"

"I don't think I'll ever marry, but Tyler's a great guy. True, we're different in just about every way. And lately there've been issues over Tae. And it doesn't help when my sister shows up unannounced. Plus, I think he believes his grandmother is still alive, and I have to admit, it does seem like her ghost lingers…" Maggie clears her throat before changing the subject. "I didn't know you knew Caroline," she says, all too casually.

The last time there was a Sulie sighting, Maggie was pretty sure she'd seen her talking with Caroline in a doorway on a side street off Main. It had been late, and too dark to tell for sure, and Maggie hadn't wanted either of them to see her.

"Who is Caroline?" asks Sulie.

Oh, Sulie is infinitely clever! And there is no reason to argue with her. Little reason to tell her how she'd felt afraid for their very lives while on the road… But Sulie knows. Of course she knows… Yet, to admit that now would give her the upper hand.

Maggie cannot concede anything.

Chapter 38

The flight to Washington, D.C. is delayed for an hour due to mechanical problems, and Tae has persuaded Maggie to allow her leave the boarding-gate in search of a snack. Travelers of all ages pull carry-on luggage or wear backpacks: most appear determined; some are excited, others just nervous. How do they see her? If only she were older and headed for D.C. by herself. An urge to run away sweeps over her. But where would she go? Someplace beautiful, someplace exotic… Maybe she could exchange her ticket then disappear until… When? No can do: Maggie is holding the tickets. And Maggie would never leave the airport without her. There must be some way to get hold of one of them. Maybe she and Nick could run away together someday. Two nights ago, he'd told her that he was in love with her and wanted to spend the rest of his life with her. It had taken her breath away, but she'd managed to tell him she was in love with him, too.

Maybe she wouldn't be feeling so negative toward Maggie if last Tuesday night had been different. Early in the evening, she and Tyler had been talking about Nick, and about her family in Flint. He'd mumbled how he was worried that Nick and she were hitting the sauce together. She explained how they only drank a beer, but never more than one, which was almost true. Then she got a mini-lecture. Sweet to know that he cared, but what she hadn't told him was how they'd already had sex a few times. While Nick was gentle, she didn't like it as much as she thought she would. It's gotten better since the first time, but she has a hard time feeling relaxed. And now she's almost sorry she hadn't followed Maggie's advice and waited longer. Yet she's already missing Nick, and she hasn't even left the state! Why is life so confusing?

After a few hours during the night in question, Tyler and she began to be worry when Maggie didn't respond to their calls or texts. It wasn't like her to leave them hanging. Father and daughter paced and gazed out windows. They tried calling her cell, but their calls immediately went to voice mail. They kept watch but found that they couldn't do anything but wait. Finally, well past midnight, in walked Maggie, who'd only apologized briefly *("Sorry, had my phone off...")* but then admitted that she and Sulie had met for a few drinks.

Tae wondered if Tyler felt betrayed. And she couldn't believe how Maggie had defended that crazy Sulie, even saying how it was wrong to have so quickly judged her. Maggie's 'revised' opinion (she always revises her opinions) is that Sulie is intrigued by their relationship, and she'd followed them only because she was fascinated by their road trip. ("How many middle-aged white women travel with teenage black girls?) Tae tried to catch Tyler's eye, but he'd stormed from the room after Maggie had finished explaining. Later, long after Maggie had gone to bed, Tae found Tyler at the kitchen table sipping tea. "Are you as confused as I am about Maggie meeting with Sulie? What's that all about?"

"She's a grown woman. I guess she can do what she wants."

"Yes, but..."

"I'm not going to say anything more except that I am surprised. Anyway, what are you doing up so late?" Why had he defended Maggie? Tae is still pissed off with both of them, but especially Maggie. Adults can be *so* beyond annoying.

After fifteen minutes of roaming the terminal, she settles for a packet of trail mix, Butterscotch Lifesavers, and a bottle of water. No doubt Maggie is wondering where she is by now. Good! Keep her guessing a little longer.

Tae notices a man at the snack bar—tall and large-eyed with wind-swept brown hair (slightly balding). He could be Tyler's twin, or at least his brother. She wishes—for not the first time—that it was Tyler flying with her to D.C., not so much because she's upset with Maggie, but because she would feel safer with him. Not that he could save her if the plane crashed, but he has such a—what is it? A calming presence… No matter how difficult the day, he seems to know exactly what to say to make her feel better.

So Maggie can just wait for her a little longer. She finds a seat, two gates down from theirs, and begins to silently re-read her prize winning story. Why hadn't she practiced reading it aloud before the trip? Hopefully, the judges and other writers will like her story. Looking it over, she wonders if these are really her words, words that came out of her head.

Maggie is probably getting a little worried. If so, why hasn't she phoned Tae yet? It's as if part of Maggie doesn't quite understand how cell phones work. She's definitely old-school. Sometimes Tae forgets that. Of course, it's nice of Maggie to accompany her, though Tae could have travelled to D.C. on her own. She doubts that Maggie believes this. In a few minutes she'll make her way back to Gate 37.

There was a time when she would have done anything for Maggie. Tae had let herself become convinced that a road trip to Uncle Tyler's was a great idea. She knows now, since Quintana hadn't given Maggie explicit permission, that it could be considered kidnapping, even though Tae hadn't exactly been snatched against her will. Still, the way she sees it now is that Maggie had bent Tae's will to suit her own purposes. That's the part that strikes Tae as wrong, yet she's unable to imagine what her life would have been like last summer had she continued to live with Quintana and her sisters. She still thinks of Quintana as being her mother, even though she now knows the truth. It's weird to realize that her sisters aren't really her sisters. Maybe she wouldn't have minded them quite so much had she known that they were simply her cousins. It's also weird to think that if Maggie and Tyler end up getting married, then Maggie would become her step-mother. From the start, Tae has been a willing victim, but there is no denying that she is still a victim of Maggie's…what is it exactly? An obsession? A perversion? A crime? In the end, maybe the only crime will be that Maggie has taken advantage of her. People do that to others all the time. But Maggie had planned it, had known exactly what she was doing from the beginning. At least Maggie no longer looks at her the way she did during the road trip—the way that told her that Maggie's feelings went a little too deep. And now, with this apparent change in attitude toward Sulie, it's almost as if Maggie is somehow under Sulie's spell. And who is Sulie, anyhow? Never has Tae known anyone so mysterious.

Chapter 39

Is this how a mother feels when her child wins an award? Maggie fights the urge to stand and announce that she is here with Taezha Riverton, the girl who just received the award. If she were the one receiving it, she'd feel nervous and self-conscious. And yet, Maggie has never received such a prestigious award. Her only public recognition had come as an under graduate for a group of poems about a pet pigeon. Along with the award, she had received a check for twenty-five dollars.

In the middle of reading aloud her poems to a group of twenty, a little dog had run into the small conference room; poor thing had a paper bag over its head and was trying desperately to free itself. The polite audience laughed impolitely, while one of the professors thought to help the poor puppy by simply removing the bag. The memory of that little dog has returned to her countless times over the past thirty years, as well as the feeling of having been upstaged.

Ten years after that event, her novel was published. There'd only been a few book-signings and a handful of radio interviews. *Pauline's Revenge* had been nominated for two awards. That brief moment in which she could picture an illustrious career as an author, but quickly—too quickly—it had passed...

Taezha, the rising star, now crosses the stage. She has an almost-exotic look, though her features are still dewy and sweet. Maggie had thought that she might feel envious, but she doesn't; no, only proud. Tae's simple teal dress—a perfect choice: semi-formal, and short, but not too short. The strand of pearls—which once belonged to Tyler's grandmother—gives her a sophisticated style. Tyler had given her the pearls just before they'd left.

Turns out, Tae doesn't get to read her story, or even part of it, aloud to the audience. There are too many winners and not enough time in the schedule to allow it; those who wanted to read their work, could do so in a separate room following the banquet. Maggie knows that Tae won't even consider it. Following a couple of long-winded speeches by the three judges, Tae hands over the check and certificate to Maggie.

"No, you keep them. They're yours."

"I just want you to hold on to them until after the banquet."

Each table in the banquet hall has a bouquet of quill pens in a glass vase in the shape of an antique ink holder; and at each place setting is a blank book made to look Victorian with various curlicue designs on bronze colored covers. Atop the books are pens with the festival name and year printed in Gothic lettering. "Someone certainly did well in coordinating the banquet theme," Maggie whispers to Tae, who is clearly impressed.

Tae whispers that she may have to leave due to a bad case of cramps.

"To the restroom?"

"No, back to the hotel…"

Maggie resists the urge to step on the younger author's foot.

Chatter from the other tables interferes with Maggie's ability to comprehend everything being said. Her eyes drift around the large room. This is the one place where she doesn't expect Sulie to pop up like a gopher from its hole. She feels suddenly alone, but not in a bad way, and wonders how Tyler's doing. A wave of missing him passes through her. It occurs to her, for the first time, that she doesn't have much hope for their future together, and regrets for the moment that Tae and she hadn't remained faithful to a life on the road. Those times had too quickly receded into the past, though she recalls them so clearly. Will they forever remain in memory, or fade a bit like her others? Her vocabulary's gotten worse over time. Does this mean her ability to retrieve memories is also less keen?

Chicken L'Orange is being served. It's getting late; she knows she won't sleep, or if she does, it will be in fits-and-starts. She doesn't like the way she feels in her black dress. It's clinging in all the wrong places.

Tae scowls at her and silently commands her to relax.

Maggie knows that there is more to be done: more living, more writing. Being around all these puffed-up egos is probably not the best thing for her own... Still, there are no regrets. It's satisfying to help a young writer—especially one so talented as Tae.

They make a great team!

Chapter 40

Only a few times has he peered through the half-open door to make sure that nothing has been disturbed inside Nana's room. He knocks gently before entering, almost as if he expects to see her in the flesh. He picks up her brush but sets it down before taking his usual place on the edge of her bed. Sunlight streams through the window and he is sure that her spirit is riding upon it; her presence is suddenly tangible, though he's still unable to detect her Channel No. 5.

I thought I was falling in love with her, he tells her, *but it's clearly not the case. Still, I'm grateful that she has brought Tae home. My love for Tae is unconditional—even though I haven't known her for long. I know that I missed the chance to watch her growing up—a regret I'll always have— but I'll never let her out of my life again. You know I'm true to my word. And Maggie? I hope she will remain my friend. But all those men she's lived with... She's complex and unpredictable. I guess I just want to play the harmonica and whittle my birdmen statues. Maybe someday I'll become a birdman and fly away.*

And there is another woman, a friend of hers called Sulie. Except she's not exactly a friend. Something strange about that woman—about them both. The other night they closed down a bar in town. Nothing wrong with that, I suppose. Lately, Maggie stays up late to write... Nothing wrong with that either. When she and Tae return from their trip, I'll have to find the right time to tell her that my feelings have changed.

He thinks he hears them at the door downstairs. Is that Tae laughing? Is that Maggie scolding? After listening for a while, he's forced to conclude that it's his imagination. His disappointment surprises him. Miss Sophie and Lucy Lucinda follow him as he roams through the rooms. "*What's the matter?*" asks Miss Sophie. In the kitchen he opens the liquor cabinet to see his friend there, but he quickly shuts it.

Goodbye, Jack...

Chapter 41

Hard to believe they've now been back from D.C. for two weeks. Once again, Tae spends most of her time with Nick. Maggie is aware that they're probably having sex. Little she can do about it. She just hopes that Tae is using birth control. Girls even younger than Tae are having sex these days. What does alarm her is that Alex is allowing his son to have his girlfriend sleep in the same room. (Tae admitted the sleeping arrangements on the phone.) Also, it shows that Alex likes Tae. Who doesn't?

Shortly after returning from D.C., Sulie sends Maggie a text: *Off to find locale for book museum.*

Strange days are made stranger by the change in her relationship with Tyler.

She wanders down to the giant pine standing sentry at the brook. Morning sunlight shimmers on shards of ice. The distinct outlines of trees, pond, and birds startle her into new a understanding. First night of their return, Tyler had made love to her with a new intensity. At first she thought it meant that he'd really missed her and maybe it was true love, after all. But by the next day, she realized that it had been their swansong: the kisses were goodbye kisses. Had she known, she probably would have acted the way she feels now: friendly yet aloof. Guess she shouldn't have tried to compete with Serafina's ghost. And then he told her how he cared for her, but wasn't in love with her, how she could always visit in the future.

"Playing house can only go on for so long, Maggie."

She can feel the heat from the verbal slap. He was right, of course. She should have called it off. But for a while, she'd thought that she was falling in love. But maybe she was only falling in love with security and the possibility of having a partner with whom to live out the rest of her days.

Now at this crossroad, it isn't Jocelyn's direction to which she's gazing, but Sulie's. What's wrong with a wild life? A life of unpredictability and throwing caution to the wind, no matter how wild! So what if she didn't radiate inner peace? She could laugh at herself and enjoy the crazy ride of life; except now at fifty-three, there are fewer options. Probably true for others her age and older… She could ramble around and drive further south or west to the imagined book museum in Oregon. Or wherever… If that didn't suit her, or if she chickened out, she could always move back to her old apartment building. Maybe get reacquainted with Toby. After six months or so, she could warm him to the idea of taking a trip with her. They could go out West together. No… She's got to stop having this sort of fantasy, especially after what's happened with Tae. Look where that has led her…

Inspired from sitting by the brook, she returns to the house, ready to write for the first time in a while. It's going to be a good session of some duration. But her phone rings exactly when she's about to begin her notes for a new book about a woman and a girl on a road trip: the woman is black, the girl white. (Yes, the book about the judges is on hold.) It's the second time today that she's been unable to locate her phone, but at last she does. A missed call from Quintana. It is unusual for her to call so early in the day. Maggie calls her back, not out of curiosity, but because she knows Quintana will keep calling if she doesn't return the call. She could turn off her phone, but she doesn't just in case it's Tae or Sulie.

Maggie might as well be direct. "Why are you calling?"

"Everything okay with Tyler?"

"He's fine, Quintana. Why would you care?"

"It's not easy living with a man who done time. Know what I mean?"

Maggie is aware of Quintana's tendency to manipulate and to lie in order to achieve her desired ends. "What I'm saying is that her daddy should have done even more time. A murder is much more serious, don't you agree?"

"Quintana, you know he never killed anyone. Why would you accuse him?"

"He cut Serafina's brake linings on the day of the accident. Or somebody cut them. Just wasn't enough evidence to hold him. No reliable witnesses, as far as the law is concerned, but Jayvon saw it all."

Maggie knows this isn't true, knows that Quintana will stop at nothing. Tyler had been home at the time, and hadn't heard about Serafina's death until days later from Quintana—who, at least back then, never would have made the accusation. In fact, it was Jayvon who'd been out East with a friend. He'd gone there for the sole purpose of seeing one of Serafina's shows. If anyone should have been investigated, it was him.

"You know Tyler was at home at the time, Quintana. By the way, wasn't Jayvon in New York that weekend?"

"Are you sayin' that my man killed my sister? Sure got some nerve, you white bitch!"

Maggie hangs up, turns off her phone, and then retrieves her notes which had fallen to the floor. Her hands are shaking. Tyler overheard what she'd said from the hallway. He hugs her and does his best to console her.

"You know she'll always find a new angle."

"Every time Jayvon comes back to her, she tries to pin Serafina's death on me. Serafina and I were planning to get back together, but that didn't suit either Quintana or Jayvon. Vanilla and chocolate together in one dish? No way! She knows it's likely that Jayvon cut the brake line."

"Why didn't you go after him—legally, I mean?"

"Don't think I didn't consider it. But then I ended up in the slammer for two counts of theft, and let me tell you, I found out fast that jail is no place for me."

Downstairs at the dining room table, she spreads her notes out like patches for a quilt. There are more than she thought, and she questions her ability to sew the pieces together. By doing so she will have to relive the loss of her parents, so instead she goes through her photos of doors, turns the dimmer switch on the wall one way then the other, finally leaving the chandelier lit at its brightest, and then adjusts the volume of the smooth jazz on the radio. She can't seem to get either right… She re-enters the bathroom, sits on the toilet and waits. Back to her old habits…

Then it hits her: her next book will become a banned book. Not the one about the woman and the girl. No, it will focus on erotic relationships between two sets of twins who live on an island. All will be idyllic for the two female sister-lovers, and the two male brother-lovers, until one of the females becomes aroused by one of the brothers. The stage for a murder is set. A little Shakespearean, perhaps, but she knows she has it in her to write such a tale. If only she can establish a reasonable routine. She will remain at Tyler's until the novel is written. With any luck, Sulie will return. Should she tell Sulie about her new book idea?

Next, she tiptoes into Nana's room. There is no scent. It's freezing. She sits on the edge of the bed. She senses nothing. Is it because Maggie and Tyler's love story hasn't worked out the way Nana might have liked? Lucy Lucinda chases Miss Sophie into the room. Both are surprised to see her, think better about their mischief and sit at her feet gazing up at her. Still waiting for a sign from Nana, Maggie puts her finger to pursed lips. She doesn't want their mewling to discourage Nana's presence. Both—for no obvious reason—get fat-tailed and make a beeline for the hallway.

A life she knows she can't have. She must let it go. Images of the bridge and the ledge…

"Let it go!" she commands herself as she glides across the floor to Tae's former room (the scent of patchouli still lingers), and then to her own. She slumps over the desk. If she wasn't here, maybe then Tae might return; father and daughter could have another chance to establish a relationship without Maggie the Interloper present. She's sure Caroline saw her the same way when they were growing up, as well as the men she has known. She always wound up feeling she was in the way, somehow preventing them from living their lives. Yet hadn't their needs and habits inhibited her, too? This is her day of reckoning, of realizing, and finally at fifty-three, of letting go. Not that it's a great age, but surely it is advanced enough to proclaim: *Enough!* How jealous she's been of the others in Tae's life! All of them: LeAndrea, Quintana, Tyler, and now Nick. All along she has wanted to possess Tae like a pet. What a fool she's been! Now Tae resents her more than she likes her. Yet Maggie has loved her—a different kind of love than she's had with anyone else. Maybe she could have loved Ricky (her former foster child) had he remained with her long enough. Even if she had, she's sure her feelings for Tae would be deeper and—almost—unconditional. Strike that: she has loved the girl *without* condition. In this regard, she's been like a parent to her; it hasn't mattered how Tae felt toward her. Maggie's feelings have grown, transformed.

She is about to cry because she now realizes that Quintana has felt the same way about Tae. Maggie isn't even sure of the ends Quintana will go to get her back. It would not surprise her if Jayvon came after not only Tyler, but her, too. He just might murder them both and return Tae to Quintana. Maggie could wait it out to the bitter end, but no, she's tired of the game. If Tyler is her true love and she could die in his arms knowing this, it would be one thing... Tae needs Tyler. And no one, not a soul, needs Maggie. For a time, she thought Sulie needed her, but Sulie is no longer around. If she were to wait long enough, maybe Sulie would return—only to disappear again (or Maggie would). Both a little too quixotic to be great friends... Nana's ghost is gone. Lately, she's heard zilch from old boyfriends (most of them used to contact her around the holidays)... *Who* does Maggie need? Now that's the question. She thought she knew, but now no longer.

Chapter 42

"Tell Quintana that if she continues to try to frame me, the Christmas visit is off!" Tae dips a slice of bread in olive oil, avoiding eye contact with him. He's been telling her to call him Dad, but she can't quite bring herself to do so. "Makes good sense to me…" She welcomes this advice. Too often Tyler and Maggie—and Alex, too—let her make decisions as if she were an adult. Before leaving Michigan she probably thought she was, but not anymore. For days, maybe weeks, she's been pondering about whether or not to go back to Quintana's for the holidays. (Maggie had purchased a round-trip plane ticket at the same time she bought tickets to D.C., so Tae knows she'll probably go.) What she does know is that she doesn't want to live with Quintana ever again. Since Quintana hasn't yet visited her here, and who knows if she ever will, Tae supposes she'll have to travel back to Michigan, not only for Quintana's sake, but for Tamala's sake, also. The other two, well… Part of her is curious about how they're doing, though she doesn't miss them the way she misses the sweet Tamala. She is so sick, too… And it will give Tae an opportunity to hear Quintana's side of the story, though she knows what a liar Quintana can be. She knows too that Quintana has a good heart; even if she hasn't always been the best parent, she's the only one Tae has ever known…until now. Plus, even if she spends most of her time at Nick's, Maggie is always looming always waiting for her.

Maggie has become too much of a stage mother. She just can't help herself. Also, especially lately, she's been getting in the way of Tae's relationship with Tyler: she hardly ever allows Tae to be in a room with him without her being present as well. She would like to talk to her about this but doesn't want to hurt her feelings. Maggie is so sensitive—too sensitive—for her own, or anyone's, good. Sometimes Tae feels like she doesn't need her anymore, though she does need and want Tyler in her life; in fact, even more than he's been in it lately. She's been having fantasies about doing small things with him: going to a movie, taking a walk. There's much she can learn from him. His odd but wonderful birdmen… Why does he make them? He's much more creative than either Nick or Alex.

"Do you think we could do stuff together more often, Tyler?" she asks while Maggie is out of earshot, refilling her glass of Chardonnay in the kitchen.

"I don't see why not," Maggie says, returning with a glass of wine (ready to slosh over the rim). Again, she is answering for him. Maybe Maggie hadn't heard Tae say his name.

"Sure we could, Tae, but I think you need to decide whether you're living here or with Nick. I think it's fine if he's your friend or boyfriend, but you've been more or less living there lately. I don't think you can have it both ways," says Tyler.

"Nick says he loves me." Tae is aware that her voice sounds like an insistent child.

"Aren't you a little too young to live with a guy?" Maggie purses her lips and raises her brows in a truly irritating way.

"Why are you always butting in, Maggie? Like my mom, I mean Quintana, always says: *'You up in my business!'* This is between me and my dad. So back off!"

What Tae really wants is for Tyler to insist that she move back, to tell her that her place is with him, but she knows he won't. Instead he gives her a couple of weeks to decide. He also takes the black derby, which lately had been gathering dust on an end table, and places it on her head. She smiles in gratitude. "Mine?" she asks and he nods.

She returns Nick's call. *Hunger Games* is playing in town; does she want to go? He can pick her up in fifteen minutes. "Sure, why not?" she tells him, not feeling much enthusiasm. Why does she always desire what she can't have? If only she felt more of a sense of belonging here… Maybe someday she will. At least she has something that was in short supply back in Michigan: hope.

When she glances back at the house after getting inside Nick's car, she notices that Maggie and Tyler aren't standing at the door together waving goodbye—only Tyler is there.

Chapter 43

Maggie and Tyler are drinking tea together in the living room after a soup and salad supper. The lights on the Christmas tree in the corner are off, and it doesn't help that the tree is tall and thin with few decorations. Lately, silence makes her acutely aware of her tinnitus. She asks if he misses Tae, but he doesn't answer, as he's tuning his fiddle. Tae has been in Flint for several days. It's now two days after Christmas. Tae won't be back until the end of the first week of the New Year. She could change her mind and remain in Michigan, but that seems unlikely. When they spoke on the phone earlier, Tae had said even though she was having a good time, there was a zero chance that she would stay.

"You didn't answer my question." She's not going to let him ignore her, plus she truly needs to hear him express his feelings about his daughter.

"You know I do, Maggie. Do you feel more like her mother or an aunt, or none of the above?" His question surprises her.

"Like both, but neither," she tells him. Maybe it's more like Tae is a kindred spirit. She doesn't add this. He raises an eyebrow then goes back to tuning the strings.

The new puppy—Kip the Second—stirs in his sleep on the sofa cushion. Tyler had initially acted pleased with his Christmas present, though later he'd made a couple remarks about how it seemed a little too soon for a new pet and wished that she'd checked with him first. "Then it wouldn't have been a surprise," she'd told him. Truth is that he doesn't care for surprises. She does and she'd much enjoyed the purple feather earrings he'd given her. They didn't go well with the cardigan he'd given her for her birthday.

This morning her first thought upon waking was that it was too late for her to have an ordinary life, as much as she'd thought she wanted one these past several months. It won't be long before she hits the road again. Maybe a few weeks after Tae's return. This time it will be without Tae. Maggie will have to find the right time to tell them both. Tyler will probably start tuning his fiddle, or maybe he'll shrug and leave the room. Tae's reaction will be different. Maggie will hug her and it will be hard for either to let go. There will be tears, though Maggie guesses they will do most of their crying in private. Hard to let go, but it will be for the best.

Yesterday she saw a small pale blue travel trailer for sale a couple miles down the road. It's easy to picture herself in remote campgrounds, writing during the mornings, then spending afternoons driving toward the museum—making slow but steady progress. Will she be able to write without her muse? Will they stay in touch? Maggie will do her best to write and call. She hasn't mentioned anything to Tyler, but she will before Tae returns.

She studies her photos of doors she'd taken since Tae and she left Flint—dozens of them. The last one she'll take will be of Tyler's front door.

My Gypsy Muse

Her red shawl flutters like bird wings revving for flight
She's a one-woman band and parade:
playing bongos, castanets, making birdcalls, caterwauls,
wailing in tremolo as she skips

I cartwheel the dark, follow down streets, then fields beyond
Hiccups punctuate her yodeling
Dirty feet dance in moonlit glow
"Yippee ai-yee!" she shouts as she whirls by

I'm her echo, her accompaniment
We frolic with fireflies, cavort with coyotes

Then I gape at the comet streaking my yard
The fireworks of her spirit suspend me in awe
She fizzles to a color streak—is gone

Months go by, years—
At last she returns—this young yet ancient woman
with pendulous, tattooed breasts

I never knew a voice could loop
and fill the air like twenty acrobats
Just before I grab hold of the trapeze
I hear her say, "Those who risk,
rarely regret."

It's a short visit, but YIPEE AI-YEE
for a time two muses—we!

—Taezha Riverton, 2020

Acknowledgements

A special thanks to my daughter, Sarah, for reading an early draft (and never coming up for air or taking out her red pen!); to my husband, Tom, for his continued support; to Benjamin and Mary Lynne for their encouragement; to Jane Cameron for her close reading of an early draft; and Carrie Mattern for initial editing. Also, much gratitude to David Ross and Kelly Huddleston…They were both incredible throughout the entire book-making adventure!

Made in the USA
Columbia, SC
15 January 2018